Chasing Can Be Murder

June Whyte

A Kat McKinley Greyhound Mystery
Book 1

White City

Press

Books by June Whyte
Sex on Tuesdays

THE GUMSHOE CHICK MYSTERY SERIES
Gone to the Dogs
For the Love of Dogs
Doggone It!

VETS 2U MYSTERY SERIES
Murder at Kangaroo Downs
Death at Dingo Creek
Homicide at Emu Lodge

KAT MCKINLEY GREYHOUND MYSTERIES
Chasing Can Be Murder
Muzzled
Hounded
Leashed

CHIANA RYAN CHILDREN'S MYSTERIES
The Case of the Disappearing Corpse
The Case of the Missing Dinosaur Egg

www.amazon.com/author/junewhytebooks

Chasing Can Be Murder

June Whyte

This edition published by White City Press
A division of Misti Media LLC
https://whitecitypress.com
Available in both Paperback and eBook Editions
1 2 3 4 5 6 7 8 9 10
Text Copyright © June Whyte 2024
Cover Copyright 2024 by White City Press
Paperback ISBN: 9781963479409
eBook ISBN: 9781963479256

For Jim

Acknowledgements

To start with, I'd like to thank all the *dish-lickers* I've been lucky enough to race and train over the years; noble, unforgettable greyhounds like Just Nonsense, True to Do, Flying Nonsense, True Shadow, Wotta Wizard, Truly Lightning. Dogs that could run fast enough to gain starts and even win or place in many prestigious races throughout Australia. Dogs with hearts bigger than The Great Barrier Reef. Dogs that gave me the idea for this book.

Of course I'd also like to thank the *humans* who supported me with this, the first of the Kat McKinley greyhound mysteries. I couldn't have done it without you.

First, a big thank you to my two gorgeous critique partners, Robyn Collins and Wendy Nichols, who are always there for me. And I mean *always*. Believe me when I say, friends don't come any sweeter than you two. A get-together in Tanunda again next year?

Writing buddies, Sharon Halasz, Jenny Mountfield, Tricia Stringer, Kaaren Sutcliff, and Melinda Hutchins. Whenever I need a second opinion or an original way to leap a hurdle—just ask one of these ladies, who, although busy with their own writing, invariably find time to come to my rescue.

Head honcho of the CBers, Marg McAlister, who is currently touring Oz in a Dreamhaven Crusader with her husband Rob and sharing their experiences with an Australian magazine called *Caravan and Motor-home*. Have a question about the finer art of writing? Marg is the ultimate fountain of knowledge.

And finally, I'd like to thank my family. Mum, Jim, and our three offspring, Terry, Darren, and Melissa, who, although growing up with a mother who, if not out riding her horse, had her head in the clouds or her nose in a book, still turned out wonderful warm individuals. Love you, guys. And I'm very proud of you.

1

I GAVE THE NAKED MAN BESIDE ME a suggestive nudge. No response. That'd be right. One noisy *Wham-bam-thank-you-Ma'am* the moment we collided with my king-sized brass bed and since then Lover Boy, alias Matthew Turner, had been impersonating a bear in hibernation.

A bear with appallingly bad manners.

I ticked off my complaints. Post-sex, did Matt dispose of the condom? Whisper sweet nothings in my ear? Offer to investigate the racket when my racing greyhounds woke me almost twenty minutes ago barking loud enough to put the Socceroos' cheer-squad to shame?

You guessed it. Thumbs down to all of the above.

When the dogs went into barking mode, it was *yours truly* who'd felt her way down the stairs in the dark, pressed the buzzer to switch soothing classical music on in the kennel-house and waited, shivering, for the noise to subside. Not Matt. God knows what had set the dogs off this time. Probably that mangy feral cat hanging around again—the one who'd already used up ten of its nine lives. Although, come to think of it, since giving birth to kittens under the woodpile, said cat had been more concerned with motherhood and catching mice for her babies than teasing my greyhounds. Once quiet, I'd scuttled up the stairs where my bed, not Matt, called to me; ignoring the niggle of unease prickling the hairs on the back of my neck.

And when I slipped back under the sheets did Lover Boy react to my seductive presence?

Huh. Like I wasn't even there....

I'd known Matt as a fellow greyhound trainer for over a year but since half-heartedly agreeing to go out with him two weeks ago, had been tactfully trying to let him know his presence left me feeling flatter than a warm beer on a summer's day.

Perhaps if *I* instigated the foreplay this time, pretended he was someone else—like Greyhound Training's gorgeous heart throb, Ben Taylor—who knows, I might be lucky enough to experience an orgasm before Matt's ten-second deadline expired. Before he thrust three times, hollered something unintelligible, his *little boy* went *pfft* and I was left imagining vibrators in a sex shop window while he blew the bedroom ceiling away with the volume of his snores.

Since returning to bed, his snores had stopped. Thank you, God. According to the *Guinness World Records* the loudest snore ever recorded reached 93 decibels—about the volume of a diesel engine. Whoever documented that record had never slept with Matt. And believe me, there's nothing worse than attempting to light a man's fires when the back draft from said man's snores keeps blowing out the matches.

I flopped back on my pillow and let out a sigh. *Lighting a man's fires? What was I thinking?* What was I *doing* in bed with a guy who reminded me of a basset hound, right down to his sad droopy eyes? Okay, a nice friendly sort of basset hound who'd share his last can of VB beer with you—but still a dog. Jeez, it's not like I was one of those women whose hormones were so highly charged the sniff of testosterone had me stripping down to my designer thong. In fact, I hadn't seen any action for almost six months. Not since my last boyfriend informed me in the middle of an orgasm that he was dumping me for someone younger, with a bust size of 42D. I *could* have explained to him that fifty percent of his fantasy-woman was most likely implants. Instead, I let him have it with my right knee.

The memory of Robert the Rat curled on the floor, moaning, tears streaming down his face still warms me on cold winter nights.

Yet here I was doing exactly the same thing—acting like Kat the Rat. I had no interest in the guy in my bed. He just wasn't my type. On the other hand, if the irresistible Ben Taylor, with his washboard stomach and crinkly eyed grin ever coerced his way into my bed, I'd be flying to the moon on a cloud of screaming lust and planning for multiple repeats. Warmth crept between my legs even picturing, me, bed and Ben Taylor—but let's face it, that scenario was a fizzer too. Ben, a rival greyhound trainer, the guy who starred as the hero in all my erotic dreams, treated me like I was just a good mate.

With an even deeper sigh that sprung from my chest and ended in my toes, I patted Matt's beer-gut stomach. "Okay, Matt," I told him, in a voice that brooked no argument. "You can go back to sleep now, but first thing in the morning, we need to have The Big Talk. Okay?"

Funny, the night was warm, yet Matt's skin was cold. And sort of strange. Like putty. And why was he so still? Before I slipped downstairs to quiet the dogs, he'd been tossing and turning, his snores rocking the bed like a roller-coaster ride at Dream World. I lifted my head from the pillow, one ear cocked, listening for the regularity of his breathing.

Jesus...I bolted straight up in bed and stared at the dark shape beside me. This had to be a bad dream. *Please*, let it be a bad dream. I reached forward with one hand and touched his chest. Was it rising and falling? Couldn't tell...my hand shook so much I couldn't feel a thing. Scarcely breathing myself, I slid my hand across his chest, inched forward again until my fingers connected with something hard. Something smooth. Something that felt like the handle of a knife....

Holy cat shit!

I was in bed with a corpse.

Heart banging against my ribs, I scrabbled backwards, screaming, hyperventilating, until I tumbled off the bed and hit the floor crawling. Still on hands and knees, I kept motoring until my head bounced off the bedroom door. I pulled myself up by the handle, switched on the light—and immediately wished I hadn't. For there was Matt. A long-handled kitchen knife protruded from his chest. *My* kitchen knife! I recognized it by the blue and white fake ivory handle. A thin trickle of blood and saliva had coagulated at the corner of his sagging, little-boy mouth. His glassy, slightly accusing eyes stared up at me. As I returned his stare, a curious fly, gauze-like wings fluttering in anticipation, landed on his left eyeball.

That's when the Big Mac and double fries I'd eaten for dinner the night before announced their comeback. I heard the telephone ringing downstairs but was far too busy to fully register the sound.

Stomach empty at last, I wiped the gunk from my mouth with the back of my hand and took a hesitant step closer to the bed. Was Matt *really* dead? And if so—*who the hell had killed him?*

And then an even more frightening thought slammed into my beleaguered brain. *Was the person who made him dead still inside the house?*

The fine hairs on the back of my neck reared up, one by one. I tried to swallow a lump of cement stuck in my throat. Maybe this was a joke. Maybe Matt was playing a stupid trick on me with a fake knife and ketchup. *Oh, please God, let that be true.* I shuffled closer to the bed and picked up his hand. Felt for a pulse. Oh, dear Jesus, Mary and Joseph…not a flicker…not a quiver. Mind silently screaming, I dropped the hand like it was a poisonous snake and shot backwards, flinching when the lifeless limb thwacked on the bed beside him.

I had to get away from the sight of Matt's dead, quickly cooling body. I had to hide in case the murderer was still in the house.

Bare-assed naked, I flew out onto the landing, legs and arms struggling to catch up with my body. And if I hadn't clutched the hand rail at the very last minute, I would have fallen head first down the stairs. Then, with only one thought on my mind—where to hide—I pivoted at the bottom of the stairs, undecided. The bathroom? The kitchen? The coat cupboard in the hallway?

Rejecting both the bathroom and coat cupboard as the first place a murderer would look, I dashed into the kitchen and slammed the bolt across the connecting door. Arms wrapped around my torso trying to stave off the goose bumps that shivered up and down my body, I cowered in the middle of the room. Think. Think. What do I do next? It was like a heavy weight pressed down on my chest preventing me from taking one full breath and clearing my mind.

Okay, ring the police. I'd left the cordless phone beside the walking-machine out in the kennel-house. My mobile resided in my tote bag upstairs in the bedroom and I'd rather die a lingering death involving hot oil and sharp screwdrivers than go back in there. So I had only one choice. Undo the bolt, leave the safety of the kitchen and ring from the wall phone in the lounge.

Gasping like I'd just competed in a 515 meter sprint at Globe Raceway, I made a grab for the receiver ready to wrench it off the wall and dial 000. But before I could do so—the phone rang. I screamed. And my heart performed a double somersault, tripped over its feet and landed with a gut-wrenching belly flop on the floor beside me.

Hand shaking, I lifted the receiver off the cradle and brought the phone to my ear. "H-Hello."

"Interesting collection of dog statues lined up on your dresser."

"Huh?"

The speaker was male, but that's all I could make out. It sounded like he was talking through a thick scarf.

"I owned a boxer dog once," the muffled voice went on, "just like the one in your collection. Turns out I hated the mongrel's guts, so I tied him to a tree and shot both his ears off. I guess he eventually bled to death. Never went back to find out."

I opened my mouth to speak but nothing came out.

"Since then, I've found knives much quieter than guns."

Sharp icicles broke off and clanged in my chest making it difficult to breathe. My hand shook so much I almost dropped the phone.

"Turner knew the consequences of disobeying orders. But I'm sure you won't make the same mistake…Katrina."

He knew my name.

Like the sound of a doomsday clock, a deep pounding started in my head. If Matt's murderer knew me—I must know him. "What are you talking about?" I whispered. "Who are you?"

He laughed, and it made me think of the dead chill at a city morgue. "If I hear you've told anyone about this call—anyone at all," he warned, "I will become your worst nightmare."

"But—"

"Ever felt a knife slicing into your face, Katrina? The pain as the blade cuts through the flesh into the bone, blood filling your eyes and mouth?"

I think I wet myself about then.

"Tell anyone about this call and I'll come back and rearrange that pretty face of yours. Make it so even your own mother won't recognize you."

Open mouthed, heart quaking somewhere around my ankles, I listened to the buzzing tone in my ear before the line went dead.

2

How did Matt's murderer know my name? Who was he? What if he came back? Would he come after me if I contacted the police? But surely I had no option. After all, a dead body wasn't something I could hide. Or could I? I hung up the phone, closed my eyes, drew in a deep breath, attempted to sort out the tangled chaos in my head.

Right at this moment, what I needed more than the voice of a fault-finding policeman was to hear soothing words from my best friend. Words like...*there, there, you'll be fine, Kat. The ambulance will take Matt away. We'll bin the sheets, spray the bedroom with a heavy-duty deodorizer, and hey presto, you won't even notice there's been a murder in your house.*

Tanya Ashton answered the phone on the seventh ring.

"Hunh." The noise from deep in her throat growled down the line. "It's three thirty in the bloody morning. This better be good."

"Tanya—"

"Kat?" Her voice changed to concern. "You okay?"

I sniffed. "No. Not really."

"Why? What's happened?"

My bottom lip quivered. "There's a dead body in my bed."

"A *what*?" I heard her swallow. "Gimme five minutes. Don't touch anything. Don't go anywhere. Don't. Even. Breathe."

It only took her *four* minutes. However, by the time Tanya screeched up to the house in *Phoebe*, her hot red *Toyota Yaris*, I'd covered my nakedness with the suede trench coat I'd left hanging on the back of a chair and unearthed half a bottle of vodka from under the kitchen sink. Even though I knew I needed to stay alert for the police, it didn't stop me from raiding my emergency supply for a stiff drink. For let's face it—with Matthew Turner skewered to my bed and an unidentified killer who not only knew my name but threatened to carve up my face like a Sunday roast—this was one heck of an emergency.

After letting Tanya into the house, I blinked at her pre-dawn outfit. In her hurry, she'd pulled on tie-dye skinny leggings under a flimsy green nightgown and added a ratty purple bomber jacket. But even in a crisis she'd remembered to slip on her favorite shoes—lipstick red *Chloe* stilettos.

The rustle of her bomber jacket sounded like a volley of gunfire in the silence of the room when she pulled back from a hug and studied my face. "You okay, Kat?" Although chalk and cheese, Tanya and I had been BFF from the time in second grade when we'd beat the class bully over the head with matching Barbie dolls. And we'd looked out for each other ever since.

I shrugged one shoulder. I was far from okay but if I started a pity party now the kitchen furniture would be floating in tears within half an hour.

"You said there was a dead body." Tanya's eyes never left mine. "Please...tell me you were joking."

I shook my head.

"Where is it?"

"Go look in my bed."

While Tanya climbed the stairs, I hunted up two empty roadrunner jam jars and tipped a good dose of vodka in the bottom of each before counting down.

Five. Four. Three. Two. One...

Movements jerky and uncoordinated, Tanya lurched down the stairs. For a moment I thought she was going to collapse on the bottom stair but she seemed to stiffen her spine at the last moment. I sipped my vodka and watched her. Like a sleepwalker she drifted across to the table and slumped into the chair opposite me.

"Jesus…"

I angled the other roadrunner jam jar across the table and watched her drain the contents in one gulp.

She spluttered. And then her eyes fastened on me. "It's Matthew Turner."

I nodded.

Her mouth opened, shut, and then opened again. "But…but you didn't say *how* dead he was."

"Dead is dead, Tanya. There are no degrees."

She stared at me as though I was a stranger. As though I wasn't the one who held her hand and helped her breathe and push and swear through the birth of her baby the night her lazy, useless, piece of shit, now ex-husband played poker with the boys instead of attending the birthing ceremony. "*Why*?"

"What do you mean?"

"*Why* did you kill him?" Her eyes widened ever further. "Oh, shit! He raped you, didn't he? You had to kill him in self-defense."

"Tanya…" Where were the soothing words of comfort? Where was the offer to help ditch the bloody sheets? "I didn't kill Matt. How could you accuse me of doing such a thing?"

I let my aching head drop onto the cold laminated table top with a thump. If my best friend thought I'd killed Matthew Turner what hope was there of convincing the police of my innocence? If only I could tell her about the killer's phone call. But my bowels went wonky at the thought of that psycho slicing into my face like a soup vegetable.

Tanya leant over and grabbed the vodka bottle by the neck. "Okay, okay, I'm sorry. It's just this whole dead Matt thing. It's freaking me out." She poured herself another shot. "Freaking me out big time!" She emptied the fiery liquid down her throat, spluttered and gasped, and poured another. "And what about whoever stabbed Matt? What if he's holed up in the house waiting to pounce on us? What if he finds another knife?" She covered her mouth with one hand and barreled to her feet. "Oh, Jesus! Do you think we should hide your kitchen utensils?"

Without waiting for an answer she was off again like the steam from a boiling kettle. "No, no, we better not do that. If he can't find a knife he might find something worse to kill us with."

I blinked up at my best friend who was supposed to be comforting me. "Tanya, would it really matter what he used if we ended up dead anyway?" I shook my head. "What am I saying? If whoever murdered Matt wanted me dead I'd be upstairs going stiff and cold right now."

"You're right. Of course." Tanya flopped into her chair again, picked up a cardboard coaster from the table and fanned her face. "So, have you rung the police?"

Both hands on the table I pushed my chair back. "I'll do it now. I was just waiting until you—"

"Don't ring the police."

The kitchen spun as I jerked my head up and gave her a disbelieving stare. Did Tanya know about the killer's phone call?

"What I mean is," she continued, evidently unsure of her ground, "we could er... you know, get rid of the body, so we don't get involved."

I let out a breath. No, she didn't know about the phone call. She was just on a different wave length to me.

"Look, I'm not saying we drop Matt in the river, or leave him in the middle of the railway tracks. Nothing tacky like that." She took another swig of vodka before continuing. "Hell, Matt was a good guy. Pathetic, but still, a good guy. All I'm suggesting is we drive him home and quietly leave him on his front doorstep." She shrugged one purple-clad shoulder as if to signify the simplicity of the operation. "Then no one knows he was murdered in your bed."

"Yeah, but—"

"After we arrange him neatly, you know, with his hands covering certain naked limp and ugly appendages, we come back here, clean your bedroom and no one will know he's been here."

"Yeah, but—"

"That way, one of Matt's neighbors finds the body and rings the police and you're in the clear."

I hesitated. Her plan did sound tempting. "Well, I suppose we could, but…"

Something about the image of dragging Matt down the stairs, his head banging reproachfully on every step, of jamming his stiffening body parts into the boot of his car, made my stomach clench in protest.

Tempting—but no cigar.

Instead, I patted my best friend's hand. She meant well. Boy, did she mean well. "Thanks for the offer Tan, but we'd better give the Thelma and Louise act a miss. There's no way we can do that to poor Matt."

"Why? Poor Matt wouldn't feel a thing."

I shivered at the reality. "I know, but it doesn't seem right, does it?"

"Your call."

"Talking of calls…" I stood up and moved toward the phone.

"Anyway, how come Matt was in your bed at all?" Tanya followed me into the lounge room, drink in hand. "You were supposed to dump the guy."

"I did try to put him off but he was like a damn puppy. You know all eyes and tongue and little-boy grin."

"Little-boy grin? God, Kat, you're twenty-eight years old. If you want to catch a *real* man it's time you started playing with the grown-ups."

I sighed. Why couldn't I say no?

My mother's words bounced censoriously around in my head: "*Katrina McKinley, you're the world's biggest pushover. If a guy in a hoodie told you he needed money to pay for his dear dad's heart operation you'd direct him to the nearest bank then offer him your car keys.*"

And once again, I'd been comprehensively sucked in. Not only had Matthew Turner talked me into training his incessantly howling greyhound—he'd also talked his way into my bed.

"Easy for you to say," I growled, "but I don't have a lot of *real* men in my little black book at the moment." And then it hit me. "This is my fault Matt's dead, isn't it? I should have refused to let him in."

"Not necessarily." Tanya shook her head so hard she almost fell over. I glanced at the vodka bottle. Almost empty. "Whoever killed Matt wasn't worried about his location," she went on, righting herself. "He'd have stabbed him in his own bed if he hadn't come here."

A silence followed.

Tanya, who seemed to be studying a picture of the indestructible roadrunner on the front of her jam jar glass, finally looked up.

"Kat…" Her voice scraped against her throat as she spoke. "What if the police charge *you* with Matt's murder? What if they take you away to jail?"

"Don't be ridiculous. Why would they charge me?"

Tanya's face twisted in an apologetic grimace. "Well, you *were* in the house with Matt at the time."

Oh God. She had a point. My heart hammered in staccato at the thought of me, black-eyed criminals, and a cold jail cell. "But I had no reason to stab Matt," I croaked, my voice struggling to make its way through my tightened throat.

"I know that, but the police…"

Tanya stopped and slurped another large gulp of vodka, her eyes blinking at me as if she'd suddenly lost her train of thought.

Unable to stand still, I began to pace up and down the room, afraid not only of the murderer's threats but of what might happen when the police arrived.

While I paced, Tanya drained her glass, sucked in a deep breath and reached for the phone. "Okay, here's what I'm gonna do. I'm gonna ring the police and tell them you didn't do it and I'm gonna…" Waving the phone, she staggered a couple of steps and gazed around, her expression confused. "*Whoa…* I don't feel so good."

I removed the empty glass from her hand and placed it on the coffee table. "Perhaps it's time to ease up on the medicinal alcohol, Tan," I said and snaffled the phone from her limp fingers. "This always happens when you drink too quickly."

"I know. I know. But hey, in case you didn't notice, there's a dead body in your bed."

"Yes, I *did* notice."

Tanya slid slowly down the wall until she was sitting on the floor. "And I'm *so* not into dead bodies."

I knew exactly how she felt.

Taking a deep breath, I dialed the police. "I need to report a murder," I told whoever answered the 000 call. While "whoever" wandered off to fetch someone higher up the food chain, I joined Tanya on the floor.

By the time Detective Inspector Garry Adams came on the line and introduced himself we were both sprawled on the black-and-white carpet tiles, backs to the wall.

"Are you the woman who rang to report a murder?" he shouted over Tanya's rendition, his voice a lump of steel crashing against a galvanized iron fence.

"Er…yes. But it wasn't me, Detective Inspector. I didn't do it. I didn't stab Matt."

"Calm down, madam, and tell me exactly what happened."

If the vodka had been closer I'd have drained the bottle and joined Tanya in oblivion right about then. Instead, I had to convince this detective of my innocence.

I drew in a deep breath and let him have it. "See, I've got this dead friend called Mathew Turner in my bed and I don't know what to do with him—or how he got that way. Okay, I admit he was a bit of a damp squib while we were having sex, but hey, that was okay. Well actually it wasn't *really* okay because it only lasted ten seconds, but all I'm saying is it wasn't a dirty great knife sort of not okay…I mean I didn't *stab* him just because he rated a minus five in bed."

Okay, I know. I was jabbering. But how else was I supposed to get my innocence across before we got onto specifics?

"Ms. McKinley." DI Adams broke in, his voice rock hard. "Tha*is* your name?"

"Yes, but—"

"And you are ringing from?"

"Um—" My gaze slid across my comfy sofa and two chairs and my newly purchased LCD digital television. I frowned. "I'm ringing from my lounge room."

"Of course. And your address is?"

"My address is..." I bit my lower lip and forced my brain to concentrate. "My address is eighty eight, Downes Road, Two Wells."

"We're on our way."

With that DI Adams hung up.

The wall at our backs, Tanya and I sat and stared at our feet. While my best friend gazed at the red leather straps on her designer shoes, I concentrated on the slimy thing adorning the knuckle of my big toe. Was it a gherkin or a piece of pickle? Could even have been a regurgitated slice of tomato.

Tanya was the first to break the silence. "Who do *you* figure killed Matt?"

"No idea."

"What about that weasel-faced guy with the long beard and big ears? You know the bloke who punched Matt in the stomach at the track last night."

"That was Matt's Dad."

"Right." Tanya went back to studying her shoes for a few moments. "Well, what about the big bruiser who lives next door to Matt? What's his name? Pipsqueak?"

"Peewee."

"Yeah, that's the guy. I heard Matt telling one of his mates that Peewee chucked a brick through his window and threatened to do him in if he didn't stop his noisy freaking dog from keeping him awake at night."

"They came to an understanding," I muttered. "Matt talked *me* into training his noisy freaking dog so his neighbors could get some sleep. That was right before I let him come inside my house and he ended up dead in my bed."

"Riiight."

3

A THUNDEROUS KNOCK ROCKED THE HOUSE. I cranked my head carefully around to blink at Tanya.

"Did you lock the front door, Tan?"

She shook her head.

As neither of us had the energy or inclination to leave the comfort of the floor, the police let themselves in.

The first one shouldered his way through the lounge room door and stood regarding us with one of those disparaging for-*this*-I-left-a-warm-bed scowl. He reminded me of that PI character, Columbo, from the eighties television series shown occasionally on Fox Classics. Short. Scruffy. Long, daggy overcoat. Five o'clock shadow worn like a badge of honor.

"Ms. McKinley," the Columbo-lookalike said bearing down on us with his shuffling gait. "I'm Detective Inspector Adams. Did you ring about a murder?"

"Yes, I did." I grabbed a deep breath in an effort to focus. "It's my friend, Matt. We were sort of in bed together and—and—when I woke up—he was dead." I sniffed, wiped my nose with a scrunched up tissue, before continuing. "He'd been stabbed."

"And whoever killed your friend Matt didn't stab you?"

Was this guy seriously blind? I gave him a no otherwise-I-wouldn't-be-sitting-here-talking-to-you-now, eye roll and shook my head.

"Well, in that case," he went on, hard black eyes staring into mine so intently they were escalating my headache, "can you explain how an intruder entered your bedroom, stabbed your lover and then escaped? All without waking you?"

I pulled my coat down further over my bare legs and tried to block out the more difficult questions he'd brought up. "Matthew Turner wasn't my lover."

"No?"

"He was merely a friend."

Detective Inspector Adams didn't comment, just raised his thick dark eyebrows a couple of centimeters.

"And I-I guess I didn't wake up when it happened because I was tired."

He just kept that cynical eyebrow thing going. "Oh?"

"If you'd been up since five in the morning training a team of greyhounds and didn't get to bed 'til midnight you'd be wiped out too."

"Not too wiped out to hear the person beside me getting stabbed to death."

Exactly. He'd hit on the piece of the puzzle I couldn't figure out either. Together with the other stray segment which went something like, how close had I come to being used as a pig-sticker too? In an attempt to clear my befuddled brain I took a deep breath and let it out in one long drawn-out sigh.

And then it struck me.

"You know, whoever killed Matt must have snuck into the bedroom while I was playing Tchaikovsky to the greyhounds."

His eyes glazed over and I detected a slight tick in his left cheek. "Let me get this straight. You were outside playing an instrument to your dogs while your friend was inside being murdered?"

"It's not an instrument." I shook my head. "All I had to do was press the buzzer at the bottom of the stairs." His eyes remained glazed, so I went on, eager to fill him in on the finer details of the situation. "See, this salesman, George someone or other, who I'd read about on the notice board at the Gawler dog track, set this gizmo up inside the house for me. When my dogs bark, all I do is go downstairs to the landing and press a buzzer. Immediately a Tchaikovsky CD starts playing in the dog-shed."

"I see," he said in that tone of voice that's really saying, yeah-yeah-pull-the-other-one.

"It really works," I assured him, intent on proving my point to this granite-nosed cop with the hard black eyes. "It definitely stopped my dogs barking when they woke me at around three o'clock this morning."

"Are you trying to say you weren't in bed when your friend was murdered?"

"Yeah, I guess that's the only explanation."

"So it was only later, when you returned, that you discovered he was dead?"

"That's right." *Thank God we'd got that all sorted out.*

"Was the bedroom light on when you came back in the room?"

"No."

"Well how did you know your friend had been stabbed?"

"I was…um…like, feeling around and…um…"

Heat spread across my cheeks and charged down my neck. Okay, I was way past the age of consent but no one likes to have their pathetic sexual exploits laid out on the table and examined in minute detail. While fanning my face, I watched a second plainclothes detective enter the room and walk across to Columbo. They began a whispered conversation in which the only two words I heard clearly were, *naked* and *dead.*

The second detective could have been cast as the main character in the next James Bond movie. Poised, good looking and somewhere in his mid-forties, this guy had clearly been born with a magnetism that drew women to him like fish to white bait.

"Good evening, ladies. Or should I say, good morning?"

The vision, dressed in an immaculate silvery grey suit with a pale blue shirt and darker blue tie, smiled. Every gleaming, perfectly aligned tooth sparkled and glinted like an advert for some super-duper, new-age toothpaste.

"I'm Detective Chief Inspector Tad Stevens," he said, stretching one beautifully manicured hand toward me.

Inhaling his spicy cologne like a wine connoisseur, I reached up to meet the proffered appendage. But before my sweaty fingers could adhere to his cool flesh, Tanya gave a gasping, choking sound, staggered to her feet and snatched the hand out from under my nose.

"Hi, I'm Tanya and I'm divorced."

I could tell by the way her eyelashes fluttered she was imaging herself and Inspector Gorgeous alone on a desert island together. There'd be a two-man tent, enough coconuts to keep them alive for a couple of years and no mobile phones or rescue boats to spoil the scenery.

Still clutching his hand like she wanted to chop it off at the wrist and stash it in her pocket, Tanya plastered a grin on her face. I don't know whether it was the grin or the frenetically fluttering eyelashes, but both men reacted as though she'd produced a weapon of mass destruction from her waistband. Columbo whipped out a set of handcuffs while DCI Stevens wrestled his fingers from her grasp and took several hurried steps backwards.

"And *you* are?" Columbo swung the flashing hardware in front of Tanya's button nose.

"Tanya Ashton" she squeaked, her eyes seemingly hypnotized by the swinging cuffs. "I'm Kat's friend."

"And you are here because?" This time his supercilious eyebrows almost collided with his hairline.

I scrambled to my feet, propelled myself off the wall. "Tanya's here because I rang and asked her to come."

"Before you bothered to phone us?"

"Hey, I was scared."

"All the more reason to ring us first, Ms. McKinley."

Columbo was starting to irritate me. Big time. Although his boss had paid his respects to the deceased, Short Dark and Scruffy hadn't moved from the kitchen. "I'm sorry if my actions don't meet with your approval," I told him in my best schoolmarm voice. "But I suggest you stop with the verbal assault and go look in the bedroom upstairs."

"Verbal assault?" He repeated, eyes narrowing to slits.

"Because that's where you'll find the victim, Matthew Turner."

I leant closer, all the better to breathe my vomit-enhanced, vodka-fuelled breath into his disapproving face. "Just don't expect *him* to answer any of your insinuating questions, either."

4

AFTER DI ADAMS RETURNED, Tanya and I were separated for further questioning. Tanya to the comfort of the lounge room—me to the hard, straight-backed wooden chair in the kitchen.

And you guessed it…Tanya won Inspector Gorgeous in the raffle and I ended up with the booby prize…DI Adams, the Columbo lookalike in the daggy long overcoat.

Twenty minutes into questioning, DI Adams produced a crumpled packet of cigarettes. He gazed at them hungrily, then, with something like a snarl, stuffed the packet back into his pocket. I let out a sigh. That's all I needed. Verbal wrestling with a grumpy nicotine addict in the throes of trying to kick the habit.

As it was, things weren't going well. Every time I opened my mouth I seemed to dig a bigger hole. I'd find myself popping up in China if this went on much longer. My head drooped, my brain was out to lunch, and if I could dredge up the energy, I'd go hunt up a couple of paper-clips to prop my eyes open. The big question of the moment was: *How could an alleged killer get into the house when there was no sign of a break and entry?*

The Inspector leaned closer. I winced as his thick nicotine-stained fingers gripped the tabletop. "Were all the windows and doors locked before you and the deceased went upstairs to bed?"

"Yes, Inspector, I locked up personally, as I do last thing every night.

But I've already told you this. At least six times." My fingers, unable to keep still, fastened around the loose button on my suede jacket. Twisting and tugging. Tugging and twisting. I knew, deep down where the scary maggots and worms eat away at your insides, if this relentless inquisition continued for much longer, I'd scream—and somehow, once started, I didn't think I'd ever be able to stop.

Unaware of how close I was to unraveling, DI Adams leant both elbows on the table and continued to chip away. "And does anyone else have a key to your house?"

I shook my head. Why waste words? The man wasn't listening. I'd already told him no. Perhaps I should try answering in Pig Latin. *Onay. So… ogay umpjay in the akelay.*

"Well, what about a spare key? Do you have a spare key that you hide in some obvious place like under the mat or under a pot plant?"

"I hide my spare key inside the gnome's mouth in the front garden."

"I see." DI Adams pushed his face so close to mine I got a whiff of what he'd eaten for supper. Something involving curry…with perhaps a touch of basil. On closer inspection, I even made out the faint coffee moustache from his last caffeine fix. "And why didn't you advise me of that important fact earlier, Ms. McKinley?"

I shoved my face back at him, almost exchanging nose fluids. "Because I bring the spare key inside before I lock up at night," I said, enunciating each word with tongue. "I'm not a complete ditz, you know."

His bushy eyebrows speared downwards somewhere in the vicinity of his slightly crooked nose—probably broken as a baby when he poked it into another toddler's affairs and got it battered with a rattle.

When he spoke again, his clenched teeth made the words difficult to decipher. "So, let's get this new information completely clear, Ms. McKinley. Am I right in saying you not only locked up before going to bed last night but you also brought your spare key inside the house?"

My reluctant nod barely registered on the up-and-down meter.

"Which means no one could get into your house. Right?"

Suddenly I didn't like where this conversation was going.

"And...if no one could get in, that also means you were the only person in the house other than Matthew Turner when he was killed."

I sagged deeper into the chair. Visions of prison bars, black-and-white striped uniforms and toilets resembling buckets swam through my mind. "No, that's not right," I protested, the loose button on my jacket finally coming off in my hand. "Obviously the killer was in the house too."

"How could he be, Ms. McKinley? There was no sign of a break in. You locked up. You brought the spare key inside."

Okay, stripes and bucket toilets weren't my thing. I sat up straighter, grabbed a mouthful of air and jutted my chin forward. Time to climb out of the deep dark hole I'd managed to dig for myself. "For the last time, I did not kill Matt," I said looking him squarely in the eye. "What if someone stole my spare key while it was in the gnome's mouth, had a copy made and then replaced it before I could discover it was gone? And last night that someone let himself in the front door while we were sleeping."

DI Adams surprised me. Instead of hurling my idea out the window like a smelly cigarette butt, he burrowed deep inside his baggy overcoat, finally producing a notebook and silver biro from one of his many pockets. "Right," he said, flicking the notebook open at a new page. "I need the names of anyone who knew where you kept your spare key during the day."

Faces of friends, acquaintances and delivery guys played like a movie before my eyes. Who out of my friends hated Matt enough to run a knife through his heart? Surely I'd know a murderer if I saw one. Perhaps the kid from the supermarket who delivered my groceries on Fridays inadvertently mentioned where I hid my key to a bad-ass customer? I rubbed the back of my neck to ease the growing tension before answering. "Actually, quite a few people know where I hide my spare key, Inspector."

"Names, Ms. McKinley."

"Well…there's the tradesmen, because I'm always busy out in the kennels whenever they call around and…well, I do have heaps of friends who come and go…and the local protesters meet here in my kitchen every second Wednesday night while I'm off trialing dogs at the Gawler track and once a month the—"

"Stop!" His fingers gripped the tabletop so tightly when he stood up I half expected the laminate covering to rise with him. "So the fact that you lock up at night and bring the spare key inside is really a wasted exercise."

Geez…this guy was in dire need of anger-counseling, maybe even the services of a full on shrink. "Um…" I cracked a tentative smile and nodded. What else could I do? He made me nervous. "I guess if you put it that way…."

Ten minutes and fifty-one names later, I looked up to see Tanya pushing her way through the kitchen doorway. She waltzed across the room, Chief Inspector Gorgeous trudging wearily at her heels. The Chief Inspector appeared ragged around the edges. He had a mumbled conversation with DI Adams. Adams scowled, dug out his crumpled packet of cigarettes and offered one to his superior. Then, glancing across at me, he gave an exaggerated eye roll and lit one up for himself. I shook my head at him and frowned my disapproval. Finally they exchanged a few more mumbled words and left the room.

"How'd it go?" Tanya asked as soon as the door closed behind them.

"So-so. And you?"

"Not good," she said scowling at a policewoman who marched into the room and stood, arms folded, watching us. "For a while there I had the Chief Inspector eating out of my hand but then I discovered he's married with five kids and two mortgages. It sort of went downhill after that."

To cheer myself up I drew a love heart on the table using the liquid from a puddle of vodka. First I put *K. Mc.* at the top, but before I could add initials to the bottom, the love heart ran into itself and changed back into a puddle. I let out a sigh. Typical. Especially for a girl whose bedside drawer contained a packet of vibrating panties as opposed to a much used packet of condoms.

"I'd better push off now, Kat." Tanya's words broke into my thoughts as I looked up to see her slipping her arms into the sleeves of her ratty purple bomber jacket. "The Chief Inspector has arranged for me to be driven home. I told him I only live around the corner but he wouldn't listen. Anyway, after I sleep this vodka headache off I'll ride my bike back and pick up *Phoebe*. I need my car to get to work."

I *really* didn't want Tanya to go. Not with the police taking over the house. "Sure you can't stick around a bit longer?"

"Sorry," she said shoving the empty vodka bottle into an overflowing pedal bin. "I would, but I need to get home and grab a couple of hour's shut-eye. The black coffee helped but I need to sleep and sober up. Thing is, I have to pick up Erin from her father's before work. Dan reckons his transmission's stuffed so he can't drop her off at school this morning."

I pushed away the dead chill that threatened to take over my limbs and turn me into a zombie. Of course Tanya had to get on with her life—just like I had to go out there and start working my dogs as soon as the police had finished with me.

"Sure your ex isn't a vampire, Tan?" I asked aiming at eliciting a smile from her before she left. "Dan never gets out of bed until the sun sets."

Tanya's chuckle came from deep in her throat. "Dan throws up at the sight of blood so he's hardly likely to be a vampire—but you're right about him being allergic to work."

The longest Dan had ever held down a job was two weeks—and the shortest—thirty seconds. He walked into a car factory one day, discovered a worker with actual sweat on his forehead and broke the speed record getting out of there.

"Sure you'll be okay, Kat?"

"Of course," I said forcing my smile muscles to work. "Go on. Go home and get some sleep."

After all, I only had Matt lying dead upstairs, the police on the verge of charging me with his murder and the real killer threatening to carve up my face.

Why *wouldn't* I be fine?

*****

Tanya's breezy voice, asking someone she referred to as PC Plod whether he was her allocated chauffeur and if so where the heck was his limousine, drifted back to me. A car door slammed. The motor sprang to life. And my one-person support team was gone.

What now? I perched on my hard wooden chair in the kitchen with a burly policewoman guarding the doorway and sniffed. My energy levels were down and dirty and mixing it with pond scum. And to make it worse, the two glasses of medicinal alcohol I'd consumed after the killer's phone call had changed my brain cells into lumpy porridge.

However, before my mother's voice started yakking away in my mind, ordering me to get a backbone, I dashed the back of my hand across my eyes and cemented my bottom lip. Okay, Mum. I know. No more pity party…if I wanted to survive this nightmare I had to toughen up. Inhaling a deep breath, I glanced at the kitchen wall clock before coercing my soggy limbs to push off the chair and support me. My greyhounds were howling, which meant, although it was only 4:30 a.m. it was time to take a shower and start my day.

After all—with such a murderous beginning—surely my day had to improve.

I settled the chair back under the table but before I could drag my dishrag body toward the bathroom, a smiling blonde policewoman entered the room, a mug of black coffee in one hand. The sixth brew she'd boiled up in the last half-hour. I shook my head. "Bladder's ready to explode," I explained and headed for the stairs.

Immediately the burly policewoman standing guard flung herself away from the doorway and appeared at my side. Unlike the smiley blonde, P. C. Hilliard looked like she'd been caught sucking a lemon when the wind changed. Pumped-up authority and no-nonsense seeped from every pore as she thumped up the stairs behind me, her breath like exhaust fumes searing the back of my neck.

I paused on the landing. I could hear low voices coming from behind my bedroom door and the horror of what lay on the other side of that door hit me all over again. My stomach swirled. My legs buckled. I made a grab for the banister to steady myself. Then, panting like an old dog on a five-mile hike, I scuttled past the crime-scene tape, praying no one would open the door. I didn't want to see inside my room. I didn't want to see Matt's dead eyes, smell blood or urine or hear the click of police photographers' cameras as they took snaps of Matt's final indignity.

When I reached the guest room at the end of the passageway, I slipped inside, propped myself up against the side of the wardrobe and caught my breath. Ever vigilant, my escort tagged me all the way. I snagged a pair of jeans and a faded T-shirt from inside the wardrobe and stomped across the room to the old-fashioned dresser given to me by my Granny McKinley. The policewoman shadowed my every move, so close she bumped against me. I glared at her, beetling my brows into dark storm clouds. What the heck was she expecting me to do? Pluck a homemade bomb from under a pile of my ratty sweatshirts? When she stepped closer, peering over my shoulder as I opened my underwear drawer, I actually snarled. "You want to choose my panties, constable?" I gestured with one aggressive thumb at the open drawer. "If so, go right ahead."

All I wanted to do was empty half a bottle of coconut shower gel over my skin, scrub the vomit from my feet, the sweat from my body and the stink of fear from my armpits. And I wanted to carry out said ablutions alone. Was that too much to ask? Gritting my teeth in frustration, I whipped knickers and matching bra from the drawer and headed for the bathroom.

So did my shadow.

"I *can* take a shower without you holding my hand," I growled attempting to shut the bathroom door on her shiny black size tens.

"Ms. McKinley." Her voice was cool, almost disinterested. "I'm only doing my job." She elbowed past me into the bathroom and stood beside the pale pink washbasin, arms folded across her Amazon chest. "And until we have finished our enquiries I cannot permit you to shower."

"Not shower?" I stared at the woman as though she'd just told me the earth was square. "But I *have* to shower."

"Forensics may need evidence to verify whether there's any of the victim's DNA on your body."

"Of course I have the victim's DNA on my body," I told her and sat down hard on the toilet seat. "What do you think Matt and I were doing in bed—playing Monopoly?"

Her responding smirk made me want to slap her. "Well, I certainly hope you kept the get-out-of-jail-free card," she quipped. "You might need it."

That's when a blurred movement from the corner of the bathroom caught my eye. It was a bristling scrap of golden fur emanating get-lost vibes more potent than heat waves from sizzling tar. Tater, my Chihuahua had woken up. Born the size of a postage stamp but with the heart of a stegosaurus, Tater was a birthday present from my Dad five years ago. A week before the road train came blaring out of nowhere on the country road and smashed Alex McKinley into oblivion.

I watched P. C. Hilliard glance down at the time-bomb ticking away on the pink and white bathroom tiles. Evidently unfazed by the diminutive size of the aggressor, she returned her cool gaze to me.

"*I have* to shower," I protested again, raising my voice to be heard above the now growing list of threats spewing from Tater's yapping mouth. "I stink. I vomited on my feet and my fingers touched Matt's body and–"

"Not my problem."

It could have been her apathetic shrug that sent Tater into a final tailspin. Either that or my whispered, "Go get 'er, boy!"

Anyway…one minute Tater was using the floor as a trampoline, the next he'd wrapped his front paws around the policewoman's leg and was doing what he did best—humping his little heart out.

I quickly shucked out of my suede jacket, turned on the shower and left them to it.

5

THE REMAINDER OF THE MORNING passed in a frightening blur.

My house crawled with forensics and men with flashing cameras and a buzzing hive of uniforms and plainclothes detectives. Early afternoon was no better. After I'd finished working my dogs, a policeman drove me to the police station where I was questioned again and subjected to the stark detachment of a fresh-faced constable who stole my fingerprints and entered them into the computer system. Made me feel like a real life character from *The Gangs of Oz*.

But by far the worst moment of the day was when two uniforms carried a bright orange body bag down the stairs on a stretcher. I think that's when it truly hit me. My friend, Matthew Turner, was dead. Never again would I see him at the track, leaning over the rails, urging his dogs to victory. Never again would I return his shy grin or share a laugh over a cold can of VB beer.

By four o'clock in the afternoon I was a wreck. All I wanted to do was curl up in a ball and suck my thumb like a baby. Instead, I hitched my overflowing tote bag over one shoulder, crossed to the station wagon and opened the driver's side door. Even with a baseball cap jammed on my head, I could feel the heat from the sun eating into my scalp, irritating a headache that four Panadol in as many hours hadn't dented.

"I'd better push off or I'll be late for kenneling," I told my young dreadlocked assistant, Jake. Between us, we'd loaded six greyhounds into the dog trailer, checked registration papers against ear brands and packed leads, muzzles and kennel bedding into the tack box for the night's racing. Too much physical labor for someone whose head felt as though it might explode at any time. "You okay to finish off here, Jake?"

"Sure, dude. I'm rocking. Our protest march doesn't like move off until seven."

"So what's the protest about tonight?" I eased behind the wheel, wincing when an army of fencing contractors began hammering hundreds of steel posts into my already tortured brain. "Save the whales? Save the trees? Save the dun beetles?"

Jake's slow grin lit up the silver nose rings that matched the hardware through both eyebrows and his right ear. "You can scoff, dude. Today's march is against microwave ovens."

"You're kidding me."

"Did you know the radioactivity coming from your microwave can like kill you and all plant life in a ten meter radius?"

I gave a weary eye roll. Even though Jake was a fruitcake of the highest order and came highly *un*-recommended, my greyhounds adored him. As well as helping out in the mornings, it was his job to return around four in the afternoon and let each dog into a separate run for a final gallop, then feed up before going home to his pad, where he lived in happy squalor with six other professional protesters.

"I'll leave you to it then," I told him, ignoring the rhetorical question re microwaves as too much strain on my already comatose brain.

Overflowing with caffeine and paracetamol, I took off with my team of racing dogs for Globe Raceway. .

As it turned out, I may as well have stayed home and gorged on caramel bears.

Four hours later, after maneuvering the wriggling black greyhound into the No. 1 starting box, I closed the door on her squirming rear end, straightened up, stretched my aching shoulders and thought, what a lousy night to complete a lousy day. Make A Dollar, my entrant in the first race of the night managed to finish third but my other four dogs were, as they say in the racing game…still coming.

As the starter placed his hand on the manual lever, in the off chance the automatic trip start might malfunction, I crossed my fingers. Last chance for a win tonight. My little black dog, Tempting Fate, known to her friends as Lucky, was odds-on favorite.

"They're off and racing!"

The ping of the lids had me watching seven jostling, straining greyhounds fly the boxes and chase the lure in a moving mass of colored racing rugs.

But the eighth dog…the odds-on favorite from box one…Tempting Fate…was nowhere to be seen.

Damn!

Of all nights for Lucky to stay in the starting boxes—why tonight? I slapped the leather lead against my leg and let out a long drawn out sigh. Anyone would think I'd smashed a mirror into a thousand pieces then deliberately walked under a ladder while six black cats slunk across the path in front of me.

When was it going to end? This latest drama would have me fronting up to the stewards for sure. And if Lucky was suspended again for failing to pursue, her owner might pull the plug on her.

Double Damn!

A cheeky black face peered around the side of the metal boxes, small ears cocked, dark eyes full of mischief.

"Oh, Lucky," I moaned as the rest of her shiny black body, clad in a formfitting red lycra rug, followed. "Why?"

Perhaps she deciphered this as a comment on her ingenuity and beauty because, tail wagging, she sprung into the air and banged me on the nose with her wire muzzle. Her way of saying, *I love you too, Mum!*

"No wonder ya mangy mutt don't wanna race. Like all sheilas, you're too soft on 'er. I bet ya a boiled sweet to a fruit cake that fleabag sleeps on your bed at night." The snide comment from Art Basset, a grizzled trainer in his early seventies, grated in my ear. And he wasn't done yet.

"Although, from what I've 'eard around the track tonight," he continued, his voice sly. "Your bed ain't safe to sleep in—even for a mollycoddled mamma's dog."

Instead of informing the old geyser where and how far up he could shove his opinions, I let it ride. Just didn't have the energy for a fight.

I sensed more than saw six-foot-two of toned muscle amble up beside me. It was Ben Taylor, the guy who treated me like a mate. The guy I'd most want to be having sex with if the world ever came to an end. He stood so close my nostrils inhaled his scent and decided to store it for later fantasies. Fresh air, earth and sunshine, mixed with the natural smell of a musky hot male.

"Zip your lip, Basset before both your muddy boots end up in that big gob of yours?" Ben's voice was as sharp as gravel. "Why do you think every trainer's wearing a black armband tonight?" he went on. "Not because we barrack for the Kiwis, you silly old fart—it's because we're mourning a mate. Some lowlife gorilla swung out of the trees early this morning and did Matt Turner in." The furrows in Ben's forehead deepened. "And here you are having a go at Kat. Jesus, she's lucky we're not wearing an armband for her too."

"But—"

"But nothing. I hear any more crap outta you and I'll confiscate your bloody walking-stick."

"Humph…" Art pursed his shriveled lips and turned away.

My hero. "Thank you, Ben."

"No worries, mate."

I resisted the urge to jump up and down waving both arms in the air, yelling, *Hey, look at me, Ben, I'm a girl—not a mate. I even have boobs. Two of them.* It was only pride and the fact that my boobs were the size of flat tennis balls that stopped me.

"You little beauty!"

Huh? I swiveled around with a dazed smile—but Ben wasn't referring to me. His eyes were honed in on dog number eight as it burst through the pack and careened to the front.

That'd be right.

Shoulders hunched, I tightened the collar around Lucky's neck while the rest of the field swept into the home straight. For me the race was over. Watching Ben's mouth split wide open in a triumphant grin, I knew the number eight dog had won. It was Ben's second winner for the night.

The air whooshed out of my chest in another giant sigh.

Ben and I had a personal bet between us. $200 plus a meal at a swanky restaurant for whichever one of us finished with the most winners for the season. Until tonight, I'd been in the lead. Now, with only a month to go, Ben had inched past me.

I removed Lucky's race rug and tucked it under my arm. Funny thing, beating Ben didn't seem as important as it had twenty-four hours ago. And the black band around my sleeve was a grim reminder of why my priorities had changed.

Unable to control his grin, Ben punched me on the arm. "Don't worry, mate. There'll be other race meetings for you."

My arm cringed involuntarily as I pretended I was made of steel. "Congratulations. I guess that means you're on top now."

"My favorite position," he agreed, lips twitching, eyes dancing. Then, with a mischievous wink that had my heart flopping and floundering like a fish on a line, he sauntered off toward the run-on lure to pick up his dog for the catcher.

"Ms. McKinley. I'd like a word." Barney Thompson, the tall string-bean steward who operated the starting boxes brought me back to earth with a terseness he usually reserved for guys who boxed dogs under the influence of too much of the amber stuff.

"Yes, Barney." I started to smile but decided against it when I noticed the razor sharp glint in his eyes.

"The chief steward wants to see you in the stewards' room immediately after re-kenneling your dog."

"Right."

"And I wouldn't be surprised if the punters express their

appreciation by throwing rotten eggs at you."

I blinked. "Why?"

"Because there was big money riding on your dog," he snapped slamming the two-way receiver back into its cradle beside the boxes. "You shouldn't have nominated the dog for the race if you weren't a hundred percent sure she'd jump. Punters did their money cold."

Okaaay. Was I missing something here? Barney's comments were strangely out of whack. The steward was normally talkative and pleasant to all handlers. Not mean like this. I tugged on Lucky's lead and headed toward the kennel-house. Why was there big money riding on Lucky tonight? Did Barney know something I didn't?

After ten minutes spent defending the little black bitch in the stewards' room, Tempting Fate still ended up with a six-month suspension from racing. It was her third offence. One more transgression and she'd be suspended for twelve months—which is virtually a life sentence for a racing dog.

But how could I be angry with Lucky? Always pleased to see me, always fun to be with; if she was human, she'd be one of those bubbly girlfriends who dress in faux leather and knee-high boots and giggle at your most pathetic jokes. It wasn't her fault she sometimes didn't feel like competing.

Sometimes I didn't either—especially on my worst PMT days.

Tiredness descended on me like a thick airless quilt. What else could go wrong today? I emerged from the stewards' room, closing the door carefully behind me. And that's when I ran slap-bang into Peter Manning, the Tire Man, current owner of Tempting Fate and four other greyhounds in my kennels. With an effort, I straightened my shoulders and dug up a smile to offset Pete's *not-happy-Kate* expression.

One of my most generous owners, Peter Manning was also one of the hardest to train for. He paid top dollar for his dogs and expected them to win—every time. If not, he wanted to know why. Tonight, gazing up at his pugilistic face, I swear I could see steam erupting from both ears.

"Not good enough, Kat." His lips, usually ready to charm their way out of a paper bag were tight and leaf thin. "You told me you'd fixed that bitch's problem."

"Jesus, Peter, I'm a trainer, not a miracle worker. And anyway, you've won heaps on Lucky over the last couple of months."

"And gave every cent of it back tonight. Plus more."

More fool you, I thought, but knowing I was treading on dangerous ground settled for diplomacy instead.

"Come on, Peter, the time off will do Lucky good, get her mind off racing for a while. In six months' time, she'll be itching to run again."

"I will *not* pay training fees for a dog that's not racing. She'll have to go."

"How the heck am I supposed to find a home for a dog with a six-month suspension hanging over her head?"

He shrugged. "Give her away as a pet. Take her to the vet and get her put down. Put her in the Greyhound Adoption Program. I don't care. I'm not paying for a useless mutt to sit in the kennel for six months." He cleared his throat. "Anyway, I've bought another dog for you. Big Mistake. Good type and only two years old. He won the final of the Puppy Championship at Sandown last night."

Any other time I'd hug Peter and dance a jig at this news of acquiring a good dog. Tonight, like Rhett Butler…I didn't give a damn.

"Okay, give Lucky to me. She's lost interest in racing so I'll breed a litter from her and you can have the pick. Won't cost you a cent." As I made this offer, my mother's words rang in my head again. The ones that kept insisting I was a first-class sucker.

"Do what you like, Kat." He spoke over his shoulder while stomping off toward the exit. "Just don't add her name to my account."

I frowned at his receding figure and swore under my breath.

Soft in the head—that was another of mum's delightful character descriptions of me.

And she was right. I needed another house pet like I needed a dose of castor oil. A vision of Tater who thought he was a Doberman and

Lucky the soft black marshmallow eyeing each other off for first dibs on my bed brought a smile to my face.

Until I remembered what happened to my last bed warmer.

"Hey, Kat, how you doing?" Tanya came bustling up from the direction of the cafeteria. A good distance behind her, dragging two-hundred dollar cross-trainers and a sulky bottom lip along the ground, was Erin, her eleven-year-old daughter.

"Do you want the true answer or the sanitized version?"

"Uh! Oh! The stewards suspended Lucky."

"Yep! Three months."

Erin, better known as *Devils's Spawn*, gave an exaggerated sniff and kicked at the ground. "Muum… I'm bored. When are we going home?"

"Shut up, Erin."

"Yeah…shut up, Erin," I echoed.

Erin and I got on like oil and water. Whenever Tanya coerced me into babysitting, I was ready to tie and gag the kid five minutes after her mother left.

"What did Tire Man Pete have to say about her suspension?" Tanya flicked her hair from her eyes. White combats, teamed with a Diesel candy pink T-shirt and matching high heels was a definite improvement on the green nightdress and purple bomber jacket from this morning.

"Let's just say I now have another pet to share my bed. Big-hearted Peter gave Lucky the chop."

"Talking about your bed—"

"My *bed*?" I did a double take. Amazed at how Tanya wasn't a shaking mess after this morning's trauma. Then again, she always did bounce back better than me. "Oh, why not?" I said and threw up my hands. "Seems like it's the topic of conversation on everyone's lips tonight."

Erin stepped closer, her eyes two glowing orbs of excitement. "My friend Jamie says you stabbed Mr. Turner in the guts and kept stabbing him until he was dead. Did you, Kat? Did blood spurt out? Did he scream when the knife went in?”

“Erin!” Tanya gasped.

“This is *so* cool knowing a murderer,” Erin continued as though we weren’t both regarding her with horror. “All my friends at school will be *so* jealous. Can I have your DVD collection and your digital camera when you go to jail?”

I shook my head at Tanya. “Are you sure they didn’t switch babies on you in the hospital, Tan? Sure you didn’t end up with Ned Kelly’s great-great granddaughter?”

“Sometimes I wonder,” she muttered then scowling, took a step toward Erin. “Hey, back off! Now! Unless you want the job of cleaning the toilet every day for a month.”

With a dismissive shrug, the kid voted most likely to end up as leader of a biker gang, twirled a lock of her straight blonde shoulder-length hair around one finger and carefully readjusted her face to its normal bored expression.

“As I was saying, Kat,” continued Tanya turning away from her eleven-year-old with that *why me* expression shared by all mothers throughout the world. “You’re welcome to use my spare bedroom. Why not settle the dogs down for the night then come on over? There’s a six-pack of Vodka Cruisers in the fridge and I can pick up some Chinese on the way home.” She lifted one candy pink shoulder. “Hey, after what we went through this morning we could do with a bit of relaxation.”

“I’ll see how I go, Tan. It’s just that…I don’t know…someone used *my* key to get into *my* house and stab Matt. I feel like it’s up to me to find out who did it.”

“Up to you to find out who did what?” Ben Taylor, tight black trousers emphasizing his one hundred percent masculinity, joined us. As he passed Erin he tipped her baseball cap over her eyes.

“Dooon’t…” Erin grumbled pushing the cap back onto her head and stamping her foot.

Ignoring the kid’s drama-queen act he fixed his eyes on me, waiting for an answer. When I studied the ground and shuffled my feet, he reached out and lifted my chin with one finger. "Find out what?"

"Find out who stabbed Matt," I blurted. "I'm scared shitless but I have to find out who snuffed out his life as though he were a pesky mosquito on someone's arm."

Ben gazed at me as though I needed a shrink—or a brain scan—or both. "Why? That's what the cops get paid for. Matt's murder doesn't concern you."

If Ben knew about the phone threat he wouldn't say that. Hell, the police needed all the assistance they could get to catch this maniac before victim number two—*yours truly*—was found with her face shredded like fish bait. Maybe I should confide in Ben and Tanya.

"Don't tell anyone about this phone call or I might have to rearrange..."

Then again—maybe not.

Ben slung one well-muscled arm around my shoulder. "So, where you figure on sleeping tonight, babe?"

"Whoo…hoo!" Tanya, grinning like a sheep on steroids, let out a whistle.

"Is that an invitation to sleep with *you*?" I fluttered my eyelashes at him and mentally shoved the killer's words to the back of my mind. Instead, I replaced them with an image of Ben, wearing a leopard skin loincloth stretched out on a king-sized bed. He was smiling up at me while I fed him juicy black grapes and fanned his fevered brow with an open race book.

"Huh?" The loinclothed vision sent me a sickly grin, grabbed another grape and promptly disappeared. "I only meant if you're nervous about staying on your own, you're welcome to bunk down at our place."

Ben and his older brother Nick lived with their widowed father on a large property on the outskirts of Gawler and while Nick ran cattle, Ben trained greyhounds for a living.

The grin on Tanya's face changed to a smirk. "Aha! King-sized bed…Kat in the middle…Ben on one side…Nick on the other. Now *that* sounds like a cozy threesome."

"Nick has his own bedroom and I'll be sleeping where I always do—in the caravan beside the dog kennels."

Tanya pursed her lips in a show of disgust. "Ben Taylor, you're about as much fun as a wet dishcloth. Anyway, I've already offered Kat a bed for the night and been knocked back, so unless you can offer extra bonuses that I can't match—?"

"Drop it guys. I'll be fine," I insisted, suddenly too tired to keep up with the banter. "I'm off to collect my dogs from the kennel-house now and then I'll call it a night. I'm bushed."

When both Ben and Tanya looked ready to persist, I held up one hand, palm out. "Look, I really appreciate your concern guys, but I'll be fine."

What I didn't add was that I'd probably sleep in the broom cupboard curled around a baseball bat, the kitchen knives under my pillow and a super-sized lock on the door.

6

Home isn't always a place you can trust.

Knots tied and untied themselves in my stomach as I angled the car and dog trailer off the roadway and crawled to a stop. The Holden's piercing headlights picked out the silver of my wire mesh gate. I could see the rusty scratch mark on the left-hand post caused the day I was in a hurry to get to the track and misjudged the width of the opening. Strangling the wheel, I narrowed my eyes and read every painted word on the sign, *McKinley Greyhound Kennels*. All familiar. All homely. Yet, out there, on the other side of the gate, shadows loomed. Shadows that could easily hide a man with a knife.

Muscles primed for action, I set the hand brake in the on position and climbed from my car. What was I doing here? What was my problem? Why did I need to prove to everyone I was like Sidney Bristow from *Alias*, when in reality I was more like the field mouse from *Alice in Wonderland*?

As usual, my mother was right—I was *soft in the head*.

Fingers numb, I unhooked the heavy metal chain and gave the gate a shove. It swung open with an eerie screech that ripped through the night air. An involuntary shiver launched a rush of goose bumps up my arms. As Grandma McKinley always said, *like someone had walked over my grave*.

"Katrina McKinley?"

One hand still on the gate, I yelped, lashed out with a closed fist in the direction of the voice and connected with what felt like hard bone and soft tissue.

"Oooomph!"

Ready to follow up with a knee to the groin if necessary, I swiveled on one foot and peered at the man who was bent double, holding his nose.

Oh, crap. I'd punched a cop.

That's when I noticed a junior officer scrambling from a nearby patrol car hidden in the shadows. All legs and arms, he galloped towards us. "Sir! Sir! Are you all right, Sir?"

After a quick check of his injured senior officer, he turned to me, keeping a long arm's distance away. Probably worried I'd let fly with another wild punch. "Sergeant Gregory didn't mean to startle you, Miss. We're here patrolling the area because DCI Stevens instructed us to maintain a 24-hour surveillance."

I touched the still-moaning Sergeant Gregory on the arm and flinched when he ricocheted away from me like I was a live electric wire.

"I'm sorry I thumped you Sergeant, but you shouldn't sneak up like that. You scared me half to death." I flashed the man a wobbly smile. "Lucky I wasn't carrying a baseball bat, hey?" His answering scowl sent my smile scurrying for cover. "Um… how about you come inside the house and let me put an ice pack on your poor nose? I could brew some coffee while I'm about it."

Exactly what I needed—a couple of uniforms to accompany me through my front door. Detective Chief Inspector Stevens was not only gorgeous he was a living legend for sending these two guys around to guard my house.

The young policeman looked at his superior expectantly. "What do you say, Sarge? I wouldn't mind a hot drink."

"Who wouldn't, standing out here in the cold night air," I cajoled, the idea of going inside that front door alone getting scarier by the second.

A grunt, followed by a distinct, "No way!" came from the direction of the police car. The Sergeant leant against the bonnet and stemmed a flow of blood from his nose with a large handkerchief. "It's our duty to prevent intruders from entering your house and we can't do that from inside your kitchen."

Damn.

I didn't bother arguing, just hefted myself back into the car and rattled down the driveway toward the kennel-house. After all, with two nice policemen installed at my front gate no murderers could get in. Perhaps I'd even catch up on some sleep.

No sooner had I unloaded the dogs from the trailer and loosed them into the emptying yards than I heard Tater going off his tree inside the house. He must have heard my car pull up.

To save disturbing the other greyhounds, I quickly settled my charges into a smaller kennel-house built next to the dog kitchen and fed each dog a sloppy meal of beef and vegetable stew with a kidney flush thrown in. Then I paused to listen. Why was Tater still barking? It wasn't his "hello" bark, or his "hurry up and feed me" bark, or even his, "Ooh goody, my mum's home—now I'll have a lap to lie on" bark.

No. It was his alarm siren.

I crept up the path toward the house, heart cowering in my black leather flatties. If I refused to acknowledge the trees and bushes that changed into aliens and reached out at me with their twisted gnarled fingers as I passed—it meant they weren't there.

Or that's what I figured.

The moment I inched open the front door, a miniature hurricane flew through the air and landed at my feet still storming and raging, then catapulted another ten meters up the path. Hair on his back standing on end, he let rip with another volley of frenzied barks before strutting back to me, tail curled high over his back, mouth open in a wide grin.

It's okay now, Mum, he seemed to say. *Reckon I scared 'em off!*

But *whom* had he scared off? And what was *whom* doing inside my house? And how the hell had *whom* got in with Cop1 and Cop2 guarding the fort?

With Tater trotting importantly beside me, I tiptoed through the open doorway, switched on the hall light and, leaving a trail of lights behind me, proceeded to check every downstairs room. Geez…this was worse than the shower scene from *Psycho*. At least Janet Leigh didn't know the big scary guy dressed as his mother was a murderer so she didn't die of fright before he killed her.

One foot in front of the other, I shuffled up the stairs and stood in front of my bedroom door. Did I really want to go inside? Did I really want to know if the murderer was on the other side of the door waiting for me? *Don't be ridiculous*, I chastised myself, drawing a deep breath and letting it out slowly, *no one could have broken into the house with the police on sentry duty. It was more likely a feral cat knocked over a pot plant and set Tater barking.*

Eyes scrunched closed, I turned the door knob and edged into the room feeling along the wall for the lightswitch. And when I opened my eyes—there it was—in all its three-dimensional ordinariness. My queen-sized wooden, IKEA bed. And when I snatched a hasty peep inside my mind, I could still see Matthew sprawled on top. His eyes blank, his mouth slack, one of my well-sharpened kitchen knives protruding from his chest.

The police had removed the bed linen for evidence and all that was left was the bare mattress. They may as well have confiscated that too. It was ruined. And even if it had been in pristine condition there was no way I could ever sleep on it again.

I edged my way across the room to the window and peered outside. A faint half-moon had slipped from behind the night clouds and I could just make out the police car parked by the front gate. From the kennel-house, Matt's dog, Queen of Egypt, known to her friends as Cleo, short for Cleopatra, let out a high-pitched howl. Like a cry of mourning.

I sniffed the air. Was that a faint smell of spice? Had Matt been wearing a spicy aftershave last night? I couldn't remember. Too many other memories crowding and jostling around in my already overcooked brain. With a shrug, I closed the curtains, walked across to my dressing table and absently studied the collection of dog statues displayed on top.

My favorite was a shiny black greyhound with two snow white front feet. I picked it up, ran a finger lovingly along the length of its china back and moved it further down the line, next to the brown-eyed golden cocker-spaniel.

As I turned away, determined not to ever sleep in this room again, I caught something in my peripheral vision that made all my childhood nightmares seem tame. At the end of the line, its tail pointing jauntily towards the sky, stood my cheeky brown and white boxer dog. And next to it, like two tiny pebbles, lay the dog's broken ears.

I owned a boxer dog once…hated the thing…tied him to a tree and shot both his ears off…

The room spun. Nausea ate into my bones, turned my limbs into useless lumps of soggy mush. To keep myself upright, I grabbed for the dresser and held on.

The murderer had been in my bedroom.

Again.

And just like last time…

He'd left a calling card.

A scream caught in my throat threatening to choke me. I swallowed it down then forced my eyes away from the mutilated statue. Who or what was I up against? The doors and windows were locked. The police had been crawling all over my house like blowflies on a carcass until a couple of hours ago. And even now—two men-in-blue were staked out by my front gate.

Drawn against my will, I gazed down at the two broken ears and almost gagged. What if they'd been Tater's ears? What if this monster had tied my darling little Tater up and shot off his ears?

If the killer's aim was to scare me off, he'd sure as hell succeeded.

Mouth dry, I stuffed the broken statue into the back pocket of my jeans and headed for the open doorway. If this psycho intended using my bedroom as a drop-in centre, there was no way I was hanging around waiting for his next visit. And as for reporting the incident to the police—what could I say? I'd found one of my dog statues with its ears broken off? I'd be laughed out of the station. And if I blabbed about the threatening phone call I'd be demoted from chief suspect to victim in a body bag.

Poker stiff, breath escaping in short raspy gasps, I descended the stairs. Was the killer waiting in the shadows? Was he hiding in the linen cupboard ready to spring out at me? Jesus…it would only take someone to say *boo* right now and there'd be no need for a sharp instrument to the left ventricle. I'd die of fright.

At last I reached the front door. But as my damp fingers closed around the white plastic knob, I caught a blurred movement off to the right.

Tater.

Scooping the scrap of brown fur up under my arm, I yanked the door open and not taking time out to either lock up or switch off lights, stumbled outside. The little dog wriggled in my arms, wanting to get down. I tightened my grip. Cleo let out another mournful howl from the kennel house. It hung in the air, making the hairs on the back of my neck prickle.

Mouth open, panting like I'd run a marathon, I tossed Tater into the passenger seat of my car, scrambled in behind the wheel, jammed the locks down on all the doors…and burnt rubber.

Didn't even stop to let my two protectors at the gate know how completely bloody useless they'd been.

7

BODY RIGID BEHIND THE WHEEL OF MY CAR, I stared at Tanya's front porch. Forced myself to pull in a deep breath. *That monster had been in my bedroom again.* The bare light globe hanging on a cord set high in the roof of the porch swung in the breeze, throwing more shadows than light. *His creepy fingers sliding everywhere.* Long formless shadows moved across the red brick path leading up to Tanya's front door. *The same fingers that likely rifled through my underwear, smoothed the fabric on the clothes in my wardrobe, selected the sharpest knife from the drawer in my kitchen and savagely plunged the blade deep into Matthew Turner's heart.*

I choked back a sob. Tasted raw fear as it flooded my mouth. With Tater clamped in the crook of my arm, I manhandled the door open and threw myself out of the car. Knees weak, I staggered, righted myself, then made a dash toward the light. Desperate to shed the paralysis of my thoughts. Desperate to see a friendly face.

"Kat?" A face not so much friendly as downright scary confronted me the moment I hammered on the front door. "Jesus, you look awful." Tanya's face, covered in this thick greeny-yellow glop had hardened into a mask, but when I opened my mouth to inform her she didn't look so crash-hot herself—no words came out.

"I heard you pull up. Did you change your mind about sleeping here tonight?" When I didn't answer, Tanya blinked, then reacting to my glazed expression, scooped Tater from my arms and set him down on the floor. "Come in and sit down."

Like a zombie, I followed my friend into the kitchen. When she pointed to a big old faded green armchair that not only radiated coziness and much loving use but had the added bonus of smelling of cats, horses, dogs and my best friend, Tanya, I moved toward it.

"You'll be okay now, Kat," Tanya crooned as she shooed Sweetie, her large ferocious ginger feline that looked more tiger than housecat off the chair. Even as I sat down I knew I'd never be okay again, but it was comforting to have Tanya fuss over me. Exactly what I needed to chase away the nightmares.

"Erin, put the jug on to boil and take care of Kat while I dig up a blanket. She's shivering."

Left to the mercy of *Devil's Spawn,* I turned away and watched Tater swagger across the kitchen toward Tanya's hairy grey lurcher, Petunia. When he nipped her on the end of the tail, she butted him away, then gently rolled the little dog onto his back and proceeded to clean his underparts with devoted thoroughness. Tater, drooling in ecstasy, responded with a wriggle.

"Yuk! That's totally gross!" Erin regarded the two dogs with a curled upper lip. "You're a *girl* dog, Petunia. Where's your pride?" She perched on the arm of my chair and chewed gum with her mouth wide open. "Is that what Mr. Turner did to you last night, Kat? Is that why you killed him?"

When I didn't rise to her bait she sighed, stood up, then sauntered back to her jug-boiling duties.

"Hey, look what I found?" Tanya, face now scrubbed clean of her garish beauty mask, bustled back into the kitchen, arms full of red tartan quilt, which she proceeded to tuck around me. But even huddled under the quilt I couldn't stop shaking. And when a hot-water bottle landed in my lap and a mug of hot chocolate in my hand, for a moment, I couldn't work out what to do with either of them. I could see both Tanya and Erin peering at me like I'd morphed into a six-headed creature from Outer Space, but I could only blink in return.

"Talk to me, Kat. What's going on?" Tanya looked worried. Erin highly fascinated.

Instead of answering, I cuddled the hot-water bottle and concentrated on breathing. In…out. In…out. There was a heavy weight crushing my chest, making every breath painful. It was like trying to breathe underwater. I wanted to tell Tanya about my intruder but couldn't seem to form the necessary words in my head.

Gnawing at her bottom lip, Tanya crouched beside my chair. She reached out, one hand massaging my arm as though she could reassure me through the tips of her fingers. "How am I supposed to help if you won't talk? Are you hurt? Did someone threaten you?" She hesitated for a moment and then I watched her eyes widen to dinner plates. "Oh, no!" She shot to her feet, both hands flying to her mouth. "You haven't found– *please* Kat—don't tell me you've found another dead body!"

When I didn't answer, she marched across to the telephone, back straight, shoulders tense. "Okay, I'm ringing Ben Taylor. If anyone can snap you out of this weirdness—he can."

*****

His lips tasted of mint-flavored chewing gum. His aftershave hinted of pine forests on a fresh misty morning. When the kiss deepened, my breathing slowed to a ripple on a lake and I found myself floating, freewheeling, lost in the magic of pure sensation.

With a moan, I wrapped my fingers in his hair, dragged him closer. Heat or hunger or just plain unadulterated lust pooled in the pit of my stomach. And when his tongue slipped inside my mouth, claiming every nerve end, fireworks exploded in my brain and a bonfire raged in my groin.

Hell, I'd been waiting my entire life for this kiss.

"Oooh, yes..." I moaned and transferred my grip from hair to shirt, prepared to rip off the buttons in one jerk if necessary. "Don't stop! Don't *ever* stop!"

"Hey, she's talking!" Tanya's exclamation seemed to be coming from a long way away. "You've done your job Ben, so you can unplug your lips now."

Oh, no. Come back. Don't go. The fiery tongue and minty lips withdrew, leaving me cold, lost and disorientated.

Devastated, I clutched at Ben's shirt as he slowly disentangled himself, straightened up and flicked a raised eyebrow in my direction. "Hmm..." he said, running an exploratory tongue over his lips. "Not bad."

Tanya tapped him lightly on the arm with her fist. "Hey, I didn't know you were such a good kisser, Benjamin. I might even try you out myself one day."

"Sorry, but you'll need to get on the end of a very long queue."

She punched him again, this time, harder. "Don't get carried away, lover boy. If Kat had been remotely on the ball tonight, she'd have bitten both your lips off and fed them to her dogs."

Mind whirling, I gazed up into Ben's teasing brown eyes and wished I could swallow a "drink me" potion. You know, like Alice stumbled across in Wonderland. Shrinking to the size of a flea sounded a pretty good option right now. A flush warmed my skin as it rose from my toes and travelled all the way to my hairline. If only the floor would lift so I could slide underneath, pull the boards back over me and disappear forever.

Ben turned to me, lips twitching. "Not a bad technique for treating shock. Even if I say so myself."

Ben had kissed me and I'd responded. Boy, *how* I'd responded. But while his kiss had switched on every one of my fairy lights it meant nothing more than medicinal psychotherapy to him.

"You know," he said, hooking a thumb into the front of his jeans like the Neanderthal he was. "I should market fridge magnets. *When you need the kiss of life don't call 911—call Ben Taylor.* I'd make a fortune."

If I had access to a water hose, I'd drown the big lug. Who needed Ben Taylor anyway?

Me...a little voice bleated.

I gave myself a mental slap. *Don't be so bloody pathetic. There are billions of guys out there waiting for a special girl like you. Who needs Neanderthal Man?*

Of course, by now, Erin was hanging over the armrest of my chair, nose twitching, eyes the size of hubcaps. "Did you see that, Mum? Ben and Kat were kissing with their mouths open. Ben's tongue went right inside Kat's mouth. Right down her throat. It was totally gross*!*" She puckered her lips and did a stinky imitation with her nose to show us exactly *how* gross. "Why were you moaning, Kat? Did Ben's tongue get hooked on your tonsils?"

"Erin. Bed."

"But Muuum…that's *so* not fair. You always make me miss the good stuff."

"You'll miss the school trip to Monarto Zoo next week if you're not in your room by the time I count to ten. One…two…three…four…."

Ignoring the everyday mum-daughter battle of wills going on behind him, Ben dragged up a chair and sat facing me. "What's that you're drinking, mate? Hot chocolate?"

"Mmm…" I nodded, lips jammed together to show exactly how pissed off I was. No way was I anywhere near ready to forget or forgive the reason for that kiss.

"Hot chocolate's a drink for old ladies and insomniacs." While Tanya frog-marched Erin from the room, Ben slipped a hand inside his sheepskin jacket and produced a flat green bottle. "Now, here's a drink that'll clear your head and grow hair on your chest. Take a swig of this, kiddo, and you'll be firing on eight cylinders before you can say, Go the Crows!"

I scowled daggers at him. First *mate* now *kiddo*. What next? *Sis*?

On the proven theory if you can't beat them, join them, I snatched the bottle from his outstretched hand and took an extra long swig. Wow! Liquid fire ripped at my throat and tears ran down my cheeks.

"Where'd you get this crap?" I spluttered. "Tastes like boot polish mixed with acid."

He retrieved the bottle and made a great production of tucking it back inside his jacket. "You don't wanna know. Secret men's business."

I snorted. "Fell off the back of a truck, more like."

His answer was a slow grin that highlighted his bad boy persona and tugged at my pouting bottom lip until I found myself grinning too. "Judging by the taste, it was a Hydrochloric Acid truck."

Tanya scuttled back into the room. "Hey, come on you two, enough of the pleasantries. Time for explanations." She dragged a chair across the floor and set it up beside Ben. "Okay, Kat. What's the story? By the look on your face when I opened the door, you've either found another dead body or come close to becoming one yourself."

The broken statue in my pocket dug into my hip, wrenching me away from the warmth and comfort of Tanya's kitchen and reminding me of the threat that wouldn't go away. I pulled the little boxer dog from its hiding place and let him rest on the palm of my hand.

"I found this in my bedroom tonight."

"And...?" Lines furrowed between Ben's eyes.

"*I* didn't break its ears off."

The furrows between Ben's eyes deepened. "If *you* didn't break it—who did? Tater?"

I shook my head.

His voice became steely. "Was someone in your house when you arrived home from the track?"

Oh God...I *had* to divulge the threatening phone call, otherwise how could I tell them the killer had broken into my bedroom again? But what if my mystery caller found out? What if he came after Tanya and Ben? What if he hurt them?

"Kat, you're not making sense."

I sniffed, wiped at my nose with the sleeve of my jumper. No way could I get through this alone. Sleuthing and being threatened by a madman seemed easy, all in a day's work, for Nancy Drew and Stephanie Plum—but that was fiction—this was for real. I took a deep breath and let it out in one long drawn-out puff. "Whoever killed Matt came back tonight and broke off the statue's ears to show how easily he could get to me."

"*What*?"

By the time I'd filled them in, Tanya's wall clock chimed midnight. I hefted the quilt up around my shoulders and snuggled deeper.

"And you have no idea who it was on the phone?" Tanya squashed herself into the armchair beside me.

I shrugged. "Could have been anyone. The postman, the guy who runs the video shop. For all I know, it could have even been our local politician. He covered his mouth with a thick scarf or handkerchief so I wouldn't recognize his voice."

"Don't worry," crooned Tanya, snuggling closer. "We'll work around that hurdle. All we have to do is go over what we already know and then make plans." She shot Ben a questioning frown. "Um...what *do* we already know, Ben?"

Ben used one finger to turn my head to face him. "Kat, listen. If that bastard came back tonight it means he had a key cut."

Nodding agreement, I shivered under the quilt.

"So get your locks changed, okay?"

"I'll ring a locksmith first thing in the morning."

"Do that." Ben's fingers slid slowly off my face as he let go and leaned back in his chair. "Now, if we knew what the devil Matt Turner was up to, maybe we'd have a motive for why he got himself killed."

I thought about the one and only night I'd let Matt talk me into going on a date. We'd ended up at the Two Wells pub for a meal, but instead of studying me, he'd spent the night studying the TAB betting fluctuations and watching the races on Sky Channel.

"We *do* know Matt was a mad punter," I said. "And he could give you the breeding and likely odds of any greyhound racing at any meeting held anywhere in Australia."

"That was our Matt," Ben agreed. "So whoever's behind this is probably mixed up with gambling. There's been some weird betting plunges at the track over the last couple of months. You know, short-priced favorites going down, long-shots getting up. What if the killer is the mastermind?

What if Matt double-crossed him?" Ben, eyes shining, seemed carried away with his own theories. "What if, on the night Matt was killed, his dog, Queen of Egypt, was supposed to lose? What if Matt thought, stuff you mate, and refused to give his dog a go-slow tablet like he'd been ordered?"

Tanya, a slight crease between her eyes, shook her head. "Bit drastic, don't you think? If everyone grabbed a bloody great kitchen knife whenever they lost money at the track and went around killing owners and trainers, there'd be no race meetings." She paused, playing with a loose thread on the corner of the quilt. "Kat, shouldn't we go to the police about the freaky guy breaking into your house again?"

"I can't. They wouldn't believe me. Probably reckon I made it up to take the heat off myself. And if the murderer found out I'd been to the police…" Cold shivers made me snuggle deeper under the quilt. "He'd come back and—"

Ben reached out, caught my hand and squeezed. "For now, we keep it between ourselves. But if he threatens you again, Kat, we go to the police and demand they give you protection. This guy is dead crazy."

I nodded. The warmth of Ben's hand the only thing keeping me sane. "Thanks, guys. I knew I could count on you."

"I'm all for finding this wacko and kicking his scrawny butt up through his nose," growled Tanya, burrowing closer.

I might be *soft in the head* but I had great friends. "What say I go to Matt's house tomorrow and pick up the rest of his dogs?" I suggested. "While I'm there, I could snoop around. Casual like. Maybe even find a way inside the house to see if I can dig up any clues."

"Make it in the afternoon and I'll meet you there," Ben offered.

"Me too," put in Tanya, her voice all gung-ho and enthusiastic. And then she tilted her head and frowned. "What sort of clues would we be looking for?"

"Come on Tanya, you've watched *CSI* on television," said Ben.

"Never. It's on the same time as *Survivor*."

"Okay, here's what we do. We check to see if Matt's conveniently left the killer's phone number on a pad beside his phone. Or a betting ticket in one of his pockets telling us he'd bet thousands on some long-priced dog that won. Or maybe he wrote everything down in a diary. Wouldn't that be a scoop? We could take the proof straight to the cops." He shifted in his seat and leaned forward, dark eyes fastened on mine. "Think hard, Kat, when the killer spoke to you on the phone, what exactly did he say about Matt?"

"Not much—just that Turner knew the consequences and he should have followed orders." At the time I was more worried about the next bit—the bit that went, *I'm sure you won't make the same mistake…."*

"Okay. So, we keep our ears open at the dog track. Find out who's been placing hefty bets on long-priced dogs that unexpectedly win. Next question—who do we know that's likely to be running a betting scam?"

"What about one of the bookies?" I lifted one shoulder. "They're the guys who drive BMWs while we rattle around in our fifteen-year-old bombs."

"Possibly…but since the TAB took over, bookies aren't copping it so sweet. Although, come to think of it, Big Mick Harrison's been on a winning streak. Did you see the grin he sported when Matt's dog, Cleo, won the last race at Gawler—as wide as the bloody City Centre."

Tanya nodded in agreement.

"What about a trainer? Or a steward?" I said thinking of Barney the starting-box steward. He'd seemed royally pissed off when Lucky stayed in the boxes.

"Or even an owner," Ben added then gave me a hard look. "What about Peter Manning? He's always throwing money around."

"You're sliding down the wrong pole there, Ben. Tire Man Pete might be a gambler, but his dogs are always out to win."

A tinny rendition of *Three Blind Mice* reverberated from the mobile stuck in the top of my jeans. Instantly my heart stopped beating, yelled *for-fuck's-sake-ease-up-I'm-getting-tired-of-all-this-scary-crap* before crashing around in my chest like an aggressive drunk. I threw aside the quilt and stared down at my phone. "What if that's the killer?"

Ben casually plucked my singing cell from my waistband and handed it to me. "Matt's killer doesn't know your mobile number. If he did, he wouldn't have rung you on your home phone earlier."

Still apprehensive, I pressed OK and placed the phone to my ear.

"Hi Kat, sorry to ring so late but—"

"Peter?" I glanced at Tanya and Ben. Was Peter Manning psychic? Did he know we'd just been bad-mouthing him?

Tanya and Ben leaned closer, hanging on my every word.

"Oh, good, you're still up," Peter went on like a train coming out of a station. "Saves me leaving a message. That greyhound I told you about, Big Mistake, he's due to arrive at ten tomorrow morning—or should I say—this morning. His ex-trainer rang me a half-hour ago. Reckons the dog suffers from claustrophobia and can't be left too long in a crate. I'm flat out all morning at the tire warehouse so is there any chance you can pick him up from the airport?"

"No worries, Pete."

"Great. He'll be on Virgin Blue, Flight 562 from Melbourne, due in at 10 a.m." There was a slight pause before he continued, his voice lowering conspiratorially. "And Kat, while I have you on the phone…I lost a bundle on Lucky tonight and I've forked over a substantial amount of money for this new dog for you to train…so…any way Shifty Sue will win a heat of the John Gray Memorial on Thursday night?"

"Jesus, Peter, there you go again—expecting miracles from me. How am I supposed to guarantee your dog will win? It's not like asking for a warranty on a used car, is it?"

His voice took on a chilly edge. "No need to get snarky. I only rang to see if you could collect the dog from the airport."

When he hung up I shoved the mobile back into my jeans, shook my head and gazed into four curious eyes.

"Well?" asked Ben.

"Peter wants his dog to win on Thursday night."

"Meaning?"

"Not sure."

Ben's lips tightened. "Well, I reckon it's high time we checked up on Tire Man Pete. See what he's up to when he's not selling tires."

8

NO WONDER PETER WAS WORRIED his new dog, Big Mistake, might burst from his cage. When I barreled into the cargo shed at Adelaide airport twenty minutes after the plane landed, I was greeted by the biggest greyhound I'd ever seen. And the ugliest. Feet splayed like a claw-bath, one ear up, the other drooping. And as for the Roman nose…I bet his mother even winced when she spotted *that* nose sliding from her womb.

"G'day, Lofty," I said, reading his nickname on the name tag attached to the door of his shipping crate. Immediately, the dog's kangaroo tail thumped against the wire, threatening to send the crate into orbit. His cavernous mouth opened revealing a wet, never-ending tongue and teeth the size of tombstones.

The freight attendant, grinning broadly, passed a document across the counter for me to sign. "Figure you might need a horse trailer to transport that one."

"I was thinking maybe I should hitch him to the car. Let him pull me home," I said and swung the door of the wire crate open. *Big mistake.* Planting a front paw on each shoulder, the excited dog proceeded to give me a sponge bath, seeking out the infinitesimal layers of dirt up my nose and deep inside my ears.

"*Down*, Lofty!" I told him, reaching around the tree-trunk neck to fasten a lead to his collar, all the time dodging that fat, slurping tongue.

When all four paws were back on the ground, I patted the big head and led the dog over to the station wagon. "Okay, in you go. Your carriage awaits you, big boy," I said, making with the cheery voice and encouraging hand gestures. "We can't hang around at the airport all day. I have plans to spy on your new owner."

Not quite ready to exchange one set of transport for another, Lofty dragged me to a nearby bush. And then, with a look of sheer ecstasy plastered on his face, he proceeded to rain on each and every leaf until I started to worry about the bush's welfare.

Bathroom duties attended to, the dog shook himself, scratched the dry airport dirt up over his back, then ambled toward to the car. One bound and he was inside examining his new mobile quarters. Evidently satisfied with the comfort of the thick blue mattress, he turned in three tight circles then settled down, his dinosaur head resting on powerful paws. I could see two large soft brown eyes watching me as I slid in behind the wheel.

After half an hour's driving through bumper-to-bumper traffic on the inner-city roads, it was a relief to hit the quieter Port Wakefield Road. Here, I could cruise at 80ks/hr, relax and attempt to calm my chaotic thoughts.

Since waking beside Matt's lifeless body, my thoughts had been like a piece of knitting caught on a barbed wire fence, knotted, snarled and so out of whack with reality that it would take a miracle to untangle them. My preferred miracle would be the killer slipping on his wet bathroom floor and breaking his neck. Of course the alternative solution wasn't quite so straightforward. It involved me as an amateur sleuth, tracking down and pursuing clues until I discovered the killer's identity.

As I drove past Globe Raceway, I slowed down. This was South Australia's new multimillion dollar multifunction complex where both the greyhound and harness racing codes shared state-of-the-art facilities. In fact, Globe Raceway was the best thing to happen to greyhound and harness racing in our state since the introduction of

TAB and Sky Channel.

From the roadway, I could see several harness horses jogging around a sandy outside training track while greyhounds, attached to their handlers by long leads, swum in a large circular pool nearby.

Once past, I forced my mind back to the present problem.

"Thing is…I'm in a bit of a sticky situation here," I told my silent travelling companion. "A friend of mine got himself killed last night and because he happened to be in my bed at the time—the authorities are inferring I might have had something to do with it."

Lofty gave a snort and I heard him shifting his bulk into a more comfortable position on the mattress behind me.

"You're right. Ridiculous idea. So it's *my* job to find out who did murder Matt."

Ice settled in my chest, as once again, I visualized myself asleep beside Matt. How close had I come to waking with a rough hand against my mouth and the pointy end of a knife slipping quietly and fatally into one of my main organs? Thank God the dogs woke me. And what if I'd come back into the room sooner and interrupted the killer in mid-kill?

Don't go there!

I inhaled deeply, held for ten and let all the nasty toxic thoughts filter out as I slowly exhaled. Feeling decidedly calmer, I continued to fill Lofty in on the story so far.

Further along Port Wakefield Road, a service station, advertising gas, hot food-to-go and ATM facilities came into view. I drove straight past. Three gaslights shone under the dash, my stomach wielded an out-of-order sign and my shaky bank balance couldn't take any spur of the moment withdrawals.

"So, Lofty," I said to my new best friend, "you can see why it's imperative I track down the real murderer. How else can I get the police off my back? Anyway, sleuthing can't be all that difficult. I've read books where frail old ladies and hairy guys with the IQ of an amoeba hit pay dirt. Me…I figure catching the crook is just a process of elimination." I eased back on the accelerator as my speed hit 100ks an hour. "Now, my mate, Ben, who I'd have sex with in a heartbeat if he'd only give me the nod, but that's another story, reckons whoever killed Matt has to be involved in some sort of betting scam. Ben says if we go after the big gamblers with a shovel we might dig up our killer. Get what mean?"

Lofty whined in his sleep.

"Now we all know your new owner, Tire Man Pete, would place a bet on two mosquitoes buzzing over a naked arm, which is why we plan to spy on him. Set up surveillance outside his warehouse. See if we can trick him into exposing whether he's part of the skullduggery going on at the track."

When Lofty's snores came close to lifting the roof of the station wagon, I shook my head. What the hell was I doing discussing strategies with a dog? Dogs couldn't keep up. Didn't offer much in the way of comments or suggestions either. Might be time I invested in a parrot. At least a parrot could talk back.

Fifteen minutes later I drove past the sign, *McKinley's Greyhound Kennels,*and parked my station wagon next to the red brick kennel-house. I could see Jake, my dude-helper, elbows deep in soap suds out the front. He was leaning over a bathtub shampooing Lucky. I guess he wanted her to smell nice now she'd changed her tag from racing dog to house pet.

"Everything okay here, Jake?" I slithered out of the driver's seat and opened the rear door for Lofty to heave himself onto the ground.

Hearing my voice, Lucky whisked her tail in the suds like an egg-beater, sprinkling white soapy flecks across Jake's black, dreadlocked hair. Made me think of coconut on licorice sticks.

Jake wiped at his eyes before reaching for a bucket of fresh rinsing water. "Yeah, fine, dude. A couple of plainclothes guys dropped in half-hour ago, but I acted dumb. They wanted to know where you were and when you'd be back."

"Damn," I grumped as I let Lofty into a nearby emptying yard to relieve himself. "What'll I do if they're parked up the road waiting for me? I can't let the police follow me to Manning's warehouse."

"It's okay dude, they cruised off back to the station after I told 'em you'd be gone all day. I said you had a couple of banks to rob and wouldn't be back till dark."

"You're a whacko, Jake."

"What's, like, going down at Manning's warehouse you don't want the cops to know about?"

"For your own safety the less you know the better. Let's just say I'm starting a new career—amateur detective."

"You?" He looked skeptical. "Hey, man, most days you can't, like, find your own car keys."

I gave Jake my most supercilious eagle-eyed glare. The one that involves narrowed eyes and flared nostrils. "Being chief suspect in a murder enquiry tends to make a person more perceptive." I watched him lift Lucky from the bathtub and wrap her in a thick bath towel. "So, if I'm gone for a while, will you be okay on your own?"

Jake nodded. "No worries, dude. Anything specific you want me to do?"

"When you've finished with Lucky can you ultrasound Cleo's right deltoid muscle?"

"Sure, man."

"And stand her wrists in ice water for five minutes then rub in that new red gunk Ben sent over. It's supposed to cure everything—or so he says."

"You'd better believe it!" Jake's metal-clad eyebrows almost connected with his head band and his cheeky grin alerted me to trouble.

Hmmm…did he know something about that horrible red gunk that I didn't? Better not to ask.

I pushed the secrets of Ben's vile smelling liniment from my mind and smiled down at Lucky. "Here you go, sweetheart." I fumbled around inside my pockets until I found an unfinished Snickers bar. Naturally it had hairs and bits of fluff stuck to it, but Lucky didn't seem to mind. Racing dogs are rarely allowed chocolate due to its caffeine content, which is probably why Lucky, new to the role of house pet, struggled to break free from Jake and explore my pockets for more of the same.

"Oh, and Jake, if you get time, ice Flynn's track leg. He can get a bit wimpy when he sees the icepack, but play his favorite Jimmy Barnes CD, *Shout!* and he'll stand for hours, no worries. Okay?"

"Roger and out, boss lady!"

Throwing a wet towel at Jake's head, I settled Lofty into his kennel with a bowl of milk, glucose and a dehydration mix.

Then flicked my magic cape and changed into Kat McKinley, Private Investigator.

9

I PARKED MY STATION WAGON BEHIND A cluster of thick bushes twenty meters up from Peter's tire warehouse. No one in sight—all clear and ready to proceed. Tanya had taken a couple of hours off work to cover the first shift while I collected Lofty. And figuring Peter would recognize our personal vehicles, our surveillance car was an ancient Holden Kingswood belonging to Ben's dad.

"Seen anything suspicious?"

Tanya jerked forward as though stung by a bee. Coffee sloshed from her open thermos onto her miniscule *French Connection* skirt. "Oh, geez…it's *you* Kat," she gasped, winding the window down. "Don't sneak up on me like that."

"Of course it's me. Who were you expecting, Jack the Ripper?"

"Not funny. There's a killer on the loose and we haven't a clue who he is."

"Any movement from Peter?"

"The only thing moving near that warehouse is the sign out the front and that's only because the wind's blowing. I don't know how Peter makes his money, but he sure doesn't make it selling tires."

"Perhaps the tires are a cover for something else."

"Like what?"

"Well, derr," I said, sounding exactly like *Devil's Spawn*, "that's what we're here to find out."

We quickly swapped cars, Tanya grumbling because although late for work she now had to go home and change her skirt.

"Why bother?" I said, burying a grin. "Just take the skirt off and wrap your scarf around your waist. No one will know the difference."

"Hilarious." Her glare could have burnt holes in steel.

After Tanya drove off in my car, I shifted Mr. Taylor's Kingswood further along the road and parked behind a sprawling bottlebrush. Being such a distinctive old heap, a passerby might get suspicious if the car stood in the same spot for too long.

From my new vantage point, I had a clear view of the front of the warehouse, but felt confident no one inside the building could see me. Satisfied, I started poking around the car's dashboard. Fair dinkum...it was out of the Ark. No CD player, no tape deck, no demister, no air-con and for some unknown reason, no windscreen wipers. I also discovered, very quickly, that there were more wire springs in the driver's seat than stuffing.

I wriggled my rear end until I found a more comfortable position. Things had been turning over at a mighty fast clip over the last twenty-four hours. There'd been no time to get my thoughts under control. Especially with the police overrunning the house, firing questions, taking my fingerprints, subjecting me to narrow-eyed suspicious looks.

I sighed. Twiddled the thick plastic wrapping on the end of the broken gear stick. I hadn't even had time to grieve for Matt. Until the killer was behind bars, there'd likely be no real closure. There again, if the killer wasn't caught soon, my friends could soon be grieving for me.

Bored, I tipped back in my seat, prepared to spend a couple of hours studying the exciting visual of wheat growing in a nearby paddock. I should be home working on the dogs. This surveillance stuff was a complete waste of time. What on earth did I expect our suspect to do? Run outside waving a large kitchen knife, yelling, "I did it! Come and get me!" Not likely. After all, I knew Peter Manning pretty damn well. Or I thought I did...until he'd indicated over the phone that he wanted a guarantee his dog would win. Or was I overreacting? Peter *always* wanted his dogs to win.

Almost asleep, I jerked upright, checked my watch for the umpteenth time and scowled at the silent warehouse. It was two o'clock. By now, Ben, using a fake foreign voice, should have rung Peter offering to sell him a new undetectable drug guaranteed to add ten lengths to a dog. If Ben had forgotten his part in the plan and was chatting on the phone to one of his bimbo girlfriends, I'd strangle him with his own telephone cord.

Another half-hour passed. I began counting magpies. Some strutted importantly along the grass verge of the road, others dug their needle sharp beaks into the dirt, searching for edible worms. The magpie-count had reached an astonishing twenty-eight, my stomach rumbled in the hope of being plied with food and if I didn't pee soon I'd end up ruining Mr. Taylor's leather upholstery.

Option one? Use the restroom in the petrol station half a kilometer down the road. I gnawed on my bottom lip. If I left my post now you could bet your last black jellybean Peter would be gone by the time I returned.

In desperation I cranked my crossed legs a couple of notches tighter.

Option two? A plastic ice-cream tub, chock-full of used golf balls, resided in the rear of Mr. Taylor's car. If I dumped the balls on the floor, I'd be left with an empty receptacle. I scanned the street. Not a movement. Not a sound. Even the magpies had deserted their roadside meal. Teeth clenched, unable to hold the inevitable off a moment longer, I clambered head first over the back of the seat, upended the golf balls and went for broke.

Oooh loverly....

No sooner had I released the floodgates than I heard a crash inside the warehouse. Bent double, ecstasy temporarily halted, I jerked my head up. Nooo! Not now! Peter Manning, shouting obscenities, came barreling through the front door of the warehouse. Frozen in midstream, I watched him fling his smartly attired bulk behind the wheel of his SUV, gun the engine and screech off down the road.

This wasn't supposed to happen.

Hair in my eyes, knickers digging into unmentionable cracks, I heaved myself over into the driver's seat, cursing all cars, killers, underwear and natural body processes.

By now, Peter's SUV had roared to the corner of the street and turned left, while I was still struggling to turn the key in the ignition. Come on. Come on. Start. After persuading the reluctant engine to kick over, I floored the accelerator. The Kingswood bunny-hopped forward, gathered speed like a tortoise with its legs tied together and then proceeded to "follow that car" at a sedate crawl. At the crossroads, anxious to see where Peter was heading, I heaved the steering wheel sharp left.

And winced.

Bugger…

Finger and thumb each side of my nose, I squeezed—just as the pungent scent of *eau-de-urine* flooded the Kingswood.

✲✲✲✲✲

Whatever was lodged up Peter's nose had him high-tailing it along the Two Wells to Gawler Road like a Formula One driver, minus the pit-stop crew. For a guy who was supposed to know his tires, he was hell bent on treating his own tread with utter contempt. If he didn't slow down soon he'd be out of sight and I'd lose him completely.

Even with my foot flat to the boards all I could coax out of the Kingswood was a sluggish 50ks an hour. May as well pull over to the side of the road and give the old car oxygen—attempt heart surgery—say a prayer over the body.

And then God looked down from heaven. He gave me a celestial wink and performed a miracle. On the road ahead, Peter's SUV Pajero did a screaming 180-degree turn and shot straight through the Taylor' open gateway.

Yessss!

Three minutes later, with a sinister hiss of smoke escaping from under the car's bonnet, I rattled along the same rocky driveway. In the paddocks on either side of me, doe-eyed cows munched cud while dreaming of whatever it is cows dream of. And daisies bloomed, their butter yellow petals rippling against a sea of irrigated pasture.

In sharp contrast, the scene taking place outside Ben's kennel-house looked anything but peaceful. Two combatants, both fine specimens of Aussie manhood but as different as fine Brie and Cheddar cheese, eyed each other off like snappy terriers over a bone. Peter, with his perfectly styled hair and matching blue tie neatly tucked inside the lapels of a dark Armani suitcoat, could have stepped straight from the pages of *Business* magazine. Ben with his slightly too long hair, dark stubble decorating his jaw, ripped jeans, scuffed work boots and a red-and-black checked shirt secured with one button, was an advert for VB beer.

I hopped from one foot to the other in a dance of indecision. Should I dive in between the two of them? Act as referee? Strip off my clothes in an attempt to distract? When we'd discussed setting a trap for Peter the night before, I guess we hadn't thought our plan through to its full conclusion.

I wasn't the only witness to this highly charged exchange. Ben's older brother Nick, his hands covered in either engine oil or black cow diarrhea, popped out of a nearby milking shed. He gave me a definite I'm-not-getting-involved-in-this, eye roll and just as quickly popped back inside again. Cindy, Nick's grey-muzzled sheepdog slunk under the tank-stand and lay, one eye open, one ear cocked forward, observing the fallout. While farm cats of every color and shape in the cat spectrum dove for cover.

"What the fuck do you mean by questioning my integrity?" Peter snarled, a vein pulsing in the side of his neck. Fine spittle sprayed from the corners of his lips as he spoke, exemplifying the up-until-now vague term, *foaming at the mouth.*

"Questioning your integrity? I don't know what you're on about, Peter." Without looking up, Ben dipped an old rag into a half full tub of Leather Combo and carefully applied the thick orange goo to the length of the dog lead he held in his hand.

"Don't play the innocent with me, Taylor. I know it was you."

"Sorry, mate. You've lost me."

Peter's hands closed into fists so tight each knuckle stood out like ribs on a skeleton. "So you're too much of a chicken-shit coward to admit it?"

Uh! Oh!

I watched Ben stretch his neck, slowly rotate his shoulders then place the lead over the hitching rail beside six others. He turned towards Peter and smiled. All teeth and no eyes. "Better watch it, mate," he warned, his voice as soft as the fur on a charging bull.

"Watch nothing!" Peter spat. "You're a dipshit, Taylor, and I'm going to knock that stupid grin off your face and into the next paddock."

Double Uh! Oh!

Ben's eyes flickered and narrowed. He carefully scratched behind one ear, his grin set in a concrete mask. "Look, I don't want to hurt you, mate." He carefully screwed the lid back onto the Leather Combo container and placed it on an outside shelf. "What say we go inside, grab a beer and talk about what's bothering you?"

"You can stick your beer up your ass!" Peter took two steps toward his opponent and pushed his puce-colored face closer. "Ever heard of caller ID…mate?"

Ben raised one eyebrow and glanced across at me with an expression on his face that clearly said…*bummer.*

I quickly made a mental note of our *faux pas* in my sleuthing diary.

Eyes chips of frost, Peter sent a thick yellow globule of spit dancing across the dirt. "Why ring *me*? Why pretend to be some foreign git instead of yourself?"

"Um…caller ID, eh? Fancy that."

"And why would you think I'd be interested in buying drugs?" Peter drew himself up to his full height, which was still a head shorter than Ben's six-two, and quivered. "Answer. Me. That." Emphasizing each word, Peter poked Ben in the chest three times.

May as well have tried breaking his finger on a brick wall.

"Watch it, mate." Ben's retaliatory shove sent Peter reeling backwards until he stumbled and went bum first in the dirt.

"Aw…Ben…I don't think you should have done that."

These guys were going to kill each other. Wringing my hands and saying, "Aw Ben" wasn't going to cut it. Ben's brother, Nick, was as much help as ice cream in a blizzard. And my fighting skills were up there with Pooh Bear's.

Peter sprang to his feet and immediately adopted the traditional boxing pose. Hands chest high, fists bunched, narrow eyes focused. For several minutes they danced around each other, huffing, puffing, snorting, spitting and trading testosterone vibes like a couple of ten-year-olds in the school playground.

"You're a prat, Taylor!"

"You're a thug, Manning!"

"*I'm* a thug?" Peter's voice skidded upwards. "You offer to sell me drugs and then call *me* a thug." Another phlegm-laden globule of spit hit the dust a few centimeters from Ben's feet.

Ben tossed an exploratory fist in Peter's direction and then danced backwards. "Does the name Matthew Turner mean anything to you?"

"Of course it does. We all knew Matt…" And then the subtext behind the question must have registered. Peter's jaw dropped. "You bastard—"

"Hey, come on. This isn't getting us anywhere. Break it up, fellas…" Palms face out in the global gesture of *I-come-in-peace*, I stepped between Ben and Peter at the exact moment Peter swung a lethal right uppercut. And somehow, on the upward arc, the point of my chin got in the way.

Or that's what Ben told me afterwards.

At the time, I didn't see the fist coming, can't remember the punch connecting and didn't feel my head bouncing along the asphalt.

It was pretty much good-night and sweet dreams….

10

I woke to a jackhammer excavating the inside of my skull, scooping out my brains and replacing them with burning coals.

Warily, I unglued one eye.

It was daylight. I was lying in a hospital bed. And a nurse was entering the room. I went to sit up but my head felt like every member of the Two Wells football team had kicked it during their recent Grand-Final match.

I lay down again.

The smiling nurse placed a water jug on the table beside my bed. I didn't return her smile. During the night, every time I drifted off to sleep, this blue-and-white starched figure complete with flashlight, thermometer and clipboard, appeared by my bed. Always with the same questions:

How many fingers am I holding up, Ms. McKinley?

What day is it, Ms. McKinley?

When did you last use your bowels, Ms. McKinley?

Still wearing her artificial smile like a badge, Florence Nightingale lifted a biro, poised it over her clipboard. "Good morning, dear. Sleep well?"

"Four fingers. It's Saturday morning. And not since you inspected the contents of my bedpan last time and commented on the size, consistency and color of the contents."

Undeterred, the nurse smiled at her clipboard, added three ticks then slipped a thermometer between my lips.

Why had I given in and let Ben drive me to the Gawler hospital? When I regained consciousness after being knocked out, I'd assured the dithering trio I was fine, just had a bit of a headache. But did the three wise men listen to me? You've got it. An apologetic Peter Manning, bowing and scraping and virtually promising me his first-born child, helped lift me into Ben's car while Nick handed me two frozen packets of Country Fresh baby peas. One for my jaw and one my head.

And two hours later, when the doctor shone a torch in my eyes, asked a few questions and decided to admit me overnight for observation, Ben was still by my side. Of course I told the doctor I couldn't accept his hospitality as I had dogs to feed. But Ben, being the good Samaritan he is, promised to send one of his own workmen over to help Jake, so I reluctantly agreed on the sleepover.

Florence Nightingale, still fussing beside me, brought me back to the present. "You're one of those greyhound training ladies, aren't you, dear?"

I nodded. What else could I do with a cylinder of plastic that tasted of disinfectant denting my tongue?

"We had a greyhound training gentleman admitted here last night. Looked like he'd been beaten up," she went on, puffing my arm up to near-bursting point with the blood-pressure gizmo. "He's next door, in room 32B. Name's Barney Thompson. Do you know him?"

The tall string-bean steward who operated the startingboxes at the track?

I spat the thermometer from my mouth. "Barney? Is he okay? What happened to him?"

"No, no, no," she protested, jamming the hard plastic tube back in place. Assured that the thermometer was cemented between my lips, she shook her head. "Mr. Thompson has a fractured skull, three broken ribs and a broken arm. He told the doctor he fell out of a tree, which doesn't make sense. I ask you, what tree inflicts bruises to over eighty percent of your body?"

I bit down hard on the plastic. This was getting scarier by the minute. Even stewards weren't immune. Had Matt's murderer put Barney Thompson in hospital? Or was the killer only one member of a well-organized gang?

Lots of questions. No answers. But one thing I did know—reclining in a hospital bed dressed in nothing but a starchy white gown with a dirty big slit down the back made me a sitting duck for anyone to walk in and blow me away.

I handed the thermometer to the nurse and swung my feet onto the floor. "Look, I'm fine," I told her, gritting my teeth against the sudden dizziness. "I'm checking out."

"The doctor will be doing his rounds in a couple of hours, dear. Let's see what he says, shall we?" She inspected the thermometer, wrote on her clipboard then placed a cold hand on my arm. "You have visitors waiting to see you, dear, so hop back into bed like a good girl and I'll let them in."

"Do my visitors have names?"

"It's that nice young gentleman who brought you in yesterday and a flashy woman dressed for the beach."

Tanya must be wearing two handkerchiefs stuck together with chewing gum. "Okay, I'll see them now, thank you."

"Back into bed first, Ms. McKinley," she said in that sickly sweet sing song voice nurses all over the world use on their patients, "or we'll have to tell your visitors to go away, won't we?"

I closed my eyes, allowed my imagination to run riot for a moment. Pictured a red-nosed circus clown riding a miniature bike into the room and knocking Florence Nightingale head first into a recently used bedpan.

Okay, bizarre, I know, but at least it stopped me from screaming.

"G'day, mate? Ready to go another three rounds?" I opened my eyes and couldn't help smiling. It was Ben. He'd brought the scents of the outdoors with him along with my favorite smell of dogs and early morning freshness. His long fingers, calloused but gentle, traced a line down my cheek before tilting my chin upward to get a better view of the damage. "You'd better have a good story ready," he advised with a wink. "No one's gonna believe you ran into a door."

The cool touch of Ben's fingers on my skin chased tingles up my spine. A sensation I knew I'd play over and over in my head, later tonight. But first, I needed to persuade my friends to help me escape.

"What took you so long?"

"And it's lovely to see you too," drawled Tanya who was definitely dressed in her work clothes. Miniscule denim skirt, six inch, knock 'em-dead apple red Fendi stilettos and a matching red halter top no bigger than a birthday card. She thrust a large packet of peanut M&M's at me, folded her arms and scowled. "What's with you, Kat? Are you suicidal? Why else would anyone step between two big bruisers intent on killing each other?"

"Cute nurses," Ben broke in before Tanya could get wound up any further. He tossed his akubra hat onto the bed and parked his butt in a chair. "Especially that nurse in reception. You know, the one with the eyelashes like hairy fish hooks. Tell you what, she could be a twin to—"

"Get me out of here!"

"Eh…hang on, mate." Ben blinked his confusion. "You have to wait for the doc to discharge you."

"Not an option." I swung both feet onto the floor, suddenly remembered the slit at the back of my gown that exposed more skin than I was willing to show in mixed company and dragged the sheet around me. "What if *the doctor's* the murderer? Everyone knows doctors are experts at using knives."

Ben and Tanya exchanged a wary, she's-losing-her-marbles glance then stared blankly back at me.

"I'm not going nuts," I assured them, dabbing at a layer of sweat dampening my top lip. "But I *have* to get out of here. While I'm in hospital I'm an easy target for both the psycho *and* the police. What's stopping the killer from sneaking into the room while I'm asleep and smothering me with a pillow? Or Columbo from barging through that door brandishing his handcuffs and reading me my rights? Don't you see?" My voice rose and I waved my arms in desperation. "I have to be free so I can prove my innocence?"

"Okay. Okay." There was a note of exasperation in Tanya's voice as she tried to sit on my bed. Her minuscule skirt prevented this maneuver so she perched on the edge instead. "Maybe you're not going nuts but you can't be serious about Dr. Bernard. How could you suspect him of being a murderer? He's a sweet, grey-haired, family man with eight children and twenty-three grandkids and he's almost ready to retire." She shook her head. "The reason I know is because one of his grandkids is a regular at The Luv Bug. Gavin's always trying out our newest gadgets—especially the male vibrators."

"Male vibrators?" Ben lifted one eyebrow and leant closer. *All ears,* as Granny McKinley would say. "Anything I might be interested in?"

"Benjamin, you do not need a vibrator. Vibrators are for those who *aren't* getting it. Now, Kat," she said, dismissing Ben with an eye roll and turning to me, "Dr. Bernard will be doing his rounds soon. Can't you at least wait until he gives you the all clear?"

I gripped the sheet tighter to stop my hands from shaking. "I'm scared," I whispered and sucked on my bottom lip. I wanted to go home. I wanted to lock myself in the house with a baseball bat and two dozen guard dogs. "Barney Thompson got beaten up and admitted to hospital last night."

"Barney? Beaten up?" Ben froze in the act of unfolding his body from the bedside chair.

"He's in the room next door with a fractured skull, broken ribs and a broken arm."

Tanya gasped. "Who did that to him?"

"Who do you think?" I chewed on a nail and nodded when Tanya's eyes widened, evidently on the same page as me. And then I remembered the task I'd set Ben the night before. "Ben, did you ask Peter where he was the night Matt was murdered?"

"We can cross Peter off our list. He was in Melbourne watching Big Mistake win the Puppy Championship at Sandown Park. He spent the night at the trainer's house and drove back to Adelaide the following morning." Ben gave a one-shoulder shrug as he straightened up. "He even made me ring the trainer to verify his alibi."

"Good. And did he accept our apology for doubting him?"

Ben's lips curled up at the corners. "I'd say he was more worried about you charging him with assault."

"Hey, it was an accident."

"Peter will be relieved to hear that," Ben said and rammed his akubra on his head. "Now, if they've attacked Barney, it's not safe to leave you here. Get your clothes on and we'll break ya outta the joint." Indiana Jones in grubby jeans, scuffed R. M. Williams' boots and a checked flannelette shirt with the sleeves rolled to his elbows. "I'll stand guard outside the door while you get decent."

When Ben left, Tanya's frown deepened. "Why would they do that to Barney?"

Before I could hazard a guess, Ben's familiar face popped around the doorway.

"If you need any help, give me a yell. You know—zips that won't zip, buttons you can't reach. And by the way, I'm a dab hand at hooks."

"Out!" Tanya growled and made a shooing motion with her hands.

The moment Ben closed the door I let my sheet drop to the floor. "Grab my clothes will you, Tan? They're in the cupboard."

While Tanya rescued my crumpled jeans and T-shirt, I shrugged out of the hospital gown and arranged two pillows under the blanket. In case Florence Nightingale paid another visit.

It took no more than three minutes to dress and rejoin Ben. Then, like three characters from a "Carry-on Detective" movie, we flattened our backs against the off-white corridor wall and crept forward. Edging past an X-ray room, I couldn't help noticing a huge colored poster displayed outside. Painted in glaringly graphic colors, it was the ugliest, sickest, creepiest picture of a clapped-out pair of lungs I'd ever seen.

Scary enough to put any sane person off smoking for life.

The corridors at this time of the morning were decidedly empty. We only spotted two people. An old man on a walking frame dragging a beeping machine behind him and a harassed looking doctor, so frazzled, so out of it, he wouldn't have noticed us if we'd been a bunch of green-skinned aliens with horns.

Almost to the end of the second corridor, with a tantalizing view of the hospital entrance, Ben came to a sudden stop. My face slammed into his back, almost adding a broken nose to my list of injuries.

"Sorry," he said and grabbed my elbow to keep me upright. "You okay?"

I rubbed my tender nose. "No thanks to you. Why are we stopping?"

"We have to go back. Talk to Barney before we leave."

"Why?" Remaining in this hospital a minute longer than necessary was way down on my priority list. Even below hammering nails under my finger nails.

"To find out who beat the crap out of him, that's why."

Ben had on his mule face. The face he presents to owners who tell him how he should train their dog—just before he asks if they also offer advice to the plumber as he's shoving an arm down their blocked toilet.

"But—"

"That way we'll know who to look out for."

"Who to steer clear of, you mean," muttered Tanya.

I knew when I was beaten but opted for one more shot at the prize. "But Barney's room is way back where we started."

"Elementary, my dear Watson."

"What if Florence Nightingale spots me?"

"McKinley, I'm surprised at you," Ben chided, shaking his head like a disappointed headmaster. "And here's me thinking you'd leap at the chance to sharpen your sleuthing skills."

"I'd rather go home."

"What if Barney can point us in the killer's direction?"

That's what worried me.

Room 32B was a mirror image of 32A, the room I'd recently vacated. Smooth off-white walls, dark grey and white tiled floor, functional cupboard in the far corner, hospital-issue metal bed pushed against the adjoining wall. In fact, Barney and I must have slept head-to-head during the night.

As we entered the silent room I took one look at the man stretched out on the bed and the fear roiling in my stomach became a tidal wave. His face was as white as the mummy-like bandage wrapped around his skull and his long string-bean body hardly made a bulge under the covers. Both eyes were blackened, and judging by the unnatural bend, the swelling around the top, and the dried blood clinging to both nostrils, his nose had obviously been busted. Monitors blinked busily beside the bed while intravenous drips snaked their way purposefully from a tall pedestal stand down to a multitasked needle implanted in his good arm. The other arm was thick with plaster.

"How's it going, mate?" Ben sat on the metal chair next to the bed, his powerful jean-clad legs stretched out in front of him, his bedside smile warm and comforting. Geez this guy did weird things to my insides when he smiled. Things that left me with an uncontrollable urge to sit on his lap, wrap my legs around his waist and kiss the stuffing out of him.

There was only one catch. I knew if I ever showed my real feelings Ben might instantly back-off, so I had to suffer in silence. At least, as a mate, there was always the chance that one day he'd look at me, suddenly discover a desirable woman under the freckles and messy hair and take me seriously.

Or *un*-seriously.

Or any damn way he liked—

As long as he *took* me.

Reluctantly, I dragged myself out of my fantasy world and returned to the stark reality of Room 32B, where I had a job to do.

"Barney, tell us who did this to you."

He opened his eyes, stared up at me, but didn't answer.

"What did he want you to do?" I gently straightened the sheet under Barney's chin. "Tamper with the starting boxes? Hide a cyanide cylinder inside the favorite's box?"

Whatever it was…Barney evidently hadn't followed orders.

"Kat?" I could read the fear in Barney's voice and see it in his bloodshot, half-drugged eyes. "Kat," he croaked again, a dribble of spit forming at the corner of his poor bruised mouth. "What are *you* doing here?"

"I asked you first, Barney. Who did this terrible thing to you?"

His head moved feebly from side to side and when he spoke his throat sounded drier than month-old bread rolls. "No, no," he protested. "I…fell out of a tree. Stupid thing to do. I was pruning…saw a bird's nest…baby had fallen out…tried to put it back in."

Ben lifted a glass of water to Barney's parched lips. "Come on, mate, you're among friends here. Tell us who beat the crap out of you and we'll pay the mongrel a visit. Remember, we've got a score to settle too. Turner's dead and McKinley's been threatened. We need to stop this scumbag once and for all." He placed the glass back on the bedside stand, never taking his eyes off the man in the bed. "Did you recognize the guy who beat you up?"

"I-I told you… fell out of a tree." He closed his eyes, either to sleep or shut out any more questions.

Tanya, whose job it was to stand guard outside, poked her head into the room. "Let's go, guys. Nurse approaching from due north."

Ben unfolded his long frame from the hard metal chair, said goodbye to Barney and strode across to the doorway.

Before following, I patted the steward gently on his good arm. "I hope you feel better when you wake up, Barney."

His eyes opened. "Be careful, Kat," he croaked, his voice barely loud enough for me to hear. "Whatever they ask—do it! They're like animals. No…worse than animals."

I felt an arctic chill slice into my heart as it pounded against my ribcage. "They?" I repeated slowly. "I thought there was only *one* psycho. Who do you mean by *they*? Barney, you've gotta tell me. I need to know who's out to get me."

As though he'd been pricked by a pin and lost all his air, Barney's eyelids closed and he lost consciousness.

"Kat!" Tanya grabbed me by the arm and towed me to the door. "The pillow under the blanket trick didn't work. The nurse knows you're missing. Unless you want to sign out, we have to go."

"But—"

"Ms. McKinley? If you are hiding in the bathroom I insist you come out now."

Oh, hell! It was Nurse Nightingale on the warpath.

One last glance at Barney's pasty face and I dashed from the room. After what happened to Matt, and now Barney, I figured I'd need more than Tater and Lucky to protect me from the bad guys. I'd need a brace of ferocious Dobermans, a dozen Rottweilers and a pack of poodles hyped up on Speed.

Stepping from the dehumanizing air of the hospital into the noisy but colorful street, with the roar of cars, the swish of buses and the rush of people on their way to work was like stepping from winter into spring. I drew in a lungful of lovely crisp morning air, held it until the hospital crap disappeared from my lungs and then slowly let it out again. I figured hospitals were fine for visiting—but not for staying in.

Thing is, there was someone out there, or in Barney's case, some faceless *they,* who got their kicks from filling hospital beds—or even worse—adding to the body count at the morgue.

11

By the time Ben dropped me home, Jake was hard at work. He'd let the first six dogs into emptying yards and I could hear him singing along to something on his iPod while mopping out their kennels. What a doll. Hey, if my dreadlocked assistant was a few years older I'd ask him to marry me. That is—older—with a *real* job—the English language according to normal—and oh, yeah, a fashion sense that didn't include beads, ear-piercing and sequined head bands.

"Hi, Jake," I yelled, snaffling leads from their numbered hooks on the wall and looping them over my arm. I had to yell to be heard over the din. The moment I entered the kennel-house every dog wanted to tell me their life story. "Sorry you got left to do all the work last night. I suppose Ben filled you in on what happened."

Jake's silver rings shimmied along with his eyebrow. He grinned. "Lucky punch, eh?"

I gave him a serious *I-don't-want-to-talk-about-it-now-or-later* frown and switched on the mechanical walking-machine. It paid to warm up the motor before attaching the dogs to the equipment.

"Any problems while I was away?"

"Verity, like, came in season."

I almost stamped my foot. "Blast. I'll have to scratch her from Monday night's race. And just when she finally drew box 8." Verity was a wide runner and I'd been waiting weeks for an outside trap so the owners, a syndicate of enthusiastic young guys from the local soccer club, could have a decent bet on her. "The boys will be peed off big time," I growled.

Exasperated, I bulldozed this last piece of crappy news to the back of my mind and buried it amongst the growing pile of angst already littering the area. No time to think about it now. Instead, while fastening collars and leads to the dogs due for a free gallop that morning, I told Jake about Barney's *accident.*

Jake's eyes rounded when I described the starting-box steward's injuries. "Wow, man. That's creepy. You're not, like, hanging around here by yourself tonight are you?"

The word *hanging* didn't sit well in my already troubled mind.

"Guess so."

What was the alternative? It was fine sleeping at Tanya's for one night but with a team of valuable racing dogs in my care, my first priority was to keep them safe. Who knew what the killer might do next? What if he broke into the kennel-house and shot the ears off some *real* dogs? I started to shiver, stroked the ears of the closest greyhound, a smiling black-and-white bitch with wickedly dancing eyes, as though by putting my mark on her ears, nothing bad could happen to them. I vowed vehemently that as well as changing the locks on my house, my kennel-house would be locked up tighter than the State Bank in future.

"I've been thinking," I said. "Perhaps I should have something a bit larger than Tater to protect me. You know, until this all blows over. Is Lucky ready to come inside the house yet?"

"Lucky? For protection?" Jake's rolling eyes said it all.

"A promise is a promise. She's now a pet." I let out a heavy sigh. "But I guess you're right. If a black-hearted villain snuck in while I was asleep, Lucky would wash the guy's face, offer him one of her treasured chew-bones and then lead him to the family silver—or me. Whichever the villain requested."

Jake stopped mopping the concrete floor to scratch thoughtfully at his earlobe. His skinny dreadlocks, stiff with sweat, grazed the neckline of his scruffy T-shirt, which proclaimed in faded red letters: *Every drip counts*. "What about your Ma, dude? Could she stay with you for a couple of weeks?"

I shook my head.

Ma had left for a trip to Hawaii twelve months earlier with her latest catch, Dwayne, a weedy little man with a huge voice and an even bigger bank account. After Hawaii, they'd decided to keep going. Probably partying somewhere in Europe as we spoke. Anyway, even if available, my mother wouldn't come within ball chucking distance of, in her words, dirty smelly greyhounds. Her horrified shriek, "*Greyhound trainer!*" expressed with the same revulsion as if I'd said, "*Prostitute!*" when I told her what I intended doing with the money Dad left me in his will, still rang in my ears. As for Dwayne, her pint-sized lover, he'd be less protection than Tater. Blow on the guy and he'd drift off into space—never to be seen or heard of again.

Jake wasn't done yet. "Any brothers or sisters you can call on?"

That question earned another negative head shake.

Elizabeth, my only sibling, had run away from home at sixteen. Couldn't stand Mum's constant nagging. Before Dad's death, he had always been the one to smooth things over between Mum and Liz, but after he died, my sixteen-year-old sister refused to stick around. It was as though Mum took all her frustrations out on Liz, continually pecking away like a bird at a worm. So the day after Dad's funeral, the worm turned. Liz packed her bags, entrusted me with her favorite ruby necklace as a keepsake and caught a northbound bus out of our lives.

Now, at twenty-one, Liz lived in a hippy commune somewhere in outback Queensland. Well that's where her last postcard came from— almost six months ago. Liz shifted around so much I had to rely on her infrequent correspondence to keep up with her whereabouts. However, the letters I'd posted off since then had been returned with *not known at this address* scrawled across the front, so God knows where she lived now.

Jake squeezed the water out of his mop and leaned on the handle, evidently still endeavoring to come up with a suitable candidate. "What about cousins? Grandparents? Uncles?"

At each suggestion I shook my head. They were either dead, living in another state, or ostracized by *Ma*.

"No worries, man," Jake declared, his pigeon-sized chest visibly swelling. "Just leave it to me. I'll sort it."

I bit my lip to stop from laughing out loud. "No offence, Jake, but you're skinnier than I am. One half-hearted punch and you'd be out for the count."

"I don't mean *me*, man. You know I'm not into physical stuff. I'm a peaceful protester." He paused then nodded thoughtfully. "No…I have someone *else* in mind."

My grin quickly faded. "Who?"

"As I said, leave it to me."

Somehow that didn't make me breathe any easier.

With six greyhounds straining on the ends of their leads, I made my way toward the 200 meter galloping runs at the rear of the property. Or should I say, flew to the back runs like a kite attached to six strings, my feet barely touching the ground. Once there, I let each bouncing, barking, let-me-at-'em canine into a separate sandy run and left them to gallop up and down in a competitive effort to outdo each other, thereby maintaining racing fitness.

Leads dangling around my neck, I hurried across to the emptying yards. The greyhounds in these much smaller yards were now due for their twenty-minute walk to nowhere on the treadmill inside the kennel-house.

There were dogs to bathe, dogs to treat with different electrical appliances, dogs to check for injuries, dogs whose toenails needed clipping, dogs to visit the vet, dogs that needed a special cuddle…

It was almost three o'clock in the afternoon before I found time to ring Ben and Tanya and arrange to meet them at Matt's house. There were three of Matt's dogs to pick up so I hooked the dog trailer to the station wagon and opened the car door. Before I could slither in behind the wheel, Tater, determined to accompany me, launched his peanut-sized body in the air, skidded across the leather and braced himself, ears cocked, on the passenger seat ready to go.

Our first scheme—tempt Peter Manning with the offer of undetectable drugs—had ended badly. We'd pissed off Peter and I'd spent the night in hospital. Hopefully, our next initiative—search for clues in Matt's house—would end on a more productive note. Like a signed confession from the murderer tucked inside one of Matt's racing form guides.

Okay, I'm the first to admit, the role of amateur sleuth was a lot trickier in real life than it appeared in books. However, if I didn't want the police to roll up, red and blue lights flashing, handcuffs at the ready, I needed to soak up the entire condensed version of *How to Catch the Bad Guys 101* in the time it takes for Ben to eat a family-sized pizza.

On arriving at Matt's semi-detached, red brick, housing-trust home, I dragged the heavy galvanized iron side gate open and let Tater trot through in front of me. Tail arched over his back, ears on red alert, the little dog strutted along as though rescuing orphan greyhounds and hunting for clues were all in a day's work. Frenetic bouncing, barking, and tail-wagging from the three kennels along the fence line greeted us. Although a friend of Matt's had promised to feed the dogs, they were bored, lonely and craving attention.

I called Tater to my side and strolled toward the back door, to all casual appearances as though I had nothing on my mind except watering Matt's flowers, collecting his post, being a good friend. That is, until I found myself surrounded by a satiated swarm of buzzing blowflies. What the heck? I stopped. And that's when I noticed the source of their unflagging interest. Shoved hard against the back door of Matt's house was a large, green, graffiti-covered wheelie bin. It was emanating a stench so gross, so vile, it made raw sewerage smell like desert.

One hand completely covering my nose I approached the wheelie bin with caution. Did I *really* want to know the cause of that horrible stink? What if there was a severed head inside the bin? Mutilated fingers? Or even an entire body bent double, limbs broken? Heart careering like a motorboat at full throttle, I lifted the lid with the end of the garden rake and flipped it wide open.

Eeeuw!

Rotting kidneys, liver, chicken legs and some furry thing I couldn't recognize with a family of fat, wriggly, white worms picnicking on the entrails, greeted me. Tater indicated he wouldn't mind checking the contents of the bin more closely if I'd just be good enough to give him a bit of a hoist. I told him, no way, and with fingers still clutching my nose leaned across the bin and tested the knob on the back door.

Locked.

Cautiously, I slid my eyes over my shoulder. One never knew when a nosy neighbor might peer over the fence. If they noticed Tater and me investigating they might decide to be a model citizen and ring 000. No neighbors in sight, nosy or otherwise, so I made my way around the side of the house and checked the catches on the windows. Tater, after another sniff of the wheelie bin, wandered off to water a couple of sickly looking rose bushes growing beside the fence. Probably thought the acidity might revitalize them.

No window catches undone. The blinds on the windows were all drawn. And the only open window led into the laundry. However, being no bigger than a cereal box, the window was way too small for me to squeeze through.

What now?

In the past, whenever Matt entered dogs at a country race-meeting, like Port Pirie, Barmera or Port Augusta, he'd arrange for me to feed those dogs left behind. Could the spare key to his front door still be under the doormat? Hey, it was worth a try.

I whistled Tater, who'd gone on to test his acidity theory on the carnations, the geraniums, a rusty watering can without a spout and a three-legged deck chair and marched around to the front of the house. The heavy rope doormat was in its usual place beside a potted Winter's

Joy. Scenting success, I bent forward and hefted the mat away from the front door. Half an inch of dirt...but no key.

Plan B already formulating in my mind, I peered at the keyhole to ascertain what size wire I'd require to pick the lock—and did a double take.

Matt's front door had been jimmied.

Stomach twisted in a knot, I touched the door with the palm of my hand, watched it swing open and stood staring at the empty landing. Beside me, Tater growled. The tiny hairs along his back stood up. As though challenging an invisible foe, he cocked his head to one side, blinked his little black button eyes and swaggered in through the open doorway.

"Tater! Don't go in there!" I yelled to the tip of his tail as it disappeared into the nearest room.

Damn dog. Now I had to go in after him. If the intruder was inside he'd swat Tater like an annoying insect. I flattened my back against the wall and edged forward, eyes and ears alert for the slightest sound or movement. What I needed was one of those cute little designer guns. Which led me to thinking, where *does* a female P. I. hide her gun? Too bulky and unflattering for the waistband of a skirt. Also too dangerous if the thing went off. The mind boggled at what it could hit. And stashing the gun in a handbag wouldn't work for me. By the time I rummaged through bars of chocolate, hairbrushes, the latest John Francombe novel, a packet of condoms (one never knew when Ben might discover I was a girl), bits and pieces of make-up...

Well, hell, I'd be dead and I wouldn't need the gun then, would I?

Heart banging like the lead drummer's sticks at a rock concert, I inched along the wall until I came to the first doorway, poked my head around the corner. And my jaw dropped.

Holy catfish...

The room had been thoroughly and violently trashed. I inhaled deeply, held onto my breath and listened for sounds of an intruder. All I could hear was the *click-click-click* of Tater's sharp toenails trotting back from the kitchen, a smile on his lips and a thick dollop of strawberry jam on the tip of his nose.

I let my breath whoosh out through my nose and surveyed the mess. If the violator was still inside the house, my jammy-nosed watchdog would have flushed him out by now. DVDs had been hurled against the wall, sofa cushions slashed, dresser drawers upended, books and magazines ripped apart, ornaments smashed, bottles shattered. Even Matt's dog-racing photos had been wrenched off the wall, frames splintered and glass cracked.

Had mild-mannered Matt thrown a temper tantrum before attending the dog meeting the night he was killed? Perhaps he'd experienced a bad day's punting. Or won and then lost his winnings through a hole in his pocket.

On legs that shook like autumn leaves on a windy day, I stumbled from the lounge into the kitchen. It too was a shambles. Pots, pans, cutlery, broken crockery and bottles scattered everywhere. Sugar, mixed with crushed biscuits, honey and chocolate flavoring carpeted the floor. Chairs overturned. Tins of fruit, assorted jams, packets of soup, pasta and breakfast foods decorated the linoleum. Even Matt's precious stack of form-guides filed and religiously notarized, had been ripped, screwed up, and deposited in the middle of a thick sludge of strawberry jam.

I stumbled back into the lounge, blinked at the chaos again, and attempted to make sense of it all. Had the police been searching for evidence? But even as the thought crossed my mind, I dismissed it. No cop would make a mess like this and stay on the force long enough to claim his pension.

I guess the reality was slow to hit, but when it did, I slumped against the wall, suddenly bone weary and in need of support. The same vicious madman who'd killed Matt, threatened me, and put Barney in hospital had been at work again.

But what was he looking for?

A sudden intake of breath behind me sent my heart jerking like a frog on a hot rock. I spun around, both fists clenched and ready for action, only to find Tanya in the doorway.

"*Son-of-a-bitch!*" she gasped nudging aside the remains of a broken coffee table with her boot. "Who let the hippos loose in here?"

"Doesn't look like the work of kids, does it? Or a burglar. Too systematic."

Tanya bent to pick up a torn photo. It was a picture of a grinning Matt, his arm around one of his greyhounds. "D'ya reckon they found what they were looking for?"

They again. The faceless *they*. The *they* who had me spooking at shadows.

The violence of the vandalism impossible to get my head around, I shrugged a vague *how-should-I-know?*

"It's a wonder the neighbors didn't ring the police."

"Probably didn't want to get involved," I said.

I rescued a CD from the floor. *Dancing Queen*. Matt was such an old Abba fan. Sadly, I slotted the CD back into the empty rack. "If they were looking for something important—why kill Matt? You can't get information from a dead man."

"Perhaps they found what they were after and then followed him to your place and killed him."

"Or perhaps Matt wouldn't tell them where it was hidden so they killed him and came back here to search for it." I gazed around the room, shook my head, bewildered. "All I know is whoever did this was either very thorough or very pissed off. And you know what? Both *thorough* and *pissed of f*scare the crap out of me. I feel like I've been caught in a giant washing machine, set on a permanent spin cycle and I don't know how to get out."

Sensing my distress, Tater trotted across the room and rubbed his warm body against my ankles.

Tanya gave me a hug. "Hey, you're not on your own, girlfriend," she assured me. "Not when you have Ben and me as sidekicks. We'll kick butt, kick heads, kick balls—whatever it takes to keep you safe." She gave me another hug then moved off toward the kitchen. "But first, if I dig up a kettle, can you unearth a jar of coffee and two cups? Dunno about you, but I'm gasping for a hit of caffeine. When Ben decides to get his ass over here we'll get down and dirty and conduct our own search. Okay?"

Tater's wet cold nose prodded my ankle so I lifted him up for a cuddle, transferring strawberry jam and pickles from his face to my T-shirt in the process. One hug and he wriggled to get down again. I set him on the floor and sent a grin in Tanya's direction. Okay, a weak grin—but at least it *was* a grin. The image of my best friend, all petite 52 kilos, kicking some big gorilla's family jewels with the shiny black toe of her Marc Jacob boot went a long way towards extinguishing the nervous tension playing hopscotch in my stomach.

I stooped to set two overturned chairs right side up beside the table. "I wonder what they were after."

"Money probably."

"Maybe it was betting tickets."

She nodded. "Could be. What if Matt bet a pile of their money on a winning dog and now they're hunting for the betting tickets so they can collect their loot? As I said, it's usually about money."

"Or maybe the murderer was making sure Matt hadn't left any incriminating evidence that pointed directly at him."

While Tanya filled and plugged in the kettle I sorted through jars on the floor until I came across one that resembled coffee.

"Damn…it's generic," I grumbled, wiping sticky globs of honey and jam off the label with a damp cloth.

"Typical." Tanya took the jar from me and unscrewed the lid. "Men have absolutely *no* appreciation of fine beverages." She peered inside the jar and her nose wrinkled. "And wouldn't you know—the coffee's stale. It's all lumpy. How could Matt drink this garbage?"

Luckily, I knew where Matt hid his booze. "Fancy a drop of brandy to make the coffee drinkable?"

"Do nuns wear rosary beads?"

Taking that as a yes, I went hunting for the perfect lump-dissolver. The bottles behind Matt's bar at the far end of the lounge were smashed but there was a bottle of *St. Agnes*, with a few inches of liquor left in the bottom, in its usual hiding place at the bottom of the laundry basket in the bathroom.

"Ta dah!" Grinning inanely, I plunked my booty in the centre of the kitchen table and straddled a kitchen chair. "Let's rock and roll."

"Bloody hell!"

I looked up to find Ben Taylor filling the doorway, eyebrows up around his hairline.

"You chicks throwing a party?" he quipped. "Or have I interrupted a premenstrual temper tantrum? If so—I'm outta here."

Even scowling, Ben looked sexy. Although, to be honest, it was probably the fact that the top three buttons of his shirt were undone and the tempting flashes of smooth tanned skin peeping out from under a fine sprinkling of dark hair made me clench my stomach and sit on my hands. He'd also changed out of his grubby work jeans. Now his legs were encased in pale moleskins, so soft, so creamy-colored and so formfitting, they should be illegal.

"About time you showed up." Tanya, evidently unaffected by this mythical vision of manhood, scrounged another unbroken cup from the clutter on the floor and waved Ben inside. "Well, don't just stand there gawping like a fish on a line, Benjamin. Come in and join our Upside-down House party. I'm afraid all we have to offer is lumpy generic coffee—with or without a dash of brandy—but you're welcome to partake."

"Nah. Knock yourselves out. I'll have a poke around, see what I can find." He strolled across the room, sugar crunching under his boots with every step.

While Ben explored the kitchen and Tanya and I sipped coffee and offered advice, Tater, looking all-important and official, came trotting into the room. He dropped a rotten banana at Ben's feet then sat and grinned up at him.

"Well, thanks little mate." Ben bent to scratch the dog behind the ears. Tater sniffed Ben's boots then stretched up and licked the exposed skin between the top of his boot and the bottom of his moleskins. Which made me *sooo* jealous. Perhaps I should go find Ben a rotten banana too. Being so much taller than Tater, I could lick a lot higher. As the thought of what I could lick slid from my brain to a lower part of my anatomy, I caught my breath.

Ben flicked a puzzled frown in my direction.

Oh God… was my tongue hanging out? Was drool running down my chin? Was I that obvious?

"If Matt left a clue it sure as hell won't be here now," he said. "Whoever ransacked this joint gave it a thorough going over."

I let out a deep frustrated sigh and banged my coffee cup on the table. Ben Taylor wouldn't pick up on *obvious* if it was frozen solid and shoved down his throat. "Maybe," I grumbled. "But I still think we should do what we came here for."

Tanya drained the last of her coffee, scraped her chair backwards and stood up. "I'm with Kat. I say we follow through with our original plan."

"If that's what you want, let's do it."

We split up. Tanya took the bedroom, Ben the bathroom and laundry and Tater and I decided to look for clues in the lounge.

Five minutes into our search Tanya drifted from the bedroom, a pair of iridescent blue underpants featuring naked women in various obscene poses in one hand, a fluffy stuffed animal that could have been either a horse with a long neck or a stunted giraffe in the other. "Does anyone have any idea of what we're searching for?"

"Beats me." Ben's muffled voice came from the bathroom. "But I guess we'll know if we find it."

Recessed into the far wall of the lounge room was a brick fireplace with the charred remains of a fire in the hearth. I picked up a blackened poker and jabbed at the grate, scrabbling around in the ashes. Who knows? I might find a half-burnt diary with all the good bits still intact.

Or important letters. Or pages of a confession. In the last cozy mystery I'd read, *Murder at Mistletoe Manor,* vital evidence pertaining to the identity of the killer had been discovered in the fireplace. In that story the butler did it—naturally—although I had a suspicion no self-respecting butler would come within ten miles of Matt's house.

I blew at my bangs and leaned the poker up against the wall. The only burnt paper in Matt's fireplace was an unpaid bill from a storage depot. Absently, I picked it up by one corner, shook off the worst of the ashes and stored the remains in the side pocket of my tote bag. Probably nothing. Then not knowing where to look next I flopped onto Matt's cracked brown vinyl settee to think. What had I missed? Scratching my head, I ran analytical eyes over the room. Hmm. What about Matt's answering-machine? Perhaps if I could find his land-line there might be something worth listening to on the machine.

After burrowing into the mess like a terrier after a rat, I discovered the missing phone hidden under a brandy stained throw rug. Eager to hear any messages, I plugged it in and switched on the machine.

Silence…

Damn. The police—or whoever was responsible for this disaster—must have either wiped it clean or taken the tape.

"No clues in here and there's nothing on Matt's answering machine," I yelled and took a sip of cold coffee before spitting it out in disgust. "What about you guys?"

"Nada," came from the bedroom.

"Bugger all in here," Ben informed us from the laundry.

"Okay, you were right," I informed Ben as he trundled through the doorway, wiping grease from his hands onto a towel. "If there were any clues to start with, they're well and truly gone now.

"You know, what we really need to find is Matt's mobile," Tanya mused as she wandered into the room.

"Good thinking, Watson." Ben slung his arm around her shoulder. "Then we'd know who he's been ringing."

"And who's been ringing *him*," Tanya finished, grinning like the proverbial cream-devouring cat.

Ben turned to me and I sidled closer. "Hey, mate," he said completely ignoring my proffered shoulder. "Can you remember if Matt had his cell phone with him on Wednesday night?"

Humph! No hug for me. Just *mate*. With a sigh, I thought back to when Matt and I returned from the Gawler race meeting. We fed the dogs and settled them in the kennel-house for the night. He talked me into letting him come inside for a coffee. I tossed my jacket on the chair. Matt hung…

"It's in the cupboard in my hallway! Matt's mobile is in the pocket of his sheepskin coat and his coat is hanging in my hallway cupboard."

"Well what are you waiting for?" Tanya grinned.

"You do realize," put in Ben, rubbing one hand across the beginnings of his five o'clock shadow, "if Matt's coat was in the cupboard at Kat's house, the cops have likely confiscated it by now."

I watched Tanya deflate like a pricked balloon at a kid's party.

"It's okay, Tan," I told her barely suppressing a whoop. At last something was going right for us. "Matt's coat is still there. I noticed it hanging next to my Drizabone when I grabbed my parka this morning."

12

ALL THOUGHTS OF MATT'S MOBILE SKITTERED from my mind the moment I pulled up outside my gateway. There was a black Chrysler parked less than three meters from my front door. It hunkered down like a large cat waiting patiently beside a mouse hole. I had the sudden urge to twitch my whiskers and let out a frightened squeak. Instead, I narrowed my eyes to examine the dark figure using the car's bonnet as a prop. Was my visitor a professional knee-breaker? A hit man hiding a pair of cement boots under the back seat of his car?

The more questions I asked—the tighter my fingers clenched the steering wheel.

From the roadway side of my open gate, I eyeballed the intruder more closely. Short and scruffy. Smoking a cigarette. Dressed in a long daggy overcoat…

Columbo.

For a split second I was tempted to flatten the accelerator, do a three point turn and make a break for it. But even if I managed to escape— where would I hide? And who'd look after my dogs?

And hey, bottom line…*I was innocent!*

I parked as close to the black car as I could without actually staving in its rear end and switched off the engine. With Tater sitting expectantly on my lap, tongue out, ears up, I wound down the window and put on my smiley face.

"Well, isn't this a pleasant surprise, Inspector?"

When he didn't answer I shook my head at him in mock disapproval. "I see you're letting those nasty cigarettes rot your lungs again."

He shifted his body against the side of his car before taking another long blissful puff.

"So, what brings you to my neck of the woods?" I went on, desperate for a response. Was he stringing me along, softening me up for the sudden flash of handcuffs? "Let me guess." Although digging my nails into the palms of my hands I kept the smiley face in place. "You've found Matt's murderer, you've arrested him and now you're here to apologize for any inconvenience you've caused me. Am I right?"

The Inspector ground his cigarette out on the sole of his shoe, dropped the butt in his pocket and strolled across to my open window. The closer he came to the car, the louder Tater growled.

"Good afternoon, Ms. McKinley. I'm surprised you remember me. Last time we met, you were a little…shall we say—"

"In shock?"

"Yes. That too." The corners of his mouth flickered. "However, in case you've forgotten, I'm Detective Inspector Garry Adams." He produced his credentials and flashed them under my nose. "And this," he turned around to indicate a steely-eyed policewoman, who had slithered out of the black car, "is Police Constable Belinda Chalmers. Do you remember her?"

Remember her? Geez, how could I forget? Tater had ankle-raped the woman in my bathroom the morning of Matt's murder—and surprise, surprise—she still looked like she was sucking on a lemon.

"Out of the car, McKinley."

When I didn't jump to her bidding Police Constable Belinda Chalmers adjusted her police-issue hat at a more aggressive angle. Her eyes bored into mine. "I *said*…out of the car, McKinley."

The woman's hostility was so potent I could smell it.

DI Adams flicked a warning frown at his subordinate before opening the car door for me. "If you don't mind, Ms. McKinley, I'd like to ask you a few more questions. And as to your earlier query, no, we haven't arrested anyone yet, but we're working on it."

Did that mean I'd slipped down his list of suspects? Or he was here to officially hammer the final nail in my coffin? Muscles tense, I grabbed the open car door ready to swing my feet to the ground and that's when I noticed the policeman's gaze resting curiously on my face.

"What is it, Inspector?" I asked, rubbing at the corner of my lips. "Lipstick smudged? A dollop of mayonnaise left over from my lunchtime sandwich?"

"Forgive my curiosity. It's just…shall we say…you look…a little rumpled."

"Rumpled?" What sort of a word was *rumpled*?

He nodded then his eyes travelled slowly downward until they rested on my clothes. "Did you find what you were looking for?"

"Huh?"

How did he know I'd been looking for clues in Matt's house? What was he—a psychic?

"Have you been sorting through someone's garbage?"

I shook my head, totally offended. "Of course not."

I'd given that special job to my mate, Ben.

Curious as to what Columbo was on about, I adjusted my rear vision mirror and squinted at my reflection. The face squinting back at me had smudges of black soot on both cheekbones, another smudge on my nose—and were those streaks of sauce, strawberry jam, or blood in my hair?

I transferred my gaze from the mirror to my clothes. *Rumpled*? Geez…I could have taken out the Bag Lady of the Year award. It didn't make sense. How come I was the only one with jam and soot on my T-shirt? No wonder Ben pitched his arm around Tanya's dirt-free shoulder and gave mine a miss.

Embarrassed, I scrubbed at my face with a spit-wet finger and took another peek in the mirror. Now I looked like one of those boot-camp guys. The ones in camouflage gear who hide in the bushes and load paint-bombs ready to take out the enemy.

"Shall we go inside, Ms. McKinley?" the Inspector persisted. "I have a few more questions for you."

Standing ramrod straight beside him, PC Chalmers' sour smirk reminded me of the parson's nose. "And I intend to examine your shoe closet."

Shoe closet?

Hiding confusion behind saccharine sweetness, I replied, "I'm sorry, Constable, but your feet are much bigger and flatter than mine. I'd love to lend you a pair of shoes but nothing I have would fit you."

By now, Matt's three greyhounds were crashing around in the dog-float, scratching at the doors, yodeling and voicing their displeasure at being forgotten. If I didn't get them out soon they'd wreck my trailer.

"Okay, but dogs first—questions second," I said and snaffling three dog leads, scrambled from the car.

I opened the first berth and quickly fastened a collar and lead on the dark brindle bitch inside. When she jumped out, I passed her lead across to Inspector Adams. Hands free, I opened the door on the second berth. After tacking up a virile looking white dog that almost knocked me on my butt in his exuberance, I handed his lead to PC Chalmers.

"Just let the dogs loose in the galloping runs," I instructed, in what I hoped was a *laisser-faire* voice. I hid a grin behind the act of collaring the last greyhound. "They'll look after themselves in there."

I must admit DI Adams handled his charge like a real pro. Although, when I asked if I could give him a call next time I needed a handler at the track, he didn't respond. PC Chalmers, on the other hand, had a torrid time getting her over-friendly greyhound across to the galloping runs. Seemed like the dog wanted to hump her leg. Guess it had something to do with the woman's pheromones.

By the time we entered the kitchen, I was glad to see both Columbo and Chalmers looked a bit *rumpled* themselves. I filled the kettle with water from the Pura-tap. "Coffee? Tea?"

PC Chalmers grunted and stood in front of the door, arms folded, face like pigeon's poo. I quickly deciphered this as a no.

DI Adams settled comfortably on a kitchen chair. "Nothing for me, thank you. The reason we are here, Ms. McKinley, is because we have new evidence in the Matthew Turner homicide."

Well…well…perhaps it was the police who'd ransacked Matt's house after all.

"In your earlier statement, you indicated that when the dogs barked you woke up, climbed out of bed and walked down the stairs so you could press a button that connects with the kennel-house. Is that correct?"

"Yes. That's right. A guy called George installed the system a few weeks ago. How it works is—I leave a disc in the dogs' CD player and when I press the button inside the house it sets the music off in the kennel-house."

"Do your dogs often bark during the night?"

I nodded. "That's why I paid George to install the system. Sometimes it's possums on the roof or feral cats that get them going. However, the night in question, the new dog must have set them off. You see, I'd taken over the training of Cleo, one of Matt Turner's dogs, because she was too noisy for his backyard and his neighbors were complaining. Anyway, that night, Matt followed me home after the race meeting, settled Cleo into one of my kennels and—" I stopped, realization hitting me like a two-by-four to the ribs. "It wasn't Cleo at all, was it?" I croaked. "The dogs heard Matt's murderer skulking around outside."

"Maybe," said Colombo. "Now, this is very important, Ms. McKinley. I want you to think carefully before you answer. When you came downstairs after hearing the dogs bark, was your back door open?"

I closed my eyes, tried to picture the scene on the stairs but came up with nothing. "I'm sorry, Inspector, I really don't know. You see, I didn't turn the light on and I only went as far as the landing at the bottom of the stairs."

"And tell me again…why were you walking around in the dark?"

"I didn't want to wake Matt up."

"Yet, when you returned to your bed you discovered a knife in his chest. If you didn't turn on the light, how did you know about the knife?"

"I told you before. I felt it."

"You felt it and *then* turned on the light?"

"Yes. I couldn't believe what my fingers were suggesting, so I fell out of bed, crawled to the other side of the room and switched on the light. And there it was. The largest of my kitchen knives…and…and…it was stuck in Matt's chest."

My hand shook. Sugar sprayed onto the counter top as I added a spoonful to my coffee.

"While you were downstairs, did you see or hear anyone else in the house? Feel anything brush past you?"

I shivered as the recurring nightmare ate its way through my mind in full 3D Technicolor. "No. Nothing. The killer was already in my bedroom when I woke up, is that what you're saying?" I gulped down what felt like a truckload of concrete. "If I had turned on the light, before going downstairs, I'd have seen the murderer?"

And I wouldn't be here talking about it now.

"Are you certain it was the dogs that woke you and not a movement in the room?"

"I don't know, Inspector. I guess I merely assumed it was the dogs."

I'd been through these same questions over and over—at home and later at the police station. Why wouldn't they accept my answers and move on? Go find the murderer before he struck again?

"Any reason why the noise didn't wake the deceased?"

Oh, god, not again. I may as well bang my head against the refrigerator door.

"I don't know," I growled through gritted teeth. "Perhaps his one attempt at pathetic sex exhausted him." I crashed the kettle back on the stove, stirred the spoon around in my cup sloshing hot coffee over the sides. "Is that what you wanted to hear?"

DI Adams stood up and moved towards me, concern on his face. "I'm sorry, Ms, McKinley. I know this must be difficult for you, but we found a size 10 ripple-soled shoe print in the mud outside your front door and the same footprint and traces of mud on your bedroom carpet. This leads us to believe the murderer used the copy he'd made of your spare key to get in the front door and may have already been in the room when you woke up. It seems like while you were downstairs, he stabbed his victim, waited on the upstairs landing for you to go past and then let himself out again."

And since then he'd been playing mind games with me. "Does that mean I'm not a suspect anymore?"

He smiled. The warm crinkles around his eyes and mouth making him appear almost human. "Well," he drawled. "I wouldn't leave the country just yet."

PC Chalmers barged forward. Evidently hell-bent on breaking up this tender little interlude, she said, "I need to examine all your shoes, Ms. McKinley."

"Be my guest," I told her and tipped the dregs of my coffee down the sink. "And if you find anything that really takes your fancy, please, help yourself. But as I said, your feet are too—"

"Ms. McKinley," she broke in, herding me towards the stairs. "Your shoes! Now!"

The policewoman inspected every shoe in the bottom of my wardrobe. She got down on hands and knees and crawled under the beds. She discovered far-flung shoes in forgotten corners. She even found my long-lost hot pink wellington boots underneath a dusty upended box on the back porch.

But no muddy size tens.

The aggressive odor under the policewoman's arms grew steadily stronger, her cheeks redder, her mood blacker. At last, in clear desperation, she stomped down the stairs with me tagging along behind and banged a beefy hand on the closed door of the hallway cupboard.

"What's in here?"

"No shoes in there," I put in quickly. "That's for coats."

"Open it."

"But—"

Chalmers pushed past me and flung open the door.

"See." I shrugged. "Just coats."

DI Adam's warm breath tickled the nape of my neck. "And whose coat would that be, Ms. McKinley?" he asked, pointing to a large brown sheepskin coat squashed in between two much smaller denim jackets.

"Umm…"

"Matthew Turner's?"

I nodded.

Damn!

"Take it as evidence PC Chalmers and tag anything you find in the pockets."

Chalmers, eyes gleaming, slowly drew on a pair of rubber gloves, inserted one hand into a pocket of the brown sheepskin jacket and pulled out Matt's mobile phone.

As I said before...

Damn!

For every step forward we seemed to take three steps back.

13

Ever wondered what a mouse feels like after being mauled by a cat? Can't say I have either. That is, until standing at my front door watching the Chrysler's rear end disappear through the open gateway. However when the car turned left onto the bitumen road leading back to the police station, I put on my Sunday best smile and waved a casual goodbye to the two law-enforcing occupants.

And then collapsed in a sniveling heap.

No mobile phone meant no contacts to investigate, which meant we were no further advanced re finding out *whodunit* than immediately after *it* was done. At the rate our plans were unraveling we'd be up to Plan Z by breakfast tomorrow morning.

Resisting the urge to scream, I huffed in a deep cleansing breath and blew it out while counting to ten in my head. Focus. Concentrate on the now. It was Jake's night off and there was a heap of work to get through.

I dragged my grubby sneakers through the dirt on the way to the rear galloping runs. The rain from the previous day had leeched into the parched ground already. A strong gust of wind whipped at my T-shirt, flattened bushes and stirred up a suffocating haze of yellow dust. It hung in the air, clogged my nose and throat and made me cough. Clearly unhappy with the sudden dust storm, Matt's three dogs huddled against the wind, noses pressed to the wire mesh gate, body language imploring me to hurry up and rescue them.

As I elbowed the kennel-house door open and led Matt's dogs inside, the noise was like peak hour traffic in the middle of the city. Waste of time putting on *The Nutcracker Suite*. The only *sweet* these twenty noisy canines were interested in was the sprinkle of glucose on top of their meat and three veg.

A sudden shiver zipped up my spine.

I was alone.

A bad guy could stroll in, shoot me dead, grab a carrot from the vegetable rack to chew on and saunter casually out again.

To keep my imagination from taking me places I did not wish to visit, I grated cheese, carrots and trombone into a mixing bowl ready to spread across the dogs' teas and thought about the footprint forensics had discovered beside my front door. Inspector Adams said it matched the footprint in my bedroom. But who did the footprint belong to? Seventy-five percent of the men I knew wore size ten shoes. However, every face that appeared in my mind, I dismissed. None of my friends were capable of murder. I sighed and added a spoonful of multivitamins to each of the twenty-three dog teas lined up on the table. I guess when PC Chalmers searched my house she had grand visions of unearthing a pair of ripple-soled shoes, size ten, still covered in tell-tale dried mud, hidden under a blood-stained nightdress at the back of my wardrobe. Honestly, that woman was so keen to slip a pair of handcuffs on my wrists, I suspected her of being into covert S&M.

Unable to control the tremor in my hands I carefully cut a celery stick into thin slices, scraped the pieces into the bowl with the grated cheese, carrot and trombone, and picked up a large wooden spoon.

It always came back to the same scary fact…Matt's killer was no stranger to me.

Thoughts whirled and clashed inside my head. Should I have told the Inspector about the phone call on the night of Matt's murder? And mentioned the break-in and trashing of Matt's house? I rubbed my aching temples with finger and thumb. This was what was known as a catch-22 situation. It was the responsibility of the police to catch bad guys and protect their victims—yet Matt's forever-vacant eyes and Barney's white battered face were the reality. Protection from Inspector Adams and the grim-faced Chalmers didn't rate too highly against reality. The only good thing to come out of today was the fact that my name had plummeted on the suspect list.

After feeding and settling the dogs for the night, I hurried through the gathering darkness to the house. Normally I enjoyed living alone. Tonight, every bush had a potential murderer crouching behind it. Every movement was a psychopath with a bloody knife ready to leap out and relieve me of vital body parts.

The front door, heavy stained oak with panels, had never looked so solid and safe. Fumbling in my haste, I turned the key in the lock, darted inside and slammed the door behind me. If the police didn't find the killer soon I'd end up frothing at the mouth and laced into one of those heavy-duty white strait jackets doctors use to control the mentally unhinged.

I triple-locked the door, then, satisfied no one could get in, bent to pat my welcoming committee of two. Not only were they barking and yapping but their stamping paws and please-feed-me eyes declared I was a bad mother and they were both weak from hunger.

"Okay, okay, calm down," I told them, toeing off my sneakers and flipping them in the direction of the hall closet. "I haven't eaten either. So, let's go see what's on the menu." I padded along the passageway and into the kitchen. Lucky and Tater followed, their hard nails clicking and clacking and sliding on the polished linoleum floor.

With a flourish, I opened the fridge door and poked my head inside. A bit like Mother Hubbard's cupboard. What with the debacles of the last few days, I'd forgotten to go food shopping.

I looked down at my dogs. "How about sharing a slightly stale cheese sandwich?"

I swear Tater shook his head while Lucky wrinkled her nose in disgust.

"No? Well, what would you say to a nice bowl of tuna? I could always scrape the green mould off."

Tater dived out from under Lucky's stomach, yapping his disapproval in staccato yips. I grinned down at him as I reached for the roll of commercial dog food I always kept in the side door of the fridge.

"Okay guys, just teasing. There's savory chicken loaf for you and Chicken Tandoori Lean Cuisine for me."

It was a race to see who ate first. With the two aerobic gymnasts underfoot, I transferred the Lean Cuisine from the freezer to the microwave, set the timer for eight minutes, grabbed a Father Bear and a Baby Bear sized dog bowl from the wall cupboard and filled them both with chunks of savory loaf. Naturally Lucky, being an utter pig, hoovered her supper down in three noisy sucks. Then, before I could warn her of the consequences, she trotted over to Tater and offered to help clean his feed bowl as well.

Big mistake.

By the time I finished playing nursemaid to Lucky with cotton balls and Betadine, the microwave dinged and the aroma of Chicken Tandoori filled the room. My stomach growled, reminding me I hadn't eaten since grabbing a slice of toast before leaving Tanya's early that morning.

With Tater and the Drama Queen still grumbling at each other as they followed behind, I carried my meal on a tray from the kitchen into the lounge room. Perhaps an entertaining dose of *Dancing with the Stars* might kick aside the bone-chilling thought of how vulnerable I was. Locked doors hadn't kept the killer out before. Why should I expect them to tonight? My heart played chopsticks against my ribs as I placed the tray on the coffee table, perched on the edge of the chair and using the remote, flicked on the television.

Holy crap! What was that? The first forkful of chicken stuck in my throat. I bolted upright and cocked an ear towards the window. Sounded like something or someone scratching on the glass. A possum? The murderer? My imagination? I turned the volume on the television up to a head-thumping 25. At that level it would be impossible to hear any scratching noises…real or imagined.

Hey, what you can't hear isn't there.

Right?

Five minutes later my heartbeat had returned to normal. Costa Tzu was tangoing with his partner on the television screen. The Chicken Tandoori was fast disappearing from my plate. I'd settled back in the chair to enjoy Costa's slinky moves.

And the doorbell rang.

"On guard!" I yelled at the two dogs, surprised when my voice emerged as a throaty croak instead of a shrill command. Lucky stretched languidly, blinked, put on her plaintive *who-me?* face and promptly went back to sleep. Tater was beside me in a flash. His eyes were granite-hard. His ears flicked backwards and forwards as though waiting for permission to tear the door-ringer apart and spit out the bones.

It's okay, I told myself, muting the sound on the television. Don't panic. Ignore the bell. There's no law that says I *have* to open the door just because my doorbell rings.

I glanced at the silent television screen. The next contestants, dressed in elegant ballroom attire, were breathing into each other's faces, arms dragging their bodies closer, waiting for the music to start. I wished I was there.

When the doorbell rang a second time, my heart, already strained to the max, did a death-defying belly-flop with a one-point landing. I peered around the room for a weapon. A vintage bottle of wine Mum sent me from Hawaii on my last birthday? No…might need that if I made it through the night. The Gawler Gold Cup won by Lucky last year? No…too cumbersome to heft over my shoulder.

Finally I decided on a shiny new can of *U-Beaut* super-hold hair spray. Nothing like a well-aimed squirt of hair spray in the eyes to stop a killer in mid-kill.

"Who's there?" Shaking, I stood, canister at the ready, to one side of the front door.

"Good evening," said a beautifully articulated voice from the other side of the door. "My name is Scuzz."

"Scuzz?" What the hell sort of a name was that? And how come someone with a name like Scuzz spoke with two plums and a silver spoon in his mouth?

"Jake asked me to stop by," the voice with the rich resonant timbre continued.

"Oh yeah?"

"He indicated you were in need of a bodyguard."

"A bodyguard, eh?" Would that be before or after said body was chopped into little pieces and fed into the toilet cistern?

"That is correct. Now, may I come inside, please?"

When hell froze over.

"Here's the deal, Scuzz, or whatever your name is. How do I know you're not here to burglarize my house? Or you could even be a hit man, paid big bucks to rub me out. So, before I let you in, I have some questions for you." I rolled my shoulders which had tensed to the stage of rigidity. "What date is Jake's birthday?"

"I am sorry, but I cannot remember the date off-hand."

"One down—two to go. Three strikes and I ring the cops. How did Jake get the scar on his left buttock?"

Of course I only knew the answer to this one because Jake and I were discussing our various scars one day while waiting for the vet to arrive. Sort of adding them up. As you do. Being a tomboy as a kid, I beat Jake, ten scars to six. But that didn't mean I wanted to add to my scar-list by inviting a potential madman into my home.

The door-ringer cranked up the volume of his voice. "Actually, I have not observed Jake with his pants down for quite a number of years, so I regret I have no information on that particular scar. However, I do remember how he came by the one behind his right ear. Many years ago, Jake and I were playing a game of swordfights in his backyard when my wooden sword, which had been sharpened to a point with my new pocket knife, slipped. At the time Jake was eight and I was eleven. Jake ended up with a cut that required stitches behind his right ear and I, with a very uncomfortable backside."

I slowly undid the three bolts on the inside of the door but left the chain in place. Hey, I might be a beginner at this sleuthing business but I wasn't an airhead. This guy could still be the killer. How do I know he didn't torture Jake until he elicited that last bit of information out of him?

With Tater pressed flat against my legs, hair on end, growl deep in his throat, I peeped through the gap between the door and the jamb.

And almost choked on my own spit.

Whatever this creature called Scuzz was—he was too alien, too scary, too off-the-planet huge to be human.

I tried to swallow. Slam the door. Ram home all the locks. Instead, I froze. The *thing* on the other side of the door, dressed in black leather and a faceless black helmet, reminded me of something from one of those ancient fairytales told to small children to stop them from being naughty.

Closing my eyes, I solemnly promised God, Jesus, and whatever other deity might be listening, that I'd never, ever be naughty again.

14

"Good evening," said the monster, shuffling its tractor sized feet. "Kat, isn't it?"

"Erg…" My tongue was stuck to the roof of my mouth.

"Rather windy for this time of year, don't you think?"

Tongue still stuck…

The creature straightened to its full height of around seven foot. After removing its helmet, which thankfully revealed a rugged male human face and not something from a Freddy Krueger movie, he nudged the tire of his massive chrome and black Harley Davidson with the toe of one boot. While the beat of my heart gradually slowed to a dull roar I studied my unexpected visitor by the pale glow of the porch light. He was awesome. Shoulders like an ox. Legs like two-hundred-year-old tree stumps. In fact, this guy was big enough to scrunch an unwanted bad-ass crook into a four by four square then promptly use him to wipe up a beer spill.

I unglued my tongue and grabbed a large fortifying breath of air. Okay, time to establish who this guy really was.

"How come you know Jake so well?" I asked in my gruffest PI voice. "I've been to his apartment heaps of times and I've never seen you around. Lots of other weird life forms but not yours. For all I know you could be planning to slit my throat."

The man-mountain shook his head, placed his helmet on the seat of his ultra-powerful hog then extracted a mobile phone from his pocket. Opening it, he tapped in a number then handed the phone through the small gap in the doorway.

"It's Jake on the line. Ask him yourself."

Gingerly, as though handling a ticking bomb, I took the mobile, put it to my ear and listened.

"Hey, man, if you're after the coolest dude in SA—you've hit the jackpot. This is Jake, the man, here."

I rolled my eyes. "Listen up, you ham," I whispered into the phone. "I have the Creature from the Black Lagoon standing outside my front door. Says *you* sent him. What's the story?"

"Kat?"

"You bet your boots it's Kat. How come you didn't tell me this Scuzz guy was coming? Almost lost my dinner when I eyeballed him a couple of minutes ago."

"Scuzz is my cuzz."

"Cuzz?" I frowned and then the puzzle fell into place. "Oh…you mean he's your cousin?"

"That's what I said, dude. Scuzz's cool. See, he's driving to Cairns to meet up with Thunder, this half-sister he discovered on the net. He didn't even know she existed before he logged onto his family tree. Anyway, Scuzz only dropped in to see if I wanted to blaze the trail with him. Not my scene, dude. But I hadn't seen the big guy since we were kids, so he's like, bunking down with us for a few days. When I brought up your little problem, he offered his services as a bodyguard. Cool, eh?"

I took a couple of steps away from the front door, all the better to stop the leather-clad intruder from overhearing our conversation.

"*Cool*? Jake, the guy's a *biker*!" I whispered, my teeth grinding together the same way I'd like to be grinding Jake's head against a rocky embankment. "Or are you so absorbed in planning your next protest march you hadn't noticed?"

"Hey, man, we're marching against the destruction of trees. How'd you like it if your grandkids were born into a world without trees?"

Okay, he had a point. Except for one thing. I would never have grandchildren. One had to have a reason for having sex without a condom first. Like being in love instead of lust—and the guy you're in love with reciprocating. And then, of course, one had to go through the painful motions of giving birth to a baby. And that baby had to grow up, also having sex without a condom and give birth etc.

Highly complex.

And not relevant to this conversation.

"Anyway, dude," Jake continued, blocking my depressing thoughts re sex, condoms and the current state of my love life. "What you got against bikers?"

"They eat people for breakfast."

"How many bikers you know, Kat?"

"Umm…" I racked my brains, but all I could come up with was the eighty-two-year-old pensioner who lived in a run-down caravan at the Two Wells Caravan Park. He wore a black leather jacket summer and winter, and okay, he now rode a Gofer handicap-scooter, but I bet he'd owned a Harley somewhere in his murky past.

"Kat?"

"Okay. You're right. I don't know any bikers."

"And bottom line, you *do* need protection."

I sighed. I'd been thinking more along the lines of half a dozen fierce Dobermans patrolling the perimeter, or even a couple of hungry dingoes for protection. Anything but a seven foot biker. I let out another sigh and clutched the phone more tightly. Perhaps if I humoured Jake and let his cousin stay for the night, seeing he'd gone to so much trouble to find someone to protect me, then politely ask the scary guy in black leather to leave in the morning. Tell him, thanks, but no thanks, and hire myself a security guard. Someone I didn't have to crick my neck every time I looked up at him. "So...is this Scuzz a good guy?"

"Good guy? Hey, man, Scuzz is my cuzz!"

This conversation was getting old and the giant on the veranda was getting impatient. I touched the hang-up button and passed the phone back through the gap.

"Satisfied?"

Struggling to assimilate the educated voice with the yob in black leather, I lifted the chain and nodded. "Okay, you can come in. Just for tonight. But if you try anything remotely funny my two guard dogs will tear your arms off and bury them in the backyard. Okay?"

Scowling at the big guy on my doorstep, I picked up the now traitorous Tater whose tail was wagging a welcome and shook my head at Lucky, still snoring on the rug. I didn't know whether to be relieved about having a bodyguard or more apprehensive. After all, according to the emblem adorning his jacket, Scuzz was a *Red Dragon*.

The floorboards shuddered and creaked as the man-mountain bobbed his head to get under the door frame and lumbered towards me. I took a hesitant step backwards, noted a knife strapped to his left boot, tent-sized black leather pants and a straining black T-shirt under his sleeveless jacket. I tipped my head back and peered upwards until finally locking into two sharp black eyes set in a craggy face that, if he was to lose the wispy ginger beard, wouldn't look half bad. A red and black bandana, nose ring, matching eyebrow rings and a shaved head completed the biker image. Yet, instead of the expected odor of sour sweat, there was a hint of something masculine, even sexy, that teased my nostrils. A lingering trace of cologne or aftershave, along with the homely smell of engine oil.

I smiled wanly. "Hi."

"Good evening, ma'am. I am sorry to have caused you alarm." The leather-clad Goliath held out one hand, each finger tattooed with a bright red-and-black eye. "Allow me to introduce myself. I am Theodore Samuel Parkington the Third. But you may call me, Scuzz."

"I'm Katrina Tess McKinley—the One and Only. And you can call me, Kat." I watched in awe as my hand disappeared inside his. It was like having your hand swallowed by a whale.

"So…Katrina, where do you desire me to bed down for the night?"

Bed down? Holy crap! Hadn't thought that through. I don't suppose I could expect a biker with a plum and two silver spoons in his mouth to kip on the old sofa in the kennel-house.

Or could I?

"Umm…well…"

"If it is acceptable to you I'd like to camp here on your lounge room floor. I have my own bedding."

"Umm...well..."

"Shall I fetch my accoutrements?"

Accoutrements? Had this guy swallowed a Dictionary?

"Er…right. Go for it!"

Bemused, I watched Scuzz wheel his Harley into my lounge room with the same care and attention to placement as he would a priceless Da Vinci painting. Evidently satisfied his pride and joy was in the best position, he flipped his sleeping bag onto the floor, unzipped the front and spread a black satin sheet inside. After carefully smoothing the shiny satin with one beefy tattooed hand, he placed a pastel pink pillow on top.

Was this guy for real?

"Kat, I wonder if you have a hot-water bottle I could borrow? I seem to have misplaced mine. If I left it in Jake's apartment, I may as well kiss it goodbye. They have probably cut it up to make letters on a protester's slogan by now."

"I'll see what I can find."

If Scuzz was Jake's idea of a joke, I thought, as I marched into the kitchen, I'd slaughter him in the morning, then spread him on toast and feed him to the dogs.

With one ear tuned in to Scuzz, who seemed to be having an in-depth conversation with my two adoring canines, I dug around in the kitchen drawers until I found an ancient hot-water bottle. Okay, it had a fluffy panda bear outer covering, but I couldn't see that worrying a man who slept on black satin and rested his shaved head on a pastel pink pillow. Unable to restrain a grin, I tossed the water bottle onto the kitchen table, unearthed the matching stopper at the back of the drawer and filled my electric jug with water.

And then the doorbell rang.

Again.

My house was busier than Rundle Mall on a Saturday morning.

"Will you answer the door please, Scuzz?" I asked, endeavoring to keep my voice light. "If it's the Avon lady calling, tell her I'm not interested. I'd need more than her special hand cream to make *my* hands smooth and silky."

Adrenalin sizzled and buzzed in my brain as I switched on the jug. If the killer had dropped in to break off more ears—he was in for a nasty surprise. Even if the knife strapped to Scuzz's boot failed to prove a deterrent, the height, width and breadth of my newly acquired bodyguard certainly would.

While waiting for the jug to boil, I scuttled across the kitchen lino, put my ear to the door and listened. Muffled voices drifted in from out front. What sounded like a quarrel and what could have been several loud thumps. Or Scuzz tearing the killer apart. I smiled as I wandered back to unplug the jug. Perhaps having the man in black leather around wasn't such a bad idea after all. Ears alert for sounds of screaming, loud banging, or severed heads rolling across the polished wooden floorboards, I held the water bottle over the sink and filled it from the jug before screwing the stopper down tight.

Okay, everything had gone silent.

Time to face the fallout.

Almost afraid of what I'd find, blood, guts, maybe even mangled body parts, I slipped the cover over the rubber bottle and sailed back into the lounge.

The scene could have come from a family sit-com. Scuzz and the dogs were stretched out on the settee all eyes tuned in to the last few minutes of *Dancing with the Stars*.

"Hey, what's going on? Who was at the door?"

"No one of interest."

"What do you mean no one of interest?"

"Just some sappy guy in cowboy boots." Scuzz's eyes didn't leave the television screen. "After securing him in a hammer lock I checked him for weapons, informed him you were currently upstairs changing into something more comfortable then told him to get lost."

Oh, God. "You didn't?"

Unrepentant, Scuzz looked up and nodded. "Afraid I did."

"I don't suppose this sappy guy in cowboy boots was also wearing an akubra hat?"

"Yes."

"And did his jeans fit like a glove?"

"Well…I…can't say I noticed."

"And did he have gorgeous black brown eyes with tiny flecks of buttercup yellow running through them?"

"Kat, I—"

"And did he have cute little lines each side of his eyes when he smiled?"

Scuzz shook his head. "Believe me when I say this guy did not, at any time, smile."

"He didn't?"

"No. And for a moment there, I had the feeling Cowboy Boots was contemplating punching my lights out, but instead, after informing me several times, in a rather impolite manner, that I did not know my birth father, he drove off in a huff."

Damn. I'd never hear the end of this. "Scuzz, you chased off the wrong guy." I groaned. "That was my mate, Ben. He's one of the good guys."

Scuzz removed the hot-water bottle from my hand, pushed himself off the settee and bent to tuck the bottle deep inside his bedroll. Then, displaying a rare litheness for a man his size, he moved towards me with the grace of a wild African lion until my eyes were level with the shiny metal tag in the middle of his jacket zipper. He was so close I could see the rise and fall of his chest. Smell his expensive cologne and the strangely comforting scent of engine oil. Feel the roughness of his fingers as he cupped my chin and forced my head back to meet his eyes.

"While I am your bodyguard, Katrina," he said his voice gentle, but firm. "No one enters this house without first producing police ID, a driver's license *and* an original birth certificate."

Relief spread through me like melted toffee as the significance of this statement sunk in. And yet, I still wasn't quite ready to trust him.

Eyeing me with that unsettling look of the jungle, Scuzz brushed hair from my eyes and tucked a stray lock behind one ear. For such a big man his touch was soft. "My cousin informed me of the danger you face, Katrina."

The way his eyes devoured my lips, I wasn't sure which danger he was referring to.

"Jake has a big mouth."

"And *you* have an exquisite mouth." He dipped his head closer. For a moment I was tempted to stretch up to meet him. Then sanity intervened. I'd known Scuzz all of ten minutes. And look what happened last time I'd allowed a guy's soft-talk to melt my defenses.

I shook my head, placed both palms on his chest and pushed. It was like pushing against a ten ton truck. "Down boy," I growled, knowing if Scuzz wanted to force himself on me there'd be nothing I could do about it.

He stepped away and let both hands drop to his sides.

"Sorry, Katrina," he said with a twist to his mouth and a twinkle in his eye that completely belied his apology. "I am but a mere man and you are a beautiful sexy woman." With that, he sank onto the settee with the dogs, lifted Tater onto his lap and tuned into the beginning of *Packed to the Rafters.*

I closed my gaping mouth and shook my head. It wasn't fair. *It just wasn't fair!* Two guys in the last three days had hit on me, yet the one I wanted to notice me, that big lug, Ben Taylor, treated me like a mate. Couldn't ditch his blinkers long enough to see I not only had boobs—I was also endowed with every other piece of equipment proclaiming I was female.

According to Scuzz...I was a beautiful, sexy woman.

A beautiful, sexy woman who was going quietly insane while struggling to prevent her rampant, unrequited hormones from exploding from their cage. All Ben ever saw when he locked eyes with me was the good mate he borrowed Bone Radial from when he needed to treat a dog's sprained wrist. Or an extra person to make up the numbers in a poker game on a slow Friday night.

If only *he'd* brush his fingers through my hair and tell me how exquisite my mouth looked. Hell, I'd throw caution not only to the wind, but out the window and over the back fence. Ben only had to say the word and I'd lay myself out for him like a Playboy centerfold.

Yeah, I know. I'm pathetic. A disgrace to feminists the world over. So sue me.

"Any idea who would have had reason to kill your friend, Katrina?"

"Sorry?" I shook my head to dislodge the frustrating images of Ben from my head and blinked at Scuzz's unexpected question.

He patted the seat beside him. "Come along, tell me all about it. You must have some idea who perpetrated the crime."

I frowned, ignored his invitation and perched on the edge of an overstuffed armchair. What was going on? One minute Scuzz was all warm and fuzzy and attempting to kiss me and the next he was ferreting for information. I gave him a closer, narrow-eyed scrutiny. Was Theodore Samuel Parkington the Third *really* one of the good guys? After all, Jake hadn't seen his cousin since childhood and kids can change when they grow up. I'd heard rumors that Al Capone was a shy little boy who used to hide behind his mother's skirts.

When I didn't answer, Scuzz cocked his head to one side. "Are you certain you didn't catch a glimpse of the killer that night? Feel his presence? Smell his aftershave?"

"No." My frown deepened and a small scared little butterfly began fluttering around in my stomach. "As I told the police, I knew nothing until my fingers found the knife in Matt's chest. If I'd seen Matt's killer, do you honestly think I'd be alive and talking to you now?"

"Sorry Kat, I am being obtuse. And thank goodness you *are* alive," he said smiling at me while pulling gently on Tater's ear. "I thought he might have left a clue, that's all."

"Well, he *didn't*."

Scuzz leant forward in his seat, expression chagrined. "I apologize again, Katrina. If discussing that night distresses you, we shall not bring the subject up again. Instead, would you like to talk about your greyhounds?"

I shrugged. "If you want."

"Well then, tell me, do any of your dogs have a better than average chance of winning next Thursday night?"

Several large butterflies chased the little one around in my stomach. I felt sick. Was Scuzz really only making conversation or was there something sinister behind these questions?

"Okay, let's reverse question time." Hands on hips, I stood up and faced him. "Where were you at the time my friend, Matthew Turner, was murdered?"

Scuzz blinked. A small frown creasing between his eyes. "Excuse me?"

"Were you anywhere near this house the night Matt was murdered?"

"Of course not. I was in—"

Before he could finish, a screech of brakes reverberated from outside. Gravel spat and sprayed and bounced off the front of the house causing Scuzz to shoot to his feet, fists balled into lethal weapons.

"What the hell was that?"

I watched his lips set into a snarl as he went into fighting mode, eyes two steel traps, fists curled. Oh crap, what if it was Ben, returning to check that I hadn't been cut into morsel-sized pieces by the giant biker? The image of Scuzz sticking his fist down Ben's throat and ripping out his entrails brought me out in a cold sweat. Intent on preventing carnage, I pushed in front of the snarling biker and darted toward the front door.

"Scuzz! Stay!" I barked in the tone of voice I use on recalcitrant greyhounds and cold callers who decide to ring at mealtimes. "Don't move until I see who it is."

Amazingly, Scuzz stayed. However, the look he gave me seemed to say, *be it on your own head, Katrina!* With fumbling fingers I undid the three bolts, turned on the outside light, and warily poked my head through the open doorway.

No Ben.

Instead, a dark colored car, lights off, was hurling itself, kamikaze style, out through my gateway.

And sitting on my front porch was a large bunch of flowers.

All dead.

In the eerie glow from the single-bulb porch light they reminded me of flowers left on a grave until they'd become dry and brittle. As dead as the person whose remembrance they'd originally commemorated.

I took three rubbery steps forward and felt a sour burning spasm jam my stomach muscles. The flowers were tied together with what looked like a dog's tail. Blood still leaked from the stump and where the tail was knotted, a large roofing nail kept the wet ends from slipping through.

Battling nausea, I bent to extricate an envelope from inside the graveyard offering. The printed letters tangoed elusively in front of my eyes. Sweat trickled between my breasts and gathered under my armpits. I forced my eyes to read the name on the front of the envelope and when I did the Chicken Tandoori I'd eaten for dinner began to flap its wings.

"On second thought, Scuzz," I croaked through a throat that had more gravel in it than a quarry. "I—I think I'll be happy to retain you as my bodyguard."

15

"HOW ARE YOU FEELING NOW, KATRINA?" Scuzz unlocked my fingers so he could close them around a mug of steaming coffee. "Is there anything else I can get you? Toasted sandwich? More blankets?" He lifted one rogue eyebrow. "A plane ticket to Las Vegas?"

From my seat at the kitchen table wrapped in a wooly tartan blanket, I looked up and shook my head, although the plane ticket to Las Vegas sounded tempting. I'd even welcome a plane ticket to the middle of Siberia at the moment. Clutching the mug, I felt the heat from the coffee gradually seep through the china and warm my fingers. As for the rest of me—I didn't think I'd ever be warm again.

Scuzz dragged out the chair next to me and sat down, his large hands wrapped around a slab of six-month-old Christmas cake he must have unearthed in the pantry. After devouring the cake in three bites, he stood up and went hunting for more. Hey, Scuzz was welcome to eat every crumb of food in the house as long as he continued his bodyguard duties. Although I'd probably need to go grocery shopping before that offer became an incentive. The fact that I hadn't fully trusted my leather-clad guardian angel had quickly dissipated the moment I'd seen the protective snarl on the big guy's face when he thought I was being attacked.

When he finished eating the second slab of cake, I passed him a napkin from the holder on the table and watched him pat delicately at the crumbs in his beard. *Some biker!* If Scuzz was dressed in a dark suit, white shirt and tie and sported a more conservative haircut and no facial hair, he'd be perfect to play the part of the butler in an Agatha Christie movie. And yet it was his explicit biker persona that made me feel safe. Hell, if Jake hadn't lent me his seven foot cousin, I'd be crouched under the bed gnawing at my fingernails and reciting the Lord's Prayer right now.

Which is probably what the flower-delivery-guy expected.

I took a sip of coffee, rubbed tense fingers over my aching forehead and re-read the words staring up at me from the sheet of paper on the kitchen table.

Big Mistake must lose—or else!

Exactly like in a mystery novel the words had been cut from colored magazines. I clutched the coffee mug to my chest. It wasn't merely the race-fixing that had me running scared, it was the reality of the *or else*!

When Scuzz gave me an encouraging wink, I attempted a smile in return. But nothing happened. Some unknown force seemed to be freezing the muscles that instigated the task of lifting the corners of my mouth upwards. I shivered. Even the blanket and the heat from my *Cheap as Chips* fan-heater blasting hot air at me from under the table had little effect.

What poor cat or dog had lost its tail and its life so the sick mind behind that deadly package could emphasize his message? Thank God all my animals were safe. Tater and Lucky were both asleep in the lounge and the security system in my kennel-house hadn't been disturbed.

Of course I should let the police know about this latest development in the saga. But first…I'd ring Tanya.

Coffee cup in one hand, threatening note in the other, I shuffled into the lounge room, trailing my blanket behind me and curled up on an armchair. As though he didn't want to let me out of his sight, Scuzz followed.

I picked up the phone, dialed Tanya's number and waited to hear her welcoming voice. I figured my best friend would be more sympathetic than the police. Sympathy I needed. Questions and innuendos about being alone in the house with a testosterone-loaded biker, I didn't need.

"Yeah. Wattcha want?"

Crap…it was *Devil's Spawn*!

"Hi, Erin," I muttered, forcing my words through clenched teeth. "Can I talk to your Mum?"

"Nope."

I scowled. Bit my already bruised bottom lip. "Stop messing around and get your mother on the phone. This is important."

"Why does your voice sound funny, Kat? Is the scary guy there? Is he standing beside you with a knife? Is he going to stick it in your throat?" She paused, evidently relishing the picture this scenario evoked. Her voice upped its level of excitement. "Hey, can I come over and watch?"

"Erin…*please*…be a good girl and go get Tanya for me."

"You just said please, so something *must* be up! This is *sooo* cool."

I quickly fought down an overwhelming urge to slam my head against the wall. Instead, I dragged out my pleasant *jam-with-cream-on-top* voice. "Erin. Darling. If Tanya is not on the phone in exactly thirty seconds I am coming over to cut all your hair off." I paused to let my threat sink in. "And—I won't cut your hair with scissors. I'll use blunt gardening shears."

"Oh, didn't I tell you? Mum caught a plane to Melbourne an hour ago 'cause Granny fell down the stairs and broke her leg."

"No…you *didn't* tell me," I growled into the phone. This kid had perfected the technique for yanking my chain from a very early age.

Don't let her get to you, I told myself, *you're already chief suspect in one murder case.* Before continuing, I deliberately sucked in a deep breath, picked up my coffee mug and swigged several mouthfuls of caffeine.

"Sorry to hear about your Gran," I commiserated. "So, who's looking after you while your mother's away?"

"Dunno why everyone thinks I need looking after. I'm eleven—not two. I can take care of myself."

"Who. Is. Looking. After. You?"

I could almost hear her sulky bottom lip go *thunk* as it hit the floor.

"Well," she said, letting loose a dramatic *why-me?* sigh. "Dad is. I guess. But his car broke down. I told him I'd be okay on my own, but he's sending this guy he met in the pub to pick me up."

Typical Dan. "How well does he know this guy he met in the pub?"

I could hear the blasé shrug in her answering tone. "How should I know? Hey, there's someone knocking on the front door. That must be Dad's friend, now. See ya, Kat."

"Erin—"

Too late. All I could hear was the smug purr of the dial tone.

Growling deep in my throat, I slammed the receiver back on its base.

"Well?" Scuzz raised both be-ringed eyebrows in query.

"Tanya's in Melbourne. Her mother fell down the stairs and broke her leg."

"So, are you going to ring the police now?"

What could the police do about the note? Some psycho wanted to stop Lofty from winning, which made me madder than a hen whose chicks had been gobbled up by a passing fox. The warning was on plain white paper and the letters cut out of a magazine. As for fingerprints— whoever did the artwork sure as hell would have worn gloves. And if I went to the police—who's to say Lofty wouldn't lose *his* tail or maybe his tail *and* his ears, in payback? Nope. Not worth the risk.

"Katrina?" Scuzz persisted and heaved himself off the sofa. "If you are not going to ring the police, at least let *me* help. I have connections."

Hmm...biker connections? I took another sip of coffee before attempting to get my head around that one.

Too strong, no sugar, but what the hell...

The man-mountain's dark eyes held mine. "When you opened the front door, did you see the number plate on the car?"

With an effort I forced the cobwebs from my mind and focused on Scuzz's question. "All I saw was the shape of a car screaming through the gateway."

"Was the vehicle a sedan, van, utility, SUV...?"

I sighed and shook my head. At the time I'd been too mesmerized by the bloody bouquet to notice anything else. "I *think* it was a van. But I'm not a hundred percent sure. It was dark."

"Damn." His scowl could have sent Genghis Kahn scurrying for cover.

He looked up, must have seen the fear in my eyes, because his voice immediately gentled. "Hey, don't worry, Katrina." He laid his hands on my shoulder and squeezed. "The sick bastard was probably driving a stolen car with a bogus number plate anyway."

"If I had my way I'd wrap his bogus number plate around his bogus head." I banged my fist on the table, slopping coffee onto the offending note. "I can't drug my dogs, Scuzz. It goes against all my principles."

"Easy, my darling," he crooned, continuing to knead the muscles in my shoulders.

"I can't do anything that might hurt Lofty. He trusts me." I sniffed, wiped my nose with the back of one hand.

"Come here." Scuzz took me in a bear hug. Along with the comforting feel of soft leather nestled against my cheek, his hard safe muscles made me wish I could stay wrapped in his arms forever. Of course I had to finally come up for air and when I did he offered me a handkerchief the size of a tablecloth.

"Why me?"

Even to my own ears that whine sounded like one of Ben's bimbos? Especially the blonde ones with the big hair who bleated *why me* every time they broke a fingernail. Still, with a madman looking to break not only my fingernail but possibly an entire set of fingers, I guess whining was permissible.

"I do not know why he's fixated on you, Kat. But I can promise you one thing—this monster will not get near you while *I'm* around."

I stood on tip-toe and kissed him on the cheek. "Thanks, Scuzz."

"Thank *you*." He winked and sat down. "Now, why don't you give that sappy boyfriend of yours a call? See what he suggests."

"Boyfriend?"

"The cowboy. The one with the boots and the hat and jeans that fit like a glove."

"Ben's not my boyfriend." I sighed. "He's just a good mate."

"Oh." Scuzz lifted a quirky eyebrow. "Well, do you know your good mate's telephone number?"

"Does the sun set in the west?" I said and picked up the phone and dialed Ben's number.

16

Finally Ben's answering machine kicked in. It advised me that he, Benjamin Taylor, was in the shower and to leave a message after the beep.

"Ben. It's Kat. I—"

He picked up before I finished, his surly *Yeah* making my stomach twist in apprehension.

"Ben, I need to talk to you."

"So… talk."

Damn…he sounded grumpy. Probably still upset over Scuzz humiliating him. Or was he jealous because he imagined the giant biker and I were into something a little more intimate than the mutual admiration of his black-and-silver Harley?

In your dreams, McKinley…

"Sorry if I've caught you in the shower," I told him. "I did try ringing Tanya but *Devil's Spawn* reckons her Mum's in Melbourne. She says her Gran had an accident—fell down the stairs and broke he leg."

Ben didn't answer so I snatched a breath and plunged onwards, spurred on by the murderer's blood-stained threat staring up at me from the coffee table. Mismatched letters cut from a magazine.

"It's just—"

"Kat, I know you regard me as a mate," Ben broke in, his words tight and clipped. "But if you plan on discussing a blow by blow description of what happened in bed between you and that gorilla—leave it until Tanya gets back. *She* might be interested in your sex life. *I'm* not."

Sheesh! I sighed and ran a weary hand through my hair. I was tempted to make up a sizzling story where Scuzz and I performed every position of the *Kama Sutra* while covered in chocolate syrup, then thought, why bother.

"Ben, there's nothing going on between the biker and me." I frowned across at the cause of our current misunderstanding. Stretched out on the settee, blatantly listening to every word, Scuzz's dark eyes sparkled with amusement.

"Personally, I don't care if you have sex with a telegraph pole. But what I *do* care about is being told to shove off when I offer my assistance. Then, to kick a man when he's down, you ring up later wanting to tell me how King Kong performed in bed."

"What the hell are you on about? Scuzz is my bodyguard. There was no all-night orgy between him, me and his bloody motorbike, you moron."

I heard what sounded like throat clearing. "Another thing," he went on in a quieter voice, "why didn't you ask *me* to be your bodyguard?"

Holy Catfish! This guy was sending out so many mixed messages I was drowning in the backwash.

"Because you distinctly told me you had a hot date with the Petrowski twins tonight. That's why." I paused to let my words sink in. "Which reminds me, *Benjamin*, what are you doing at home at this early hour? Twins stand you up, did they?"

"Not that it's any of your business, *Katrina*, but I decided on an early night."

"Wow! Should I send for a doctor?"

"Always the comedian."

"I'm merely surprised, that's all."

"And I'm standing here dripping water and freezing my butt off," he continued, voice tighter than a screw top jar. "So—what's up?"

Geez... the possibilities were endless.

In fact, the image of Ben, naked, with *what's up* being in the realms of fantasy, had me choking on my saliva. Okay, as I said before—I'm pathetic—I'm a masochist—I know he'll never reciprocate—but that doesn't stop me from transferring erotic images of Ben into a special folder in my brain where I can drag them out and examine each frame in minute detail. Under the cover of darkness. In the privacy of my own bed.

Like a pin-pricked balloon, the reason I'd rung Ben brought me back to earth. "I'm scared, Ben, that's what's up. Matt's killer paid me another visit tonight."

"Bloody hell!" His yell was so loud I held the phone from my ear. "Why didn't you say so in the first place? Where's that useless King Kong? If that gorilla chickened out instead of protecting you I'll fry his liver and throw it to the dogs. I'm sorry, mate. What happened? Are you hurt?"

I was back to being a mate. Still, that was okay. At least now we could talk to each other without emotions driving a wedge between us.

"I'm fine." I sighed. "Well…not really. Some lowlife left a graphic message on my doorstep about half an hour ago. It involved a warning note, dead flowers and animal body parts."

"Oh, crap!"

"It was awful, Ben. The dead flowers were tied up with this…this…tail…and it was all slippery with blood."

"What was on the note?"

"Big Mistake must lose—or else."

There was a moment's silence before he spoke again. "Give Lofty a loaf of bread or a sedative. Whatever it takes. Just make sure the dog loses."

"I don't know," I bleated still unsure of this part. "It doesn't feel right."

"Listen to me, Kat, nothing's worth getting your head smashed in for."

I ran my fingers over the letters, vaguely noting the only colors used were red and black and they'd been cut roughly, as though in a hurry, or anger. "But Scuzz says, if I follow this psycho's orders, I'll never get out of his clutches."

"It's not the gorilla's head on the chopping block here. It's yours."

"But—"

"No buts. Have you forgotten what happened to Matt?"

Forgotten? Every time I dropped off to sleep, the image of Matt's blank lifeless eyes invaded my dreams.

"Of course I haven't," I answered, the chill stirring deep in my gut. "But Matt didn't have a bodyguard. I do."

"And what do you know about this...bodyguard?"

I hesitated. Flicked another glance at the man-mountain spread out across my settee. "Not much. But he seems sort of nice. And he's Jake's cousin."

Ben snorted. I guess I hadn't won him over. "Listen mate, if you want company tonight, I could be dressed and at your place in less than ten minutes."

Suddenly exhaustion hit me, so profound it ate deep down into my bones. I slumped in my chair and closed my eyes. No way could I cope with the open hostility raging between two testosterone-charged combatants tonight.

"Thanks Ben, but I'm whacked off my feet right now. Think I'll take a sleeping tablet and go to bed. Don't worry, I'll be safe. Scuzz and the dogs are camped in the lounge." I paused to allow this vital information to register. "But, hey, can we get together tomorrow morning? Plan what to do next?"

"Sure. Make it ten o'clock. I'll have my dogs worked by then and don't figure on leaving for the track until twelve. Like you, I have a dog racing in the Derby qualifiers tomorrow afternoon."

"Okay."

"But, Kat, you *do* know, if you need me before then, I'm as close as a phone call away?"

"Thanks Ben. You're a real good mate."

"Yeah, I know."

Hmm…did that sound like Ben sighing? Nah. Just experiencing a painful twinge of indigestion.

"Now," his voice took on a hard edge. "Before I get back under the shower, let me have a word with King Kong."

"His name is Scuzz."

Ben's deep throaty chuckle came down the phone line. "*That's* a name? Thought Scuzz was something you threw away with the garbage. Okay, pass the phone to the gorilla so I can warn him if he lays one finger on you I'll cut off his main appendage and feed it through my mincing machine."

Well, what do you know? My good mate, Ben was prepared to defend my honor. Pity after defending it he didn't fancy keeping it for himself.

I handed the phone to Scuzz and settled back in the armchair. Tater scaled my leg and made a nest in my lap. As I stroked his soft fur, kneaded the tiny muscles along his neck and listened to his blissful sighs, my tension slipped away. It's strange how animals have this almost magical power to relieve human stress.

My head fell back onto the head rest while I concentrated on following Tater's example, relaxing my muscles one by one from my neck, down to each individual toe. Eyes closed, I smiled as I listened to the one-sided conversation between my biker bodyguard and near-naked mate. Geez, if things didn't cool down soon they'd be calling for dueling pistols at dawn. Which would probably prove painful for me.

While secretly removing the bullets from both their guns, there was every likelihood I'd shoot myself in the foot.

*****

Perhaps the sleeping tablets were past their use by date. Perhaps I was allergic to the ingredients. Whatever the reason, sleep didn't come easily that night and when it finally did I had the sort of nightmare you normally only have after gourmandizing on pizza half an hour before bedtime.

131

A horde of maniacal garden gnomes with concrete smiles and bloody pitchforks were chasing me around my garden. Well, it felt like my garden—although it didn't look like it. My taste in flowers doesn't run to giant snapdragons with sharp pointed teeth. Anyway, these crazy gnomes kept grabbing at me and laughing. Not nice laughing either. It was that scary horror-movie sort of laugh where you grab a handful of popcorn and shove it in your mouth to stop from jabbering. Their eyes spun, their painted fingers reached for me and their spine-chilling laughter grew louder and more feral as I scrambled to get away. Underfoot, dead flowers with bloody tails coiled around my legs, tripping me over.

And there, nonchalantly leaning against a post and rail fence was my good mate, Ben. Thing is, when I called out to him for help, he didn't move. I called out again, this time more frantic. But still he didn't move. He'd pulled his akubra hat down over his face. When I looked more closely, I could see two dark eyes. Not Ben's eyes. These were flat and cold and remote.

"You're on your own, mate. I would have helped but you chose King Kong," the Ben lookalike hissed, just before turning into a snake and slithering away into the underbrush.

On the roadway ahead, hundreds of motorbikes quivered restlessly, all roaring, rumbling and spewing smoke. Astride each bike sat a black leather-clad creature with no head. Thick crimson blood gushed freely from the severed necks, oozed down over the headless bodies and pooled on the bitumen below.

I tell you, sometimes it doesn't pay to have an active imagination.

Thankfully, the insistent clamor of barking dogs ripped me from my nightmare. I squinted at the bedside clock.

7:36 a.m.

I groaned. No wonder the dogs were making a racket. I'd slept through the alarm.

While my quilt lay in a heap on the floor, my body seemed to be wrapped mummy-style inside the sweaty sheet. And I was bursting for a pee. Cursing the inherited genetic pool responsible for my pathetically weak bladder, I kicked my way to freedom. Once free, I shimmied cross-legged down the passageway and into the bathroom.

Urgent ablutions completed, I dragged on a pair of faded work jeans, a black, teal and white T-shirt, proving I was a Port Power supporter, and then glanced in the mirror.

Ugh!

Blotchy face, bloodshot eyes, hair resembling a wild prickle bush. No wonder Ben had trouble locating my hot, sexy-woman persona. It was hiding behind the Wicked Witch of the West. Shaking my head in frustration, I resolved, when this was all over, to make an appointment for a complete makeover at Changing Looks, the number one beauty salon in the nearby town of Virginia. As long as the makeover didn't involve injections, unknown substances, Botox or an expensively dressed doctor waving a razor-sharp scalpel.

No man, not even Ben, was worth undergoing torture.

Intent on taming my hair into a style that wouldn't scare the dogs, I burrowed deep inside my totebag in search of a hairbrush. Toothpicks, loose change, mobile phone, half a packet of chocolate M&Ms, a spare dog lead….

As I scrabbled deeper, the bag toppled to the floor. Immediately, the M&Ms broke for freedom, silver and gold coins competed in the race and the half-burnt piece of paper I'd found in Matt's fireplace flew from the bag and landed at my feet.

I picked it up. Studied it more closely. The bottom half of the account was so burnt it was mostly unrecognizable, but the top half maintained that Matthew Turner had deposited goods in the Saftee Security Depot at Salisbury and owed the firm $52.50 for services rendered.

Why had Matt tried to burn this particular account? Why not shove it in the drawer with the rest of his unpaid bills? After all, there'd been a mountain of those. Was it because he didn't want a certain person knowing he'd stored something in a security depot? If so, what the hell *had* he stored? It didn't make sense. I shook my head in confusion. What would mild-mannered Matt have to hide? And did it have anything to do with why he was murdered?

With no time to tax my befuddled brain any further, I folded the remains of the account over carefully, slipped the paper inside the back pocket of my jeans and quickly brushed my hair, tying it off my face with a scarf. Then, ready as I'd ever be, I started down the stairs. Breakfast, as usual, would mean grabbing a slice of toast and a quick cup of coffee before trekking out to the kennels.

The tantalizing smell of crisply cooked bacon wafted past me as I clattered to the bottom of the stairs. Crisply cooked bacon? Impossible. Unless the Food Fairies had paid me a visit overnight. Juices on full alert, I skidded through the kitchen doorway and allowed the scent of bacon, tomatoes, sausages and eggs to caress my nostrils and infiltrate my taste buds. *Oh yum! Oh bliss!* Of course Scuzz must be the culprit. And considering my refrigerator boasted nothing but cheese, bread and a couple of varieties of pet loaf, I also figured he must have had an early morning rendezvous with the local 24/7 store to buy the ingredients for this surprising feast.

I smiled, imagining the big guy dressed in his biker gear wielding an egg-flipper, my frilly apron like a little pink dot tied around his middle. Theodore Samuel Parkington the Third would make someone an excellent wife.

A note was propped up against my empty coffee mug. I picked it up and scanned the perfect copperplate writing: *Katrina, I let Tater and Lucky out for a tinkle. Breakfast is in the oven and you'll find hot coffee on the stove. Jake said to let you sleep in. He's started working the dogs so enjoy your breakfast. See you tonight. And remember, don't talk to any strangers. Your pal, Scuzz.*

Now I had a mate *and* a pal. All I needed to complete the Kat Friendship Club was a *buddy*!

17

Everyone knows the old saying: *you can lead a horse to water but you can't make him drink.* Well, there's another one in the greyhound game. *You can lead a dog to a hydro-bath but you can't always lug him up the ramp.*

I'd already clipped Lofty's toenails and treated a couple of sore muscles in his right shoulder with the ultrasonic machine but figured a hydro-bath would top off his preparations for Thursday night's race.

There was only one snag. Big goofy Lofty was averse to anything wet. When he realized the contraption we were heading toward looked suspiciously like a bath, he slammed on his brakes and I figured it would take a front-end loader to budge him. Jake had already left for a protest meeting, something to do with the rape of the River Murray, or maybe it was the rape of the parklands.

Whatever…

I was totally on my own here.

"Come on, Lofty, darling," I wheedled, trying to tempt the reluctant dog up the ramp with a piece of cheese. "You'll love the hydro-bath. Honest. Not only will the warm water relax your muscles, but this fabulous shampoo I picked out especially for you, is guaranteed to leave you smelling like rose petals."

There was a grunt behind me. "Huh! Rose petals? No wonder the big guy's refusing. I'd object to smelling like a girl, too. Kat, when are you going to learn that guy-dogs, like guy-people, do not appreciate flowery shampoos? They prefer to smell more masculine. You know, like dustbin lids, or footy sweat."

I took a quick glance over my shoulder and tossed a grin at the speaker. "Is that why your hair sometimes gives off that fragrant, washed-in-a-mud-puddle bouquet?"

Ben looked exactly like he did in my dream. He wore that same tight-lipped smile, raised eyebrows and pissed off, *you-chose-King Kong-over-me* expression. But thankfully, his eyes were normal, the color of rich dark chocolate and twice as enticing.

"Okay, Lofty," I gasped, struggling to prevent the dog from slipping his collar and darting back to his kennel. "If you behave yourself, I'll buy a special bottle of Testosterone shampoo tomorrow—especially for you."

"D'ya need any help there, mate?" Ben's voice was slow, almost drawling, as he watched me pit my muscles against the 42kg dog. Lofty had suddenly worked out that if he lay on the floor and played dead, it would take *two* front-end loaders to lift him into the bath.

"No, no, I'm in total control." I glared first at Ben then down at the prostrate canine. Cheese treats weren't working so I dug in my pocket and brought out the big guns. Tasty squares of dried liver. Hey, at that point I'd have bribed him with my very last Mars bar, except chocolate, due to its caffeine content, tests positive in a swab.

And wasn't that what I was going all out to avoid? Enter a drug-free dog in the race and ignore the psycho's warning.

Lofty took one sniff of the liver and scrambled to his feet. Mouth open, tail wagging, he lumbered up the ramp and devoured the liver treats in one chomp. I quickly checked my fingers. Thankfully they were all still intact, so I slammed the hydro-bath door closed and switched on the water.

Ben ambled closer. "You okay after last night, mate?" He scratched his chin. "Sorry if I sounded a bit grumpy when you rang."

I didn't answer. Too busy preventing a wet bucking mass of dog-flesh from leaping over the side of the bath and disappearing into the horizon. Instead, while directing the warm water spray onto the dog's right shoulder, I flicked my head in the direction of the treatment table, indicating for Ben to take a look.

"Did this come with the dead flowers?" he asked, lifting the message from inside the blood smeared envelope with two fingers.

"Mmm…" Lofty bucked again. I checked the temperature of the water, noted it was still okay at 30 degrees Celsius, so directed the water pressure along his back.

After reading the note, Ben tossed it back on the table. "Sniveling coward!" he growled and slammed the palm of his hand against the wall. "Shows how low the mongrel is prepared to go."

I reckoned he'd already proved how low he was prepared to go by killing Matt, but was having too much trouble with Lofty to vocalize my opinion.

Ben paced up and down, his fists closed so tightly the knuckles showed white. "One thing this sick note proves," he said at last. "There *is* a betting scam going on. But what I don't understand is why kill Matt?"

I grunted my affirmation. I guess if we knew the *why*, we'd likely know the *who*.

Ben's voice grew thoughtful. "Could Matt have been involved in the scam, developed cold feet and threatened to expose the boss, so he had to be silenced?"

"Sounds reasonable," I agreed. At last Lofty had relaxed which allowed me to take part in the conversation.

"Anyway, what are you going to do about this?" Ben flicked the anonymous note with one finger.

"Use it for loo paper?"

He must have taken me seriously because he didn't return my smile. Instead he instructed me to put the message in a plastic bag for forensic evidence then contact Peter Manning, the dog's owner.

"Look, I'll cover the note with plastic in case we need to contact the police later but I'm not bringing Pete in on this."

"Lofty is Peter's dog," Ben insisted. "Don't you think he deserves to know what's going on?"

"That's the thing—nothing *will* be going on. I'm ignoring the message. So there's no need to tell Peter anything."

I guess I had a horrible suspicion Lofty's owner might want me to play along with the threat. After all, he could always place a bet on the second favorite in the race and win a bundle that way. Where most people had pupils in the middle of their eyes, Tire Man Pete had dollar signs.

"Anyway," I added, grinning at my fellow sleuth as I hurriedly changed the subject. "Guess what?"

"You put flea powder in the gorilla's boxer shorts before he left this morning?"

I shook my head in denial. "No, I've been nowhere near Scuzz's shorts. In fact," I mused, "I don't know if he even wears underwear. If he does, judging by his taste in sheets and pillow cases, he probably wears hot pink satin boxers with maybe a sprinkling of little yellow teddy bears gamboling across them."

Ben's grin widened into a paddock. "You're kidding. Right?"

"Well…it's only a guess."

"So what's this about his sheets and pillow case?"

"None of your business." Trust me to open my big mouth and give Ben ammunition to use against his nemesis. "And I want you to promise this conversation about Scuzz's mythical boxers stays between you and me."

"Okay."

"Okay, what?" I asked warily.

"I won't tell the big bad biker you said he wears pink satin boxers with yellow teddies."

"Ben…"

"*Your* words not *mine*."

Resisting the urge to spray the big lug with the hose, I gave him a raspberry before continuing. "If we can leave Scuzz's underwear alone for a couple of minutes, what I've been trying to tell you is…I've found a clue. In fact, it's a real ripper of a clue." I turned Lofty around inside the hydro-bath so I could spray the muscles on his left side. "With any luck, this clue might even lead us to Matt's murderer."

"Go on then…fill me in."

"There's a piece of paper in my back pocket. Think you could get it out for me? My hands are wet and the paper's fragile." Ben sauntered up behind me, his closeness making me almost drop the hose. "Um…be gentle now."

I closed my eyes and breathed in the smell of pine trees and fresh air emanating from Ben's body. He was so close his warm breath tickled the back of my neck. And when I felt his fingers slowly slip into the back pocket of my jeans, I had to clench my stomach muscles and hang on to the side of the bath to stop from moaning and melting into a pool of liquid lust at his feet.

"This it?" he asked, pulling out the burnt paper and moving back a step to study his find. Evidently having his hand on my bum had done bugger all for him, whereas I wanted to drag him closer, kiss him senseless, rip off his shirt, undo his belt.…

"What am I supposed to be looking at?" Ben asked.

I cleared my throat and told my unruly hormones to go take a cold shower. "Remember when we were searching for clues at Matt's house?"

"And we found zilch?" He placed the clue next to the threatening note on the table and selected a couple of thick dog towels from the cupboard.

"Well, I found that account in Matt's fireplace."

"And?"

"As you can see, it's from a storage depot. I didn't think much of it at the time, but hey, Matt must have something important stored at that depot, otherwise, why burn the evidence?"

After I undid the ramp on the hydro-therapy unit and led a much subdued Lofty out, Ben took over. He straddled the dog's body and began toweling him dry with strong circular strokes. Which was very distracting. I ran my wet hands through my hair until it stood on end like a porcupine's quills. Not that Ben would notice. He wouldn't notice if I took my head off and replaced it with a pumpkin.

"I've decided to pay Saftee Storage Depot a visit tomorrow," I told him. "See if I can sweet-talk the receptionist into letting me have a nosy in Matt's storage box." I watched the muscles under Ben's faded shirt ripple and bulge as he rubbed Lofty's coat dry. "Um…" I gulped down another load of itchy hormones and fastened my top teeth into my bottom lip to stop from visibly drooling. "Want to tag along?"

"Sure, what say I meet you here around the same time?" Ben fastened a rug around the dog's middle and handed the lead back to me. As he did so his hand brushed against mine setting the resultant flesh alive with electricity.

"Okay."

"And don't worry about getting a look inside Matt's storage box. If the receptionist at this depot is female, just leave it to the master." He winked, threw me a sexy, I'm-hot grin. The grin that invariably sent butterflies crashing crazily around in my stomach, slamming into my liver and tickling my bladder. "After all," he concluded, as he sauntered towards the open kennel-house door. "*Sweet-Talk,* is my middle name."

18

In the half hour it took to drive to Globe Raceway for the heats of the Derby, a cold gusty wind sprung up from nowhere and the sky turned to grey porridge overhead.

Hunched deep into the collar of my fur-lined denim jacket, I queued behind a dozen other handlers, all waiting to present dogs to the steward. It was the steward's job to check registration papers against the dog's ear-brands or micro-chips before allowing us to move into the kennel-house where the dog would be weighed and then checked over by the vet before being kenneled.

The ten Derby qualifying heats scheduled for the afternoon's program were for male greyhounds born two years ago, on or before July first. My only runner in the Group Two series was Wonder Boy, a chunky fawn youngster who'd already won a couple of races in the city.

Cozy in his warm tartan rug, Wonder Boy, or Clark, as he was affectionately known to his friends, stood beside me on a tight lead, ears pricked, nose flared.

In front of us an overexcited black-and-white greyhound twisted and bounced on the end of his lead, almost upending his petite handler, Leanne Jackman.

"I don't know what's got into Gumbee," Leanne groaned, pushing the dog down from around her neck for the third time in as many minutes and straightening her jacket. "It's lucky he's in an early race.

He's dribbling up a storm. Reckon if he had to hang around and wait for the last, I'd be wringing water from his kennel-mattress."

Without a spare hand to hunt for a tissue, she hunched one shoulder and used it to wipe a glob of the dog's dribble from her cheek.

"Is he normally so over the top?" I asked, gently pulling Clark from the path of Gumbee's spiraling leaps.

"He's a spirited lad—but not usually an idiot."

Nearby, I could see several trainers walking aimlessly around encouraging their dogs to squat or cock their legs on their allocated patch of grass before tacking on the end of the queue. The line shuffled forward slowly. All heading towards the official steward who read ear-brands, scanned micro-chips and checked each dog's racing papers. He stood at the entrance to a large, state-of-the-art, glass fronted kennel-house through which both trainers and punters could view the dogs in their holding cages and observe first-hand the unfolding process of a well-organized race day.

From his position behind me in the line, Dane Taylor, a professional trainer with around sixty greyhounds in work, sidled closer. "Hey, Leanne," he whispered in his *this-is-just-between-you-and-me* voice. "Are you sure someone didn't *dope* that dog of yours?"

"Of course I'm sure!" Leanne snapped. She shook her head and eyed Dane as if she thought he needed a good psychiatrist. Or a good bat over the head. "Our German shepherd wouldn't let *God* in our backyard, without my say-so. If a stranger tried to sneak in, he'd lose an arm or leg in the process." She frowned, her pixie face angry. "Anyway, what brought on a damn fool question like that?"

Dane cast a furtive glance over his shoulder then spoke from the corner of his mouth. "I hear there's a bit of it goin' on. Dopin' I mean." He paused for effect. "Did you hear what happened to old Art Basset?"

Leanne, not losing the frown, shook her head.

Art Basset was the guy who'd rubbed me up the wrong way the night Lucky decided to stay in the starting boxes. "Knowing that cantankerous old fart," I growled, moving up in line as another greyhound checked into the kennel-house, "he probably bought himself a punch in the nose. Did he tell some female her skirt was too short or she should be home cooking her man's tea instead of gallivanting around the track looking like a slut?"

"Not that I've heard," Dane answered, looking confused. "But word's around his dog swabbed positive to caffeine."

"Rubbish!" I snorted. "Art's a cranky old geezer but he's not stupid. He told me once he's been in the game for over fifty years and not one of his dogs ever tested positive to anything but good old-fashioned raw meat. And I believe him."

Jason Black, the trainer in front of Leanne, turned around to join in the conversation, his face flushed and animated. If he was a dog I reckon he'd be panting and drooling with excitement, not unlike Gumbee.

"It's not a rumor," he assured us, spittle gathering in both corners of his mouth. "It's true. You know Pitachi Gambler, that slow mutt of Art's?"

I nodded.

"Well, last week he opened up at 25/1 and then shortened to even money favorite three minutes before the race. And you know what— the bloody dog won in the best time of the day. 29.80? No wonder the stewards called for a swab. Everyone knows Pitachi Gambler can't break thirty seconds. Even on a good day when he gets a clear run, he's only a 30.50 dog." Jason paused, shifted his head close to mine and breathed the pungent odor of garlic into my face. "A mate of mine was catching another dog in that race," he went on in a theatrical whisper. "He reckons after Art's dog passed the finishing post, its eyes were rolling, it was frothing at the mouth and when it staggered and fell, he thought the dog had croaked its last."

Dane, not wanting to miss a word, shuffled closer, sandwiching Leanne and me between the two sweaty male bodies. I held my breath as I didn't fancy gassing by garlic. Leanne looked ready to knee one of them in the whatnots. Instead she elbowed her way into the clear and glared at the two offenders.

"Watch what you're at, you morons." Two bright spots of red burned her cheeks. "You could have trodden on Gumbee's foot."

"Er…sorry, love." Jason apologized, stepping back quickly. Then, too excited to waste any more time on remorse, he continued. "And a guy at the pub told me the stewards rubbed Art out for six months."

"That's gotta be right," put in Dane nodding like one of the three wise men. "'Cause both Art's dogs have been scratched from today's meeting."

By the time I'd had Clark's micro-chip scanned, I'd learned Art professed to know nothing about how the caffeine was administered. And by the time Clark had been through the weighing machine and over the vet's table, I'd discovered Art had been so upset by these accusations he'd collapsed and been rushed to hospital with a suspected heart attack.

When I emerged from the kennel-house, two of Clark's owners, Marjory and Bob Sanders grabbed me. Residents from the RSL Aged Care Facility that syndicated Clark, they always attended his races. Marjory was eighty and Bob a couple years older.

As I approached, I could see them chatting to a short dark-haired guy, who, when he turned around, proved to be Sean Basset, Art's youngest son.

"Hey, Kat, I was just telling Sean here that our boy, Clark, is going to win today." Marjory enveloped me in a bear hug that proved water-aerobics for seniors was an excellent idea for keeping elderly muscles strong. "Am I right?"

"You betcha," I replied, returning Marjory's hug. "So you'd better put a couple of dollars on him."

"Couple of dollars?" teased Bob, kissing me on the cheek. "My pockets are bulging with money. Every resident at the Home gave me a fistful of dollars to put on our boy today. If he loses, there'll be no money for pokies or antacid tablets for the next month."

"Don't listen to him, Kat." Marjory laughed. "They're so damn miserly Bob had to shame them into parting with a dollar each."

I could see Sean edging away so placed one hand on his arm to stop him. "Sorry to hear about your Dad, Sean. They tell me he's in hospital."

"Yeah." Sean gazed down at his feet.

"Is he going to be okay?"

He looked up and I got my answer. His eyes were bleak and his face drawn. "The doctors have scheduled a bypass operation for tomorrow."

"Your dad's tough, Sean, he'll bounce back."

"Kat's right," agreed Bob, slapping Sean on the back. "No need to worry, lad. A bypass op is a piece of cake these days. I had a triple bypass two years ago and look at me now. Good as new. I even won the fifty meter sprint at the Master's Games last month."

"Don't boast, Robert," said Marjory, digging her husband in the ribs and pursing her lips. "You were the only entry in the over-eighty event and I swear it took you five minutes to reach the finishing tape."

"Won't let a bloke have a moment of glory, will you, woman?" Bob flashed his toothless smile at her before gently taking his wife's arm. "Come on Marj, Clark's in the first race so we'd better get our bets on and find a good possie to watch him. See you in the winner's circle, Kat."

As they shuffled off, laughing and teasing each other, I turned to Sean. Somehow Art's youngest son had survived his father's tough upbringing and, unlike his two older brothers, was the reverse of his bullying father. A real sweetie, he'd married a lovely girl and produced a gaggle of gorgeous dark-haired kids with the same happy nature and generous smiles as their parents.

"I *am* sorry about your dad, Sean," I said keeping my voice low as a couple of trainers sauntered past, eyes curiously watching us. "I know he can be a pain in the butt at times, but he's straight as a shot from a gun. No way would he drug his dogs."

"Thanks, Kat. Appreciate that. Of course Pa's innocent but the dog *did* test positive to caffeine in the swab."

"Does your dad have any theories?"

"Not really. But he did say some lowlife rang him a couple of days before the race, insisted he drug Pitachi Gambler to win and threatened to cause Dad trouble if he refused."

"I can imagine where your dad told him to shove that threat."

"Yeah. And exactly how far up." Sean wrinkled his nose. "Then after the dog romped home at good odds and the swab proved positive, Pa swore he'd find out who stitched him up. Said when he did he'd run them over with his tractor. And he would too. In fact, when he found Big Mick, the bookie, hanging around the kennels the day after the phone call he got suspicious. Chased him off with a pitchfork."

"Mick Harrison? What was he doing there?"

"Innocent really. Turns out Mick was on his way to visit his grandmother at some nursing home and ran out of petrol. Thought Pa might have some to spare."

"Did your father mention any of this to the stewards?"

"I'm not sure, Kat. See the day of the enquiry, Pa was so angry about being accused of doping his dog, he wasn't rational. I offered to go to the meeting with him, but that made him even more upset. Said he was quite capable of telling those weak-kneed pansy stewards what he thought of them without any help from me."

"Typical." *Probably told them to go home and scrub the makeup off their wives' faces instead of wasting time harassing him.*

"Anyway," Sean went on, shaking his head. "Pa got himself so worked up at the enquiry he collapsed. They had to call an ambulance."

"Don't suppose your dad has any idea who threatened him on the phone?"

"Hell, no, if he did they'd be covered in tractor tire treads by now. The mystery caller used a public telephone and covered the handset with a handkerchief. Dad couldn't recognize the voice at all."

"Hmm…sounds like the same person who killed Matt Turner." I quickly filled Sean in on the phone call I'd received after finding Matt's body, swearing him to secrecy. "And if it *was* him—we're closing in."

"Closing in?"

"Yes. I happen to be in possession of a clue that just might point to this scumbag's identity."

"What clue?"

"Sorry, I can't tell you, Sean," I answered, shaking my head. "The less you know, the safer you and your family will be. Just hang in there, look after your dad and if this mystery caller rings again, let me know. Meanwhile…when you visit that old fossil in hospital, tell him I said he's a lazy slob. While he's in bed flirting with the nurses I'm left to do all the detective work."

Momentarily Sean's eyes lost their anxiety. "Thanks, Kat. I'm sure Pa will appreciate that."

I gave his arm a quick squeeze before excusing myself. The steward on the gate was calling for all trainers with dogs engaged in the first race to report to the kennel-house.

So—time to find out if Clark was good enough to be a Derby prospect.

19

Should i have worn a dress instead of jeans? Selected a top that displayed more cleavage? Did my new slut-red lipstick make me look cheap?

It was ten fifteen the following morning and Ben was due to pick me up any minute. Posing in front of the full-length mirror in the bathroom, I unscrewed the lid of a small heart-shaped bottle of perfume called *Grrr,* dabbed a couple of drops behind both ears and the pulse point on my wrists. According to the label, the contents were guaranteed to drive any man crazy. With Ben in mind, I'd purchased three vials at The Luv Bug while waiting for Tanya to knock off work last week.

Okay, our planned outing wasn't what you'd call a real date. We were only driving to Salisbury, a largish town about half an hour away, to check Matt's storage deposit box. Not what you'd call a romantic dinner for two. But hey, I figured a girl had to grab whatever opportunity was thrown at her and run with it.

So...I'd washed my hair with coconut shampoo and brushed every strand until it shone. I'd pulled on a newish pair of hipster jeans, a silky plum-colored long-sleeved top and even replaced my sneakers with gorgeous high-heeled suede knee-high boots. In fact, when I took a second look at myself in the mirror, I didn't think I looked half bad. Now, if only Blind Benny could remove his blinkers long enough to get an eyeful, my preparations this morning might not go unrewarded.

Ben's noisy Kombi van belched its way down the driveway and stuttered to a stop. I shook my head. If he didn't get that exhaust fixed soon he'd end up with a defect sticker. At the moment, that was the least of my worries, so grabbing my mobile, I dropped it into my bag and waltzed through the front doorway, ready to present myself for inspection.

Okay…here I am Lover-Boy. Take me. I'm all yours.

"Hey," said Blind Benny, registering my presence with a quick nod of his head before burying said head under the dashboard to fiddle with the car radio.

I gave a weary *Hey* in return and trudged towards my front gate. What was I expecting—a slow-motion love scene from *Titanic*?

"Good win by Clark yesterday," Ben yelled, nosing the car out onto the bitumen road and waiting for me to close the gate behind us. "The little bugger scampered too. 29.90. Not bad running time for a youngster."

I locked the gate and climbed into the car. "Marjory and Bob were over the moon with his win." I shouted to be heard over the noise as Ben put the van into drive and we roared off down the road. "You'd have thought Clark had won the Melbourne Cup." Smiling, I remembered the little dance the two seniors had performed when their dog went past the post five lengths ahead of the rest of the field. "And when Marjory rang me last night, she said the residents of the Home watched the replay of the race twenty times before the Chief of Staff could get them out of the recreation room and off to bed."

"Well, let's hope Clark draws box one in the semifinals next week."

I laughed. "And if he wins and gets a run in the Derby final, Globe Raceway will need to install extra handicapped spaces for the twenty-two seniors who'll be hitting the trackto cheer him on."

Ben turned off Strangways Terrace into Brother Road and drove toward the storage depot. Would the contents of Matt's storage box reveal who we were up against? We badly needed a hot tip at this stage of our investigation. Hot enough to smoke out a killer.

"Did you hear what happened to Art Basset?"

"Yeah, bloody ridiculous." Ben looked up and down the road, checking for an empty parking space. "Anyone with half a brain would know Basset wouldn't dope his dogs."

"I was talking to his son, Sean, and he's worried sick. The hospital says Art needs a bypass operation." I shivered as I thought of Art being sliced open and doctors snipping away inside his chest.

"Basset's temper has always been his downfall."

"You know, if Art dies I'd class his death as another notch in the murderer's belt. Sean says his father got a call from our heavy breather two nights before the race demanding he hit up Pitachi Gambler."

"I can imagine where Art told him to go."

I shivered as prickles of dread crept across my skin. "Yeah, but that didn't make any difference, did it? Someone still got to his dog and now Art's in hospital."

Ben's large work-calloused hands tightened on the steering wheel. "I'm ahead of you, mate." He flicked a quick look in my direction as he angled into a vacant park. "Which means you'll need to double-check your security system in the kennels until this is over. And do the same with your house. Okay?"

"You've got it." My mind drifted back to my last conversation with Sean. "Another thing, Sean said his Dad disturbed Big Mick, the bookie, mooching around his place the day after the phone call. Bit of a skanky excuse too. Reckons he ran out of petrol and was coming to see if Art could help him out."

"It's a wonder he escaped in one piece. Art hates his guts."

I pictured the scene and let out a laugh. "I believe there was a pitchfork involved and not a drop of petrol changed hands."

By now we were parked in front of No. 73 Brother Road. The long red brick building reminded me of a prison. However, according to a sign out the front, the company proclaimed itself to be a high-tech facility catering for everything: '...*from your smallest valuable to a houseful of furniture.'*

The offices near the gate were dwarfed by close to fifty or sixty large red brick garage type buildings, all with roller-doors secured by several locks and bolts. Without the appropriate key, I imagined a thief would need explosives to break in.

"Come on, mate, let's get this show on the road." Ben slipped his arm through mine and led me towards the main office. "Take note. You're about to witness a demonstration that will knock those fancy boots clean off your feet."

Aha. Progress. He may not have noticed my body but at least he'd noticed my boots.

"And what demonstration would that be—mate?"

"The Master at work."

There were two women behind the front desk. One, a film star look-alike in her early twenties, curves all in the right places, long straight blonde hair that swayed sensuously when she moved and bright red lipstick that looked as though it had been applied with a shovel. The other was a bespectacled middle-aged woman shaped like a pear, no makeup, dull mousy hair done up in a bun so tight it made her forehead resemble plastic.

Ben zeroed straight in on the film star look-alike. Of course.

"Hellooo," he yodeled, eyes sparkling with evident appreciation. "Have we come to the right place here? I thought this was a storage depot—not a film studio." He smiled at the younger woman and then put on this corny, wide-eyed, *oh-looky-here* expression. "Hey, you're not Madonna's twin sister are you?"

What a ham. I could barely stop myself from sticking my finger down my throat and emitting vomit noises.

The Madonna wannabe giggled into one perfectly manicured hand, every finger topped with inch long red talons. "No, I'm Scarlett."

"Scaaaarlett." Ben rolled the word around on his tongue like it was a fine vintage wine. "As in, *Gone with the Wind*?"

"Mummy jus *adored* that movie."

Oh God...

Ben rested both elbows on the polished counter and leaned closer. Another inch or two and he'd be near enough to lock lips with the woman. In fact, the sight of this potential intimacy had me itching to pucker up and insert my own slut-red lips between them.

"We're here to examine Matt Turner's storage box," I blurted, unable to stand the sickening performance any longer.

The boss lady at the other end of the counter looked up, suddenly alert. She peered down her hooked nose at the scene being enacted in front of her and then cleared her throat.

"Scarlett, they're calling for someone at storage area number 26. Could you see what they want, please?"

After glaring daggers of accusation at me, Ben turned to the other woman. "Excuse me, ma'am, but Miss Scarlett is busy. She's attending to us."

As though he were invisible, the dragon lady quirked her lips a fraction, just enough to send Scarlett a caricature of a smile. "Number 26 please, dear. Now, hurry along, it goes against company policy to keep customers waiting."

Ben's eyes glazed over as he watched *Gone with the Wind*'s namesake mince her way towards the door on her red strappy high heels. Her hot red dress so tight it caused her perky little bottom to wiggle with every step. But before he could make a move to follow this vision of perfection, I grabbed the tail of his flannel shirt in a death grip and held on.

"Hmmph!" The dragon lady threw Ben a poisonous, *all-men-are-assholes* glare, before dropping her head and continuing to bang away on her keyboard.

I blinked in confusion. What happened to company policy? If we weren't potential customers—what were we? Secondary characters in a novel?

Giving up, I gave Ben a nudge to remind him of the purpose of our visit. Earth to Ben...Earth to Ben. When he didn't respond, I nudged harder—almost dislocating my elbow in an attempt to get him back on track.

Finally, he shook his head as though dislodging whatever erotic thoughts had gathered for a party and slowly turned to focus on Scarlett's substitute. The horror in his eyes indicated he considered the substitute defective. His jaw tightened and he rolled both shoulders, ready to continue his *sweet-talk* demonstration.

After all—this was Benjamin Taylor and the dragon lady *was* female.

"Hello there," he drawled cranking out his *I'm-Mr-Wonderful-and-there's-no-way-you-can-resist-me* smile.

The toxic glare she hurled his way could have annihilated a plague of cockroaches. Yet it hardly made a dent on Mr. Wonderful's ego.

I smothered a grin. Could my mate finally have met his match?

Still smothering a grin, I flipped Matt's half burnt bill onto the counter. "We're here to pay an account and check the contents of a storage box."

The woman completed whatever it was on her computer that was more important than attending to customers, and then regarded me through her wire frames, small grey eyes frosty, a scowl set in concrete above her hooked nose. "And *you* are?"

I took a small step away from the counter and silently passed the baton back to *Sweet Talk*.

Clearing his throat, Ben began what looked like, to me, an impersonation of a bull-frog. Puffed chest, head high, jaw thrust forward to show off his sculpted chin. I almost expected to hear a deep *ribbett…ribbett* coming from deep in his throat. Instead, he smiled at his target and crooned, "Isn't it a lovely morning, Miss—"

"Ms.," she corrected and the temperature in the room dropped another twenty degrees. "Ms. Stratton. As you can see by the plaque on the counter."

Ben blinked. "Um…well, Ms. Stratton, as my friend, Kat explained, we have an overdue account we'd like to pay."

"Identification?"

Ben's smile sagged at the edges. "Identification?"

"Naturally. We always require identification from our clients."

Ben fumbled in his back pocket, came out with a wallet and placed his driver's license on the counter.

The dragon lady let loose another blistering scowl. If Ben was bread he'd now be toast. "This says, Benjamin Elijah Taylor. The name on the account is Matthew Turner."

"Elijah? And here was me thinking your middle name was *Sweet Talk*," I murmured, giving Ben another dig in the ribs. By the end of the day he'd have a bunch of bruises under his shirt.

Noting Ben's slightly dazed expression, I jumped in, suede boots and all, in an effort to save any further embarrassment. "Ms. Stratton, allow me to explain. Matthew Turner is my cousin. He can't get here today because he's—well, he's sort of indisposed." I crossed my fingers tightly behind my back. "Anyway, he asked me to pay his account and check his storage box."

"Identification?"

Geez…what was it with this woman and her phobia for ID? A person she trusted must have let her down badly in her dark and dismal past by pretending to be someone they weren't.

And we were copping the back-wash.

I handed Ms. Stratton my trainer's license. At least that had a slightly better photo than the unsmiling chinless thug displayed on my driver's license. I hate the way motor-vehicle department's photographers always wait until I'm thinking black thoughts, feeling impatient, or just plain glaring at some creep in the queue who's been ogling my boobs for the last ten minutes, before taking the photo.

"Your surname isn't Turner—it's McKinley."

Ms. Stratton of the snotty attitude was starting to get up my nose. "Since when has *that* been a crime?" I asked her. "As a matter of interest, how many cousins do *you* have with a different surname to yours?"

The sharp point of Ben's elbow caught *me* in the ribs.

"My dear, Ms. Stratton," he drawled, flashing another valiant smile at

Ice Woman. "A lady of your intelligence will appreciate we're not here to waste your valuable time, only to pay Matthew Turner's current account. You see, it's impossible for um...Kat's cousin to come in person, but he asked us to take care of his account and while we're here, check the contents of his storage box. Make sure it's exactly as he left it."

"I see." Was that a slight softening of the gimlet eyes behind Ice Woman's wire-rimmed specs? "That will be $52.50. Will you be paying by check or cash?"

"Cash," said Ben, his smile tottering on a smirk as he turned to me. "Right, Kat. Pay the nice lady."

"Me?"

His grin widened.

Suppressing the childish urge to stick out my tongue, I rummaged in the pockets of my jeans and brought out two screwed up $20 notes and a handful of coins.

"$46.10. That's all I have on me."

He shrugged then counted the remaining $6.40 from his back pocket before sliding the money across the counter. "So...now that's all settled, we'd like to check Matt's storage box. Merely to confirm the contents are safe."

Ms. Stratton slowly counted the money into a cash register and after making out a receipt, handed it to me. And I swear, just before she opened her mouth to speak, she *almost* smiled.

"Password?"

Ben let out a yelp of incredulity. "Password?"

"We cannot allow anyone to examine one of our storage boxes without giving the correct password. Company rules."

And I thought training greyhounds was an uphill job. If this was any indication of the problems associated with earning a living as a private investigator, they were welcome to it.

"Um—let's see," growled Ben. "Would it be...*greyhound*?"

"Sorry."

"What about *racing*?"

She shook her head again.

"*Queen of Egypt*?"

"Uh! Uh!"

"*Betting-ticket*?"

"*Race-form*?"

"*Win and place*?"

"*Quinella*?"

Ms. Stratton's head flicked from side to side like one of those painted clowns in a sideshow booth where a customer drops a ball into a moving mouth in the hope of winning a plastic comb, a Kewpie doll, or a stuffed soft animal.

The dragon lady was thoroughly enjoying herself. I could tell. Every time she shook her head, her lips disappeared inside her mouth and her eyes sparkled.

What word would Matthew have used as his password?

"I know! I know!" I yelled, flapping one arm in the air, like a school kid asking to go to the bathroom. "It's *TAB*. Matt's password *has* to be TAB."

Just as I caught the imperceptible quiver of Ms. Stratton's bottom lip, which meant I'd spoilt her day, my mobile began to trill, *Stayin' Alive*.

"Hold that password," I told her and held up one finger before answering my phone. "Kat McKinley of McKinley Greyhounds."

"G'day, Kat. Dan here. Can I have a word with Erin?"

I blinked. Confused. "Erin? No. Why would Erin be with *me*, Dan?"

There was a slight pause. I could hear a quick intake of breath before Dan spoke again. "Why *wouldn't* Erin be with you? She's staying with you, isn't she?"

"No."

"Well, if she's not with you…where the hell *is* she?"

"How should I know?" We seemed to be going around in circles. Dan could be so thick sometimes so I spoke slowly and distinctly, as to a child. "Dan, the last I heard from Erin was when I spoke to her on the phone last night. She said your car had broken down and she was waiting for some guy to pick her up. Some guy you'd met at the pub, which is pretty damn slack if you ask—"

"Yeah, yeah," Dan broke in. "But when George got there Erin was gone."

"Gone?" I went cold all over. "What do you mean, gone? And what makes you think she's with me?"

"She left a note. Said she was staying with you until Tanya got back."

The cold dribbled into my bones. "And the note was definitely written by Erin?"

"Of course, otherwise I'd have rung the cops."

That's when the shaking started and my voice box went rusty. "Dan," I croaked. "I know nothing about a note."

Had the little wretch decided to stay overnight with one of her friends and used me as an alibi? Or had something terrible happened to Erin?

I must have looked as rattled as I felt because next minute Ben's arms were around me, the rough material of his shirt pressing against my cheek.

"It's Erin," I whispered. "She's disappeared."

"No sweat," he said into my hair. "You know what a pain in the butt that kid is. She'll be at a friend's house playing games on their X-box."

Ben, one arm still around my shoulders plucked the phone from my fingers as he guided me towards the open doorway.

"Dan. Ben here," he growled into my mobile. "Listen, mate, Kat and I are on the move now. We'll ask around the streets and check the river. Meanwhile, why don't you get some mates out there searching for her and if no one's found her by 4 o'clock, we'll meet up at Kat's house. Right?" He paused to listen to something Dan said. When he spoke again his voice was softer. "Hey, don't spit the dummy mate, Erin can't be far away. Ring around and ask if any of her friends have seen her. And mate," he said before hanging up, "don't forget to give us a ring back when you find her."

As we powered through the office doorway I heard Ms. Stratton's disappointed wail following us. "TAB? Don't you want to know if that's the correct password?"

But we were too busy attempting to beat the land-speed record back to Ben's van to answer.

20

Two hours later Ben and I were still searching for Erin. We'd been to the park, we'd peered into both historical wells, which the town was named after, cross-examined shopkeepers, given joggers the third-degree and stopped locals out walking their dogs. We even poked sticks into the Gawler River. Of course the river at this time of the year wasn't much more than a trickle, but I figured if Erin was like most kids, she'd be fascinated by water and perhaps set up camp in the bushes nearby.

No camp. No clues. No Erin.

What did I expect? Erin wasn't *most* kids!

So, next item on the agenda—door-knocking. If I had a personal list of *Things I most hate doing*—door-knocking would come just below having teeth pulled without gas. Honestly, if I had to make a living as a door-to-door saleswoman I'd be sleeping under a bridge and eating dinner from restaurant garbage bins.

And if today's experience was anything to go by there was no reason to change my mind.

After banging on doors for over an hour we discovered that sixty percent of people have their televisions up so loud they wouldn't know if a hurricane hit them until their screen went static. Of the rest, ten percent hadn't seen Erin. The other thirty percent yelled "Go away! Don't want any!" and slammed the door in our faces before we'd even asked our first question.

It wasn't until we came across a group of spray-can toting kids doing a graffiti job on someone's back fence that we stumbled on a clue. Well, actually, it was Ben who stumbled on it. He was so busy questioning me about how long Scuzz intended hanging around, he didn't see this girl of about thirteen, complete with arm and ankle tats, until he stubbed his toe on her calf muscle. She was stretched across the footpath drawing stick figures in red and blue paints. And boy, what those stick figures were up to would have made a prostitute blush.

After establishing Tattoo Girl wasn't traumatized or in need of hospitalization due to the hefty size twelve to the leg, I gave the kids the third degree. Seems like Tattoo Girl, who had been sitting on her own roof sharing a bong with her boyfriend on the night of Erin's disappearance, lived across the road from Tanya. When questioned further, she told us she'd noticed this grey car with a yellow driver's side door cruise down Tanya's driveway and pull up at the house. The driver had gone inside and when he came out, seemed to be acting suspiciously. I asked her to define *suspiciously*. She said he was, *like, running from the house.*

Instantly my sleuthing antenna went all twitchy. That is until I realized the owner of the car was probably Dan's pub-mate, George, the guy Dan had sent to pick up Erin.

Still, a clue is a clue.

If we could believe Tattoo Girl, who may have been hallucinating on a bad batch of grass at the time, George was carrying something under his arm when he left Tanya's house. I asked the girl if it could have been Erin. She hesitated, thought a bit, and then said, *nah, too square.* I wasn't sure if she meant the kid he was carrying was too square to be a cool dude like Erin, or that George was carrying a box.

We seemed to have hit a dead end with Tattoo Girl so, with nothing else to go on, Ben and I decided maybe it was time to hunt down this George and have a bit of a chat.

So we set off on a pub-crawl.

Three pubs later we caught up with our quarry. He was at the Billabong, a small white-washed pub in the heart of Virginia. And it didn't take a degree in Investigative Science to figure out George was inside. A grey Holden sedan was parked out the front; its bright yellow driver's side door a dead giveaway.

It must have been happy hour at the Billabong because the pub was rocking. When Ben and I pushed through the swing doors into the front bar, the noise hit me like a physical blast.

Several curious eyes swiveled in our direction. A drunk, his clothes reeking of cheap booze, begged me for five dollars. Swore he hadn't eaten in three weeks. Instead of feeling sorry for the guy, which would have been my normal reaction, I returned his smile, pretended I couldn't hear him over the noise, and just kept on walking.

Mother would have been proud of me!

While scanning the room for George I suddenly realized I didn't know what he looked like. "How do we recognize this guy?" I whispered in Ben's ear, resisting the urge to stroke the baby-soft hairs on the back of his neck with the tip of my tongue.

"Just leave it to me, mate."

I pulled away from him, a snarling tiger. One of these days when he called me *mate*, I'd shove his words so far down his throat he'd be sitting on them.

Ben's cousin, Clappers, who was propping up one end of the bar, gestured to the empty space beside him. We muscled our way over. While Ben made subtle enquiries about which beer-swilling customer was George, I ordered two beers—a light, and a full strength—and then nodded towards my *mate*. Hey, I'd paid the bigger percentage of Matt's account—Ben could fork out for the booze.

Two beers, topped by white froth, slid easily across the grainy bar towards us. Never had a drink been more welcomed. In case you've never spent time searching for an eleven-year-old who is determined not to be found, let me tell you, on a fun level, it's up there with jumping out of a plane without a parachute. To say I was pissed off with Erin was putting it mildly.

My hand reached for the beer. A quick upward motion and the cold glass met my parched lips. *Oooh bliss...* As the amber liquid ran slowly and deliciously down my throat, I watched Ben scull his beer in one and bang the empty glass back down on the bar.

"There's our man," he said, leaning closer and nodding towards the eight-ball table at the far end of the room. "George is the guy in the baggy khaki overalls doing a con job on the Dale brothers." He shook his head and snorted in disgust. "Fair dinkum, those two nitwits wouldn't know a shark if it swam up and bit 'em on the bum. The way George is suckering them in, they'll be fleeced of their dole money quicker than the time it took to collect it."

So...that was George. Chubby face. Long greasy yellow hair. Overweight. I frowned. He seemed vaguely familiar. Couldn't quite put my finger on where I'd seen him before...but I was working on it.

While Ben ordered another round of drinks, I threaded my way through a clutch of noisy punters, all intent on watching shiny-coated horses gallop across the large screen set on the bar wall. At last I reached the eight-ball table and stood behind the guy in the khaki overalls. Up close I could see rolls of fat circling his waist line and the beginning of a bald patch skulking on the crown of his head. I waited. Timed my first question to coincide with the exact moment he pulled back his cue-arm and took a shot at the small white ball lined up with a larger striped ball.

"Hey, you Dan's mate, George?"

The cue stick missed the white ball and ran along the green baize. Mister Overweight and Flabby swung around, his reddish-purple face twisted in fury.

"Now look what you've done, bitch! You've made me miss a turn!"

"Are you George?" I repeated, outwardly cool like a professional P I, inwardly trembling like barely set jelly.

His pudgy fingers tightened and his knuckles turned white. "What's it to you if I am?"

The nasty glint in George's eye indicated how close he was to taking off my head with his cue stick. Oh crap! Perhaps this wasn't such a good idea after all. Involuntarily I lifted one arm to protect my face but was saved the ignominy of running up the white flag and beating a hasty retreat by the arrival of my good mate, Ben, who muscled his way in front of me. Ha…take that George! After whooshing out a sigh of relief, I gave the cue-wielder an infantile, *so-there,* cocky grin, just stopping short of poking out my tongue.

When Ben spoke, his voice was soft but it had that lovely hint of steel behind it. Oh, yum. "I wouldn't do that if I were you, George." Casually, as though the tension in the air wasn't as electric as a Dick Smith store, Ben handed me a glass of beer and placed his own glass on the side of the pool table, right beside a stack of twenties. Arms crossed, he gave George an up and down visual. "This lady is with me," he told him, in that orgasmic better-not-mess-with-me voice that had me crossing my legs and biting my lips.

"So?" George's knuckles remained white as he clutched his cue stick. Violence seeped out of him like a life force. I could so see this guy ramming a knife into poor defenseless Matt Turner.

"So…Dan Ashton's daughter Erin has gone missing," Ben said. "And my friend here would like to ask you a few questions about the situation. Okay?"

George's body gradually relaxed until he looked like a normal person again. "Sorry about that," he said and threw a rueful little boy grin in my direction. I pretended to miss it. "I was caught up in the game and you put me off. Of course I'll help. If I can."

"Fair enough, mate." Ben firmly extricated the cue stick from George's reluctant fingers and peered along its length. "Playing for a sheep station, are we?"

George shrugged. "You might say a bit of money's on the line."

"Mmm…I'll bear that in mind."

"What do you mean?"

Ben picked up the chalk. "While you and Kat have your little chat, I'll keep the fires burning here for you." George opened his mouth to object but before he could get a word out, Ben beat him to it. "Hey, don't worry, mate. Your cue stick is in top hands with me. I won the

Billabong Tavern Cup three years in a row." He turned to the Dale brothers, Bluey and Joe, and I saw him wink. "That right, boys?"

Joe jerked his head up, blinked rapidly and then went back to chalking the end of his cue stick. Bluey nodded vigorously.

Yes, Ben *had* won the Billabong Tavern Cup three years in a row—for sculling twenty schooners in the fastest time. Actually, I reckoned he knew less about the game of eight-ball than I did. And all I knew was if you sink your black ball into the corner hole before your colored balls, you're in deep doo-doo.

Evidently satisfied with Ben's credentials, George followed me to a less congested corner of the bar, where, over the sharp tang of disinfectant, I could still detect the common pub odder of sour sweat, spilt beer and stale cigarette smoke. I set my glass of light beer on a table covered with a plastic cloth the color of sliced watermelon, bagged a chair and sat down.

The legs on George's chair made a scritching sound as he dragged it to the opposite side of the table. "Can I get you another drink?"

"I'm covered, thanks."

"Well, let's start over again, shall we?" He leaned across the table, one pudgy hand outstretched. "I'm George Summers."

"Kat McKinley," I answered, touching the proffered soft flesh as briefly as politeness would allow.

"Kat McKinley? The greyhound trainer?"

"One and the same."

The little-boy grin touched his thick lips yet again. "How's the classical music going? Keeping those dogs of yours quiet?"

"Of course! You're *that* George. I thought you looked familiar. You're the guy who fitted the gadget beside the stairs for me. One press and instant Tchaikovsky in the kennel-house."

"Guilty as charged." His smile grew larger. Seeing all those predatory teeth made me think of Ben's earlier analogy. George Summers was a shark. "I'm sorry I didn't recognize you before," he went on. "But as I recall, our dealings all took place over the phone."

"That's right, and the day you came to set the gadget up, I was heading off to the trial track with a trailer-load of dogs. Couldn't stop, so I told you where to find the key and let you get on with it."

"And the key was in the—" He stopped, examined his bitten fingernails and cleared his throat before continuing. "Anyway, I'm glad it all worked out for you. I've had heaps of satisfied customers but if you could recommend me to your friends, I'd be obliged." He shot a quick look across the room, squinting as he tried to see what was taking place beside the pool table. "Now, how can I help you today?"

I took a sip of my beer before answering. It gave me time to think. Why didn't George say where I kept my spare key? A sudden chill spread through my limbs making me slop my beer before I could set it back on the table.

Don't be silly. This man can't hurt you. We're in a public place. And Ben's within yelling distance. I took a deep breath and squared my shoulders. "I wanted to ask you about Dan's daughter, Erin. She's gone missing."

"Little blighter done a runner, has she?"

"Has she?" I sent him a narrow-eyed frown, searching for signs of guilt.

All wide-eyed innocence, he shook his head. "The note I found when I went to collect Dan's kid said she was staying with you. If she's not— I guess she's run away from home."

"Why would you think that?"

"Well, isn't that what most kids do when they get their little noses put out of joint? Hell, when I was a kid I was always running away." He laughed, showing those predatory shark's teeth again. "Tell you what though, I always came home the next day with my tail between my legs. Too bloody cold out on the streets and I never could figure out how to eat once my pocket money ran out."

"I hope you're right, George."

"Hey, don't sweat it. The kid's probably at home as we speak."

"Dan would ring if Erin showed up." I leaned back in my chair and studied this blustering guy who proclaimed to have found no sign of Erin when he went to pick her up, yet was seen running from the house with something tucked under his arm. Funny how the little-boy grin didn't reach his shifty eyes, how the overloaded charm—when he wasn't fizzing on a short fuse—struck me as fake.

"By the way," I said as once again he craned his head to check out the happenings at the eight-ball table on the far side of the room. "Where exactly did Erin leave that note?"

He reluctantly brought his attention back to me. "Where? Um…in the middle of her bed."

The creep! "What the hell were you doing in Erin's bedroom?"

"Hey, I was trying to find her, wasn't I?" he answered, his voice getting shrill at my veiled allegations. "Go talk to Dan. He was the one who begged me to collect his snotty-nosed kid and bring her to the pub." He seemed to forcibly control himself, straighten both fisted hands, before continuing. "Okay, here's what happened. I drove to the house, knocked on the door and when there was no answer I thought, hey, the kid's playing hide-go-seek, so getting a bit uppity about wasting my time, I opened the door, went inside and yelled for her to get her grubby sneakers out here. Now. Told her I was in a hurry like. Anyway, when she didn't show herself I went from room to room looking for her. And that's when I found that note in the middle of her bed next to some mangy old teddy bear."

A mangy old teddy bear?

Stop right there. Something didn't add up. As tough as Erin was, she'd never leave home without Casper. Since the day Tanya brought her home from the hospital, a wrinkled, ugly red prune of a baby with lungs that could shatter lightbulbs, Casper had spent every night in Erin's bed.

"Think hard, George," I said. "This is important. Did the bear have one eye, no ears and a black finger mark in the middle of its stomach?"

He ran an agitated hand through his lank hair. "God, I don't know. I just saw this crappy bear on the bed next to the note."

"What did the note say?"

"Dad, I'm staying with Kat until Mum comes home."

"Okay, what did you do then?"

If this lowlife rummaged around in Erin's underwear drawer, drooling over her little girl knickers, I'd emasculate him with a pair of rusty pruning shears.

As though able to read my mind, George's eyes turned chilly and his frown deepened. "What did I do? I drove back to the pub and told Dan his kid was with you."

"And what did you take from Tanya's house?"

"Come again?"

"You heard me. I have a witness that swears you were carrying something under your arm when you left the house. Sure it wasn't a drugged eleven-year-old kid?"

"What? I don't have to answer this shit!" He stood up so quickly the chair toppled over backwards and skidded across the floor. "I just finished telling you, I didn't see Dan's daughter. I don't know where she is. And I don't like where this conversation is heading."

"You still haven't told me—what was under your arm?"

He snarled and gave the upended chair a kick that sent it spinning into the nearest wall. "I have a game of eight-ball to win. So...as from now...our chat is officially over."

I stood up slowly and gave him an *I'm-not-finished-with-you-yet-scumbag*, glare. "Thanks for your time, George. But as they say in cop shows...don't leave town."

Hey, Sam Spade, eat your heart out.

Kinsey Millhone, take a back seat.

Nancy Drew...

Oh! Uh!

George's face had turned fire-engine red. An ugly vein protruded from his neck. A tick pulsed near his left eye. I figured he was debating whether to pick me up and toss me at the bar-room mirror or simply stomp my head into the ground with his Cuban heeled cowboy boots.

"Well, it's been nice chatting with you, George," I said, edging away from the imminent explosion. "I'll um…see myself out."

On the way to the exit, I hooked arms with Ben. "Time to go, Hustler Man."

Noticing the Dale boys shoving a wad of twenties into their wallets, I smiled, and continued to drag Ben toward the exit.

"You could be right," Ben agreed, as we steamrolled through the swing doors and out onto the footpath.

Once our feet hit the bitumen we high-tailed it down the street, not slowing until we came to a skidding halt beside Ben's Kombi van.

"Funny game that eight-ball," observed Ben, almost ripping the door off its hinges in his hurry to slip in behind the wheel. "Seems like it's against the rules to pot a colored ball while you're on the large stripy ones."

"Lost George's money, eh?"

He nodded and gave me one of his bone-melting grins. "And you? Got up George's nose, did you?"

"Could say that." I piled in beside him, slammed the car door and peered back at the empty street. "Reckon we'd better get this crate on the road."

Ben turned the key in the ignition and slammed the van into gear just as the pub door exploded open. "Not that George worries me, of course," he assured me flooring the accelerator and peering into his rear-vision mirror. "It's just that we have things to do. More places to search."

"Of course," I agreed and leant forward in my seat to share the view in the rear-vision mirror of George hurling beer cans and four-letter expletives at our departing vehicle. "Think he's trying to tell us something?" I made a grab for the dashboard as Ben almost lifted the car off the road to swing onto a side street, straightened up, then gunned the car forward again. "I don't trust him. He was uneasy when I questioned him about Erin. Wouldn't say what was tucked under his arm when he left Tanya's house either."

"The guy's a shark."

"A shark who knows where I hide my front door key."

Ben's head snapped around so quickly it's a wonder he didn't give himself whiplash. "Bloody hell, Kat," he growled. "Why'd you let *that* creep know where you hide your spare key?"

"Because George Summers installed the Tchaikovsky CD system that runs from inside my house to the dog-shed."

"You're kidding me."

"He's also the guy Dan sent to pick up Erin." I paused to let the enormity of my suspicions sink in. "And now Erin's missing."

"And you think, maybe—"

"Well, let's just say, he knew my front door key was inside the gnome's mouth during the day."

The corners of Ben's lips twitched. "Hey, mate, so did the entire Two Wells football team."

"Ben, I'm serious, here."

"Okay. Okay. But why would a nobody salesman like George sneak into your bedroom at three in the morning and kill a two-bit greyhound trainer like Matthew Turner? Where's the connection?"

When I didn't answer, Ben went on in the same vein. "Unless you think Matt owed George a couple of hundred dollars for installing some techno gadget and decided to take his payment out in blood?"

"Hey, it happens." Miffed that every time I came up with a new suspect they either had an alibi or no motive, I shot a scowl in Ben's direction. He didn't bother catching it.

Instead, his eyes lit up as though he'd had a light bulb moment. "If you're looking for someone Matt *could* have been in debt to," he drawled, "how about Big Mick Harrison, the bookie? We never did get around to checking his explanation of needing petrol when Art found him on his property. What say we go visit our bookie friend now? I can engage him in man-talk in the front room while you use the bathroom and take a peek behind any closed doors on the way. See what you can find."

21

GOOD IDEAS DON'T GROW ON TREES LIKE APRICOTS. I accept that. However, what Ben forgot to mention was what I was supposed to look for while behind closed doors. Size ten boots with half my garden attached to them?

First things first, though. Question one would be had Mick seen Erin? Question two, like Little Red Riding Hood, did Mick really visit his granny on Thursday?

While Ben drove, I snaffled my cell phone from my tote bag and rang Resthaven, the aged care facility where Mick's grandmother was registered as a patient. Impersonating Big Mick's wife, when the receptionist answered, I asked her if my husband had left his mobile phone there while visiting on Thursday morning. Told her he was lost without it. "Thursday?" she queried. "You mean, *Friday*, don't you, Mrs. Harrison? I know it was Friday because Abe Potter celebrated his ninetieth birthday and your husband was kind enough to bring a chocolate mud cake for morning tea. Mr. Harrison is so thoughtful that way. A real sweetie. Always remembers patients' birthdays. You tell him not to worry, dear, I'll ask around and if his phone is here I'll have someone drop it over to your house.'

I grinned at Ben. Seems like kind, thoughtful, much-loved Mr. Harrison wasn't such a paragon of sainthood after all. Saints don't lie. So what was he really doing on Art's property on Thursday, the morning Pitachi Gambler was drugged? Knowing how handy Art could be with a rifle, I had a feeling Mick wouldn't risk a hole in the head just to steal a few daisies from Art's garden because he'd forgotten to buy his grandmother a bunch of flowers.

Five minutes later, we turned down Sunset Boulevard and Ben brought his van to a halt in front of Mick's house. Or should I say mini-mansion. Stepping out onto the footpath, I looked down at my clothes and sighed. Not what you'd call, "appropriate" for visiting. What had started out as a silky plum-colored long-sleeved top and my best hipster jeans when I dressed for a sort-of date with Ben that morning, had now metamorphosed into jeans with mud plastered down one leg and across the butt from when I slipped and fell while looking for Erin near the river and a plum-colored top with two rips in the sleeve and a beer spill decorating one breast. As for my gorgeous high-heeled suede knee-high boots—suffice to say the river mud had a lot to answer for.

Ben and I trudged up the path towards Big Mick's five-star front door, which would have probably cost more than all the doors and windows in my house plus my refrigerator and top-loading washing machine. The house itself was a rambling one-story white stucco set back off a tree-lined roadway. Like the other houses in the elite suburb of Burnside, it oozed wealth, space, and an expensive part-time gardener. However, unlike the others, this house looked lived in. A discarded tricycle, a swing, a couple of naked limbless Barbie dolls and several balls in a range of colors and sizes, including an out-of-shape soccer ball that would never stand up to a game of soccer, littered the front lawn.

Which meant Big Mick the bookie had a family. Funny how you don't think of bookmakers being like normal folk. I'd only ever seen him on his stand, shirt sleeves rolled to his elbows, setting up his board, calling out prices or transferring wads of notes from eager punters' hands to his ever-present leather bookie bag. Never thought of what he did once he folded his stand and packed it in the boot of his car.

In response to Ben's knock, a pig-tailed girl of about seven, vigorously fighting off her younger brother, threw open the front door. They were still screaming and punching each other when Big Mick strode up behind them and scooted both in the air, one under each arm.

"Ben. Kat. How ya doin'?" he boomed over the top of their screams. "Don't mind these two. Can't remember how many times I've told them not to answer the door unless they know who's knocking. May as well talk to the headlights on my car for all the listening they do." He placed his two squirming offspring back on the ground, cuffed them lightly and told them to go help feed the triplets.

"Triplets?" I squeaked and I'm sure my eyes shot open wider than a football stadium.

"Yep. Twelve months old tomorrow." He smiled the smile of a proud father. "*And* two-year-old twins. Plus the two beasties you've just had the pleasure of meeting."

Seven kids in seven years? Wow! I gazed at Big Mick with new respect. Who'd have thought this man had the wherewithal to father so many children in such a short time. I gave him a furtive once over. Beer gut. Receding hairline. Thick wet lips. Must be something about the guy I was missing. He saw me ogling him and winked. *Damn.* Was that a suggestive come-on? I scowled down my nose at him. A derisive scowl picked up from my mother who has a whole range for different situations. He licked his already wet goopy lips. I gave him a not-if-you-were-the-last-man-left-on-this-earth sniff. He wiggled his eyebrows. I thought about giving him a vasectomy, *sans* anesthetic.

Ben's choked chuckle broke up the pissing contest. He quickly turned it into a clearing of his throat but the trace of a grin danced at the corners of his lips. "Sorry to bother you, mate," he said to Mick. "Should have rung first, I guess. Hope we didn't interrupt anything important."

"Nah, as long as you're not collecting for the Trainers' Benevolent Fund. Could have built a new bloody racetrack, the money you mob rip off me during the year. Reckon I should be the one taking a collection tin around."

Ben's eyebrows hitched as he took in the vestibule's deep rich burgundy carpet and the bookie's five hundred dollar pigskin loafers, at present sinking into the pile. "Yeah. Right. And pigs fly."

Big Mick's laugh was loud and self-mocking. While he was in a good mood I thought I'd get my first question in. "The reason we're here is because we're looking for Tanya Ashton's daughter, Erin. She's missing. Don't suppose you've seen her today?"

He shook his head. "Can't say I'd know Tanya's daughter even if I had seen her. Too busy at the track to pay much attention to anyone not waving hundred dollar notes under my nose."

"Eleven years old, fair hair pulled back in a ponytail. Snub nose. Normally looking bored and put upon."

"Sorry." He shook his head. "Anyway, don't stand there blocking the sun. Come in. My kids will probably mug you but I reckon you're both big enough to protect yourselves."

"Look, we don't want to intrude on your time—" I began, deciding maybe I didn't want to know what lay behind Mick's closed doors after all.

"No, no. You're not intruding. Come in and say hello to my wife. She's in the kitchen feeding the tribe." Not bothering to hang around and see if we were following him, Mick set off down the carpeted passageway.

I pushed past the still-smirking Ben and hurried after Mick. I had questions and didn't want to ask them in front of his family.

"Why did you lie to Art?" I said when I caught up to him. Okay, maybe I hadn't perfected the art of interviewing just yet, but I figured there was no time for pleasantries. "Why did you tell Art you were going to see your grandmother on Thursday?"

Mick stopped. Swung around. His lips were still smiling but his eyes were telling a different story. "Not that it's any of your business, Kat, but I didn't lie to Art. That's exactly where I was headed."

"I know for a fact you visited your grandmother on Friday. Not Thursday."

The smile disappeared completely. He leaned so close I could smell the spices in whatever he'd eaten for lunch. "You've been checking up on me?

I didn't answer. Too busy backpedalling.

"I don't take kindly to having my personal life investigated," he warned, his voice soft and flat. He deliberately flexed his shoulders and cracked his neck. "For some reason that makes me twitchy."

I took another step backwards and found myself hard up against the wall. Not where I wanted to be. I took a deep breath, stared back at him. If I let Mick intimidate me I'd never get any answers. Just as I pushed myself off the wall, opened my mouth to ask where he was the night Matt was murdered, Ben caught up to us.

"Everything okay here?"

Mick lifted one eyebrow. "Sure. But you need to keep your girlfriend on a leash, Ben. She's likely to upset the wrong person going around firing accusations willy-nilly. Not everyone's nice-natured like me." His unsmiling eyes returned to me. "I was on my way to Resthaven when I ran out of petrol. Thought Art might have some but he ran me off with his pitchfork instead. He's lucky I didn't call the cops. And by the time I walked to the nearest petrol station and back it was too late to visit my grandmother. I called in to see her the next day instead." Without waiting for me to comment on his flatly intoned dialogue, he set off down the hallway.

Ben's fingers closed around my arm. He yanked me close enough to whisper in my ear. "Leave it, Kat. Leave Mick to me. Okay?"

I nodded. Shrugged. Suited me fine. A rollicking song Grandma McKinley used to sing to me when I was little ran through my head as I followed Big Mick down the passageway: *You can have him, I don't want him, he's too fat for me....'*

The moment I stepped into the bright sunny kitchen my teeth started rattling. I blinked. Put two fingers in my ears. *Sheesh.* If this was life with multiple children, count me out. One toddler hung over the side of his high chair singing at the top of his voice while busy stuffing spaghetti up his nose. And beside him, in an identical highchair, his sister, mouth open wider than a garage door, screamed with the force of an approaching hurricane. Not that anyone paid her any mind.

Mick, back to his effusive self, loped across the room and slipped both arms around a slim woman who looked to be in her mid-thirties. Elegant, hair cut and layered to stay in place under all circumstance, she was dressed for an afternoon at the theatre instead of feed time at the zoo. Mick bent to kiss the top of the woman's head. "And this stunning woman with the face of an angel," he gushed, "is my ever-loving wife, Beth."

Expression frosty, Beth shrugged his arm off and went on stuffing spaghetti into a series of bird-like mouths lined up in high chairs beside the table. Hmm…evidently things weren't all well-cultivated roses and daffodils in the Harrison garden.

"Sorry I can't shake hands," she said, glancing up from her task. "But as you can see, they're kinda messy." Her smile was contagious, like that of a cult leader. If she'd asked me to clean her shoes, go weed the garden, bake a cake, I'd have scuttled off to do her bidding. Instead, I smiled back. Which was my first big mistake. It meant I took my eyes off the nearest Harrison, the tow-headed baby who was glaring intently up at me from behind his Humphrey B Bear bib. Consequently I didn't see the two handfuls of spaghetti arching through the air. The stringy pulpy mess plastered my eyes and dribbled down over my nose onto to my chin and ended up on my plum-colored top.

"Eddy! No!" Beth waved an admonishing finger at the baby with the good right-arm pitch before handing me a roll of kitchen paper. "I'm so sorry," she apologized shaking her head. "It's just a phase Eddy's going through right now. He has to throw everything he picks up. I'm dreading the time when he's strong enough to lift the furniture." She let loose with that killer smile again. "Can I get you anything?"

"Er…perhaps Kat could clean herself up in the bathroom," Ben suggested giving me what he probably thought was a subtle elbow in the ribs but in reality made me wince.

"Yes, of course." Beth pointed through the kitchen doorway before returning to the job of scooping food from five baby bowls into five screaming baby mouths. The two "beasties" were assisting her by filling seven glasses with milk, which mostly ended up on the floor. "Bathroom's the last door on the left."

Adroitly dodging another fully loaded spaghetti missile, I stuck my tongue out at Eddy and hurried through the kitchen doorway, only to skid on a pool of milk. God, no way would Erin be in this house. The last thing these people needed was another child. Still, on the way to the bathroom I ducked into every room and had a quick poke around, just in case. Other than wall-to-wall kid stuff that included weird things I didn't know existed, the only item of interest was a cupboard brimming with Mick's shoes, all size 14, no mud, and branded with names I'd never afford.

A death-defying stink pervaded the bathroom at the end of the passageway. A stink so sickening I could barely breathe. Almost threw up while washing spaghetti off my face and dabbing ineffectually at my ruined top. The smell seemed to be coming from a pile of something brown in the far corner of the bath. I peered closer. Oh god, I thought, backing away in a hurry, I must ask Ben if there was any history of multiple births on his side of the family. If so, I'd join a nunnery. Abstain from sex for life. In fact, I reckon a visit to the Harrison household should be a compulsory subject on all high school curriculums.

Disappointed at the lack of clues, I glanced down at my watch while hurrying back into the war zone the Harrisons called a kitchen, so didn't see the silver spoon until it landed on its target. Pain radiated from my nose and I let out a yelp. Of course that set the up-and-coming, All-Australian pitcher laughing so hard he wet his nappy. Wiping tears from my eyes with the back of one hand, I grabbed Ben by the back of the shirt and dragged him in the direction of the passage leading to the front door.

"It's quarter to four," I told him and shot a quick smile at Beth.

"Lovely to meet you Mrs. Harrison, but we're due back at my house at four o'clock so we'd better get moving."

Before I grabbed hold of Baby Eddy's head and demonstrated the art of throwing a curve ball...

The moment Ben pulled out of the driveway and set the van in the direction of home, I shook my head and sighed. "What a total waste of time and effort."

"Oh, I wouldn't say that."

"But there was no evidence," I wailed. "No motive. Not even a stray red herring swimming around the house. Nothing, except wall-to-wall kids and a smelly pile of baby doo that put me off parenthood for life. Hell, with all that procreating, Mick Harrison wouldn't have time to *read* a good murder mystery let alone plan and execute one."

"What would you say if I told you our Father of the Year knows how to make time when necessary?" said Ben.

"Go on."

"While you were in the bathroom, I casually asked him where he was at 3 a.m. last Thursday morning, the time Matt was murdered. He said he was at home in bed with his beautiful wife."

"And..."

"His beautiful wife didn't corroborate her husband's statement. She said he didn't get home until 4 a.m., then promptly threw the remains of little Eddy's bowl of spaghetti at Mick's head." Ben's lips twitched. "That's why you only copped the spoon."

22

T~HE MOMENT WE WALKED THROUGH~ my front door, the flashing red light on the answering machine caught my eye. It would have to wait. First I needed an ultra-strong blast of caffeine to clear my head.

While I selected a largish mug from the cupboard and switched on the electric jug, Ben hooked a carton of milk from the fridge, pushed up the spout and threw half the contents down his throat in one go.

We hadn't heard from Dan—so Erin must still be missing. Hopefully Dan had already contacted the police and they were out searching for her too.

"It's not like *Devil's Spawn* to be staying out overnight," I mused shaking my head. The more I thought about Erin running away from home, the more it didn't add up. "We're talking about a kid who squirts bugs with insect spray till she drowns the critters. Can you honestly see her sleeping in someone's dirty, spider-infested garden shed, just to get back at Tanya for not taking her to Melbourne in the plane?"

Ben shook his head slowly, then with brotherly affection lobbed one arm around my shoulders and hitched my body up against his. "Don't knock yourself out, mate. Everyone's searching for Erin. And just like those crazy purple and yellow socks you reckon you lost last week—the kid will turn up."

I smiled into Ben's warm familiar face, complete with yesterday's stubble and the cute dimple he refused to acknowledge. When he didn't seem in any hurry to remove his arm, I snuggled closer and rested my cheek on the soft flannel of his shirt, let the tangy smell of his aftershave overrun my senses. The softness of his lips with that dribble of milk in one corner had me itching to reach up and lick the milk off, explore his mouth further. He returned my smile, the weather lines around his eyes crinkling. And then a strange thing happened. His eyes lost their brotherly affection, became confused and then ignited with something close to surprise. It was as though Ben Taylor was seeing me for the very first time. *Really* seeing me. He leaned in. I couldn't move. Couldn't breathe. Ben was going to kiss me.

A deep gravelly voice from the next room broke the spell.

"Is that you in there, Katrina?"

I grabbed a quick half-breath. Gave Ben a rueful half-grin as he reluctantly dropped his arm and straightened up. "Yeah, it's me. Who wants to know?"

Still floating on Ben's almost-kiss, I drifted into the lounge, the jar of Nescafe still clasped in my hand. Scuzz was parked in my largest armchair, his huge leather-clad body jammed in like a cork in a bottle. Before speaking, I bit down a curse at the guy's poor timing.

"Hi, Scuzz," I said and smiled at little Tater snoring on the big guy's lap. "Where's Lucky?"

At the mention of her name a black face popped out from under the coffee table and regarded me with large mournful eyes.

"She had an accident," whispered Scuzz from behind his hand, trying not to let Lucky hear him. "Please don't be cross with her. Remember, she has only been a house pet for less than twenty-four hours. And it was no drama. I cleaned up the mess and sprayed the room with some of that nice smelling deodorant I found in your bathroom."

"Oh, Lucky." I knelt on the floor beside her, feeling guilty as I ran my hand over the top of her head and gently pulled at her ears.

"There was no way she could get out through your Chihuahua sized doggy door," explained Scuzz.

With so much going on, I hadn't given a thought to how Lucky intended to go to the bathroom when I wasn't around. I'd get Jake to make a larger doggy door leading into the back yard first thing in the morning.

It took a tummy rub and much scratching behind both ears to return the sparkle to the black greyhound's eyes. Mission accomplished, I stood up and waved the coffee jar at Scuzz.

"Drink?"

"I hope you don't mind my presumption, Katrina, but I helped myself to a coffee when I arrived." The posh voice emanating from the rough biker body got me every time.

I smiled at him. "Hey, of course I don't mind."

"And I'm glad you're not upset with Lucky," he continued, leaning back in the armchair. "Even Short Stuff here has trouble squeezing through that doggy door." He studied the sleeping dog on his lap. "Are you sure you didn't measure a hamster when you had the door installed?"

"Thanks for taking care of Lucky, Scuzz. You're a champ." I bent down to give the biker a *thank you* kiss on the cheek, but he turned his head. My lips slid over several nose rings, brushed against soft whiskers, and came to rest on his even softer mouth. It tasted of coffee and toothpaste and heat—lots and lots of heat. The *thank you* kiss ended in a *well, hello there,* kiss that had me gasping for air and grabbing onto the arm of the chair to prevent my legs from buckling.

"Hey, what's taking you so long in there, Kat?"

I straightened up, slightly dizzy, slightly confused at how good Scuzz's mouth felt on mine and slightly anxious about Ben's reaction if he discovered me locking lips with my bodyguard.

Holy Catfish! Was I turning into a nymphomaniac? Not content with one, I'd gone weak in the knees over two guys in the space of two minutes.

Thankfully missing the highlight of the show, Ben trundled in, carton of milk in hand. He came to a sudden halt when he spotted Scuzz making himself at home in my armchair.

"Oh, it's *you!*" Ben scowled and narrowed his eyes. "Thought I could smell something off when I came through the front door." Ignoring Ben's comments, Scuzz watched me wrestle with my emotions. A smile tugged at the corners of his mouth and his eyes informed me there was plenty more where that came from. And I only had to say the word.

"Anyway, who let you in?" Ben persisted. "Or do gorillas swing through windows?"

Scuzz rolled both shoulders and cracked his knuckles, as though limbering up for a fight, and then gently pulled at Tater's tiny ears instead. This guy was such an enigma. And his mouth was so hot my lips were tingling. But I had to forget about his hot mouth and his sexy nose rings and his erotically soft beard. It was Ben I wanted.

Well, wasn't it?

"Good afternoon, Benjamin," Scuzz said quirking one eyebrow at the raging inferno framing the door. "My cousin, Jake, had some chores to attend to in the dog-shed, so he gave me the key to the house and told me to wait inside."

"Hmmph..." Ben growled.

Scuzz shifted his dark gaze onto me, suddenly serious. "Any sign of the little girl? Jake and I visited her school, but no one has seen her since yesterday."

I shook my head. "We came up empty-handed too. When Dan gets here, he'll have to contact the police, if he hasn't already. Erin's been missing far too long, and for Dan's sake, I hope he's let Tanya know what's going on."

"There may be an important message from Dan on your answering machine," said Scuzz. "It was blinking when I came in ten minutes ago."

"What? You're Kat's secretary now are you?" Ben snapped.

Grunting and twisting his unwieldy body, Scuzz managed to pull himself free from the armchair. He stood up, put Tater gently on the floor, and lumbered across the room.

"I'll make you a nice cup of coffee, shall I," he said, taking the coffee jar from my hand as he passed by, "while you listen to your messages."

"Uh. Thanks. Milk and two sugars," I called out, switching on the answering machine while eyeing his well-muscled rear end as he lumbered across the room toward the kitchen.

Back off! I scolded my hormones firmly. I was in love with Ben yet I was feasting my eyes on Scuzz and imagining him naked with his hands and his heat and his mouth all over me. *Phew!* I blamed my recently broken vibrator for the sudden rise in libido.

The answering machine crackled, spat out its usual spiel and then coughed.

"I have your friend's daughter. If you want her to stay alive do exactly as I tell you."

I froze. All extraneous thoughts evaporating as the chilly words, muffled and hoarse, echoed and re-echoed around the now silent room.

And then Erin's thin reedy voice, stuttering with fear, trickled from the machine.

"K-Kat," she said, barely above a whisper. *"I'm scared. I don't like it here. There's a mean man and he's going to hurt me real bad if you don't do what he says. Kat, I want my mum and I want—"*

"Big Mistake must lose." The muffled voice broke in. I could hear a squeaking or grunting noise in the background. *"If the dog wins you'll find the kid's tongue in the mail. Inform the police of this phone call and I won't stop at her tongue."*

With that the message clicked off.

The silence that followed was thicker than pea soup. This couldn't be happening. Not in sleepy Two Wells, where a night on the town meant eating a giant feed of fish and chips from the local take-away shop then catching up at the Two Wells pub for a drink and a chat about how well the footy team played on Saturday. Bad things like murder and kidnapping weren't part of the town's social fabric.

Face pale under his tan, Ben's gaze sought mine. "Was that the same guy who spoke to you on the phone after Matt was killed?"

I shrugged. I couldn't tell. The voice was too muffled.

Grimly, Ben turned to Scuzz, all animosity gone. "Any chance of helping us find Matt's murderer, mate?"

"I'm with you, one hundred percent."

<h1 style="text-align:center">23</h1>

Five minutes later I heard a car rumble up the driveway and come to a stop. A bundle of nerves, I tweaked the curtain to one side and peeped through the window.

Oh, no!

"It's Dan," I gasped. "And Tanya's with him. She must have caught the first available flight home."

My legs, limp celery sticks, wobbled beneath me. I leaned against the wall and closed my eyes. This was my fault. Determined to be an amateur sleuth, I'd put my best friend's daughter in danger. How in hell could I expose Tanya to the message on my answering machine? How could I stand by and let her listen to Erin's cry for help?

Ben joined me and after giving my arm a comforting squeeze, slid the curtain to one side so he could get a better view of the driveway. "Jesus! You wouldn't read about it, mate," he growled, talking over his shoulder to Scuzz. "They've brought the police with them. Exactly what we *didn't* need."

As I leaned against Ben, using his solid body instead of the wall to hold me up, Inspector Columbo's big black bear of a car, which had been following Tanya's little red *Yaris*, slowed to a halt outside. Panic bubbled up inside me. If the police discovered Erin had been kidnapped, they'd bring in reinforcements. Alert the media. Call in the SWAT team. And then what would happen to Erin? No good thinking the kidnapper wouldn't hurt a little girl—he'd already taken one innocent life when he stabbed Matt.

"*...if you inform the police of this phone call I won't stop at her tongue.*"

The words hammered away in my brain, blocking every lucid thought and leaving behind a red haze of fear and uncertainty.

I covered my face with my hands. "What are we going to tell the police?" I moaned, struggling not to break down and cry.

Ben held onto my shoulders, shook me gently. "Come on, Kat, don't lose it now. You're our rock. When the Inspector questions us say nothing about the message on your machine. Okay?"

I pulled away from Ben and staggered to the nearest chair where I collapsed in a heap.

Some rock!

Ornaments rattled and danced on their shelves as Scuzz clumped across the room toward me. He perched on the arm of my chair and stroked his fingers lightly across the top of my head, much as he would do if he was comforting one of the dogs. Tension eased from my shoulders as I pressed the top of my head into his large comforting hand. No wonder Tater and Lucky loved him.

"Hang in there, Katrina," he crooned. "Our mission is to save the little girl, which means we must watch what we say to the police. That's all. The constabulary can still go through the motions of searching for her as long as we don't tell them she's been kidnapped. You can do it. I have faith in you."

And suddenly I *did* feel like a rock—or at least one of those little pebbles you find on a nicely raked garden path. I punched him lightly on the arm, between the word *Mother* and what looked like a tattooed mermaid. "Thanks, Scuzz. I owe you one."

His answering wink, in any other circumstances, could have been construed as flirting. "No worries, babe." And then the arm of my chair groaned as he stood up and turned to Ben. "So, what's the plan?"

Ben shrugged one shoulder. "Simple. Get rid of the fuzz then let

Tanya and Dan know what's happened."

"And how exactly do we—get rid of the fuzz?"

"Well…"

"Do you even *have* a plan?"

Ben scrubbed his hand across his face. "Well…"

Time for my input. "What say we tie and gag the Inspector and lock him in the closet until after we've found Erin?" I suggested, grimacing when Scuzz and Ben rolled their eyes at me. "Okay. Okay. Thought you might object to that one, but what else can we do to get Columbo out of the mix? What if the kidnapper is watching the house right now and noting police presence?"

While Ben paced, Scuzz scratched thoughtfully at a fire-breathing dragon tattooed across his bulging right bicep.

"If only we knew where they were hiding Erin," I bleated, unable to come up with a better plan. Caller ID had shown the call came from Erin's mobile but not where she was located.

Footsteps crunched on the gravel outside and raised voices signaled our visitors were approaching the front door. Scuzz, one large finger raised in warning, leaned toward us. "Act blasé," he whispered. "Let the inspector think we believe Erin is hiding at a friend's house."

Tanya, eyes red and swollen, came slamming through the doorway into the lounge room. Worry creased her forehead and her face had that permanently startled expression you often see on a trauma victim. After greeting us with a nod, she strode across the room and stood, back to the television, anger and fear radiating from her like a force-field.

"Are you sure Erin's not hiding here, Kat?" she asked, her voice tight. "Have you searched the dog kennels? Under the bed? And what about the wardrobe in the spare room? Have you looked in there?"

I shook my head, fighting back tears. "I'm sorry, Tan. Erin's not with me. I wish she was."

"Bloody Dan!" Tanya snarled, glaring at her ex who'd followed her in. "Can't leave the pub long enough to pick up his own daughter. What does that tell you about him as a father?"

Dan looked the picture of misery. In his eyes Erin had always been his one success in life. He adored his daughter. Half the reason Erin was such a pain in the butt was because Dan couldn't say no to her.

"God, Tanya," he whined. "How many more times do I have to say, I'm sorry? You know I'd jump in a vat of boiling oil to save Erin."

"But not leave the pub to pick her up."

"I told you. My car broke down."

"If you spent as much money on that bloody car as you do on booze it wouldn't break down."

Dan sighed. Since Erin went missing, he'd probably blamed himself a hundred times. He put a comforting arm around Tanya's shoulders. "We'll find her, love," he said. "She's likely sulking somewhere because you wouldn't take her on the plane with you."

Tanya jerked away from him and stomped across the room leaving Dan standing awkwardly by himself. "If she's sulking somewhere, why haven't we found her?"

"We will, love. We will. And when we do, I'm going to lock her in her bedroom until she's at least twenty-one. No way can I go through this again."

Tanya's only reply was to snarl and turn her back on him.

DI Adams, who had followed the Ashtons, stood by the doorway, his sharp eyes assessing the situation.

"Ms. Ashton—" he began, taking advantage of the slight pause in Tanya's tirade.

Still snarling, Tanya swiveled around to face the policeman. "And you! Why aren't you out looking for my daughter? Kat's already said she's not here."

"I will, Ms. Ashton as soon as you calm down and answer some questions," he assured her. "I can't help unless I know what's happening."

Tanya's face seemed to collapse in on itself. She sniffed, scrubbed a hand over her eyes. "Oh, God, I'm sorry, Inspector. Of course I'll answer your questions. It's just that I'm so worried about Erin."

"Perfectly understandable." Columbo dug out a notebook and biro from a pocket deep inside his trench coat, opened the pad and chewed on the end of his pen. "Now...can you tell me how long Erin has been missing?"

Before Tanya could respond, I answered. "Not long, Inspector. Hey, you know what kids are like. They're always demanding attention by doing crazy stuff."

DI Adams lifted a questioning eyebrow in my direction then slowly turned back to Tanya.

"Ms .Ashton?"

Tanya sent me a confused scowl. "Dan reckons Erin's been missing for almost twenty hours. And contrary to what my *best friend's* inferring, it's not like Erin to demand attention by doing something as crazy as running away from home."

Inspector Adams wrote in his notebook before looking up. "Did you or your ex-husband argue with the child before you left her home on her own yesterday?"

For a moment I thought Tanya was going to self-combust. "Hey, hold it right there, buster," she yelled, her face and neck an unnatural shade of red. "Before I left for the airport, I telephoned Dan and arranged for him to pick Erin up. My mother broke her leg, you know, so don't go trying to imply that I'm an unfit parent."

"Calm down. I'm not implying anything. All I am trying to establish is why your daughter ran away."

"You're not listening to me!" Tanya growled deep in her throat. "Erin did not run away."

This wasn't going well. I glanced at Ben. Hands in pockets, he lounged awkwardly against the corner of the phone table while Scuzz had jammed himself back into the armchair. They'd both either gone to sleep or run out of ideas, so I guessed it was up to me to get rid of the nosy Inspector.

The cause of my discomfort chewed thoughtfully on his pen before turning to me. "Ms. McKinley," he said, giving the collar of his shirt a claustrophobic yank. The rumpled shirt attached to the too-tight collar looked like it hadn't seen an iron since the day it left the department store. "It appears you were the last person to speak to Ms. Ashton's daughter. Can you remember exactly what time that was?"

"Sorry, I had other stuff on my mind when I rang and spoke to Erin." I looked across at Scuzz. "Do you remember…Theodore?"

"I would say…around eight p.m."

Columbo took his eyes off me and let them rest on the man-mountain jammed into the armchair. He blinked, as though his more thorough examination of Scuzz had left him disorientated. "This um…*man*…was with you when you spoke to Erin on the phone?"

I nodded.

Columbo, eyeing Scuzz like he was an extra from a Godzilla movie, finally sighed deeply and returned his gaze to me. "Before she hung up, the child told you someone was at the door. Is that right?"

"Yes. But look, Erin and I bait each other all the time. It's like a game. She probably spun me that line to put me off the scent, hung up the phone, wrote a note saying she was staying with me and then took off to a friend's house."

I gazed beseechingly at Tanya, attempting to send her a telepathic message of apology. By the thunderous black glare she hurled back at me, my telepathic powers were abysmal.

The inspector passed a sheet of paper, evidently torn from a school exercise book across to Tanya. The paper was covered in clear plastic. "Is this your daughter's handwriting, Ms. Ashton?"

Tanya read the words on the paper and closed her eyes, her answering nod almost imperceptible.

"Okay, now try not to worry," he said, his voice laced with sympathy. "We get kids running off for the silliest reasons, every day of the week. Your daughter is likely hiding out and treating this as a big adventure."

"Erin is an adventurous kid," I agreed.

"Ten dollars says she's hiding in Karen's back shed or in Susanne's attic," said Ben.

"But Dan has already contacted Karen and Susanne," Tanya bleated. "They haven't seen her."

"In that case, I imagine your daughter is playing a game with one of her other little friends," put in Scuzz, dragging his huge frame from the armchair and standing up.

Tanya, apparently spotting Scuzz for the first time, looked up. And up. And up. She blinked. And by the expression on her face, didn't know whether to hide or run.

"Oh, that's right," I put in. "You two haven't been introduced, have you? This is my…umm…Jake's cousin, Theodore Samuel Parkington the Third, better known as Scuzz. He's one of the good guys." While Tanya gulped at the size of the hand stretched out in greeting, I continued with my spiel. "Naturally Erin's friends won't tell you where she is, Tan. They're probably in on the conspiracy too."

"You think so?"

I fixed my eyes on the wall behind her and nodded. I couldn't look her in the eye. How could I? I was lying to my best friend, stringing her along, encouraging her to think Erin was safe while all the time she was in unbelievable danger. Kidnapped by a monster, so evil, he would hack out a child's tongue to ensure one of my greyhounds lost at the races.

Probably sensing I was close to blurting out the truth, Ben strung one arm around Tanya's shoulders and led her towards the kitchen. "Come on, Tan, what you need is a hot drink. I'll make a gourmet cup of my famous *Taylor* brew, a recipe passed down through three generations of Taylor. Heaped spoonful of coffee, dash of honey, third of a cup of Bourbon…"

"Thanks for responding to our call, Inspector Adams," I said as soon as Tanya was out of earshot. "Now you're helping us in the search, we'll have Erin home in no time. Kids do the damndest things, don't they? But no worries, Scuzz has his biker gang out on the roads as we speak and they won't give up until they find her. Will they Scuzz?"

"I have?" Scuzz blinked, momentarily at a loss and then his eyes widened and he nodded emphatically. "Ooh yes. Of course I have.

Don't worry, Inspector, my boys come highly recommended when it comes to finding missing persons."

"You have *bikers* out there?" Columbo gulped. "Driving through our streets?"

Hmm…maybe that wasn't one of my better ideas. Maybe we'd have to revert to my original plan of tying the Inspector up. I bit my bottom lip. Last I'd seen the roll of duct tape was in the bottom drawer in the kitchen where I stored my rarely used reels of sewing thread, a pair of broken pruning shears, colored binder twine and my emergency wooden stirring spoon. I took a step toward the kitchen when the Inspector's mobile went off. I stopped. Who'd have guessed Colombo's favorite tune was *Santa Claus Is Coming to Town?* Just proves you can never tell a book by its cover.

"Goddamn daughter," he growled hurriedly bringing Santa's words of warning to a close. "Thinks she's a comedian." With the phone plastered to his ear, he grunted, assured whoever was on the other end that he'd be there in ten minutes and hung up. "Armed hold-up at Munno Para Shopping Centre," he informed us beetling a frown at Scuzz. "Three big guys dressed in black leather. All on motorbikes."

"Well, well." Scuzz grinned. "This must be my lucky day." He brushed a nonexistent piece of lint from his sleeveless leather jacket and flexed his arms, making several tattoos shiver and shake and do other unmentionable gyrations. "If a police officer should ask me where I was when the Munno Para robbery took place, I'll smile politely and say, I was with your intrepid Detective Inspector Adams."

"Mmm…" Eyes thoughtful, Columbo watched Scuzz run a gentle finger under Lucky's chin. He then pocketed his mobile and slapped his notebook shut. "If there's nothing more you can tell me about Erin's disappearance, I'd better check this robbery out."

"Of course." I smiled and took hold of his arm. "Sounds like you have some baddies to catch, Inspector."

"Oh, and Mr. Ashton," he called out over his shoulder, while I tugged more strongly on his arm, "when your ex-wife has finished her drink, I'd like you both to report to the Gawler police station. Bring a recent photo of your daughter and we'll get straight onto finding her."

While Dan nodded, I maneuvered the Inspector in the direction of the front door. I'm not sure whether Columbo suspected me of knowing more about Erin's disappearance, Scuzz of masterminding the Munno Para robbery, or he was merely captivated by the pungent aroma of Ben's special brew emanating from the direction of the kitchen. Whatever the reason, he seemed rather put-out when I bundled him through the front door and closed it firmly behind him.

I figure cops are like boulders. It's no good *asking* them to move— you have to give them a good hefty push in the direction you want them to go.

24

The message on my answering machine clicked off.

Through the deathly hush that followed, Tanya gazed at me, eyes wide with raw terror, face drained of any natural color. Beside her, Dan stood ramrod straight. The sound of an empty VB can scrunched in his hand. He snarled and his fingers closed more tightly around the tin receptacle. By the twist of his mouth and the way his brows hooded his eyes, I figured he wished the flattened can was the kidnapper's throat.

"I'm sorry, Tan," I said as I moved toward her, fearing she'd collapse. "That's why we couldn't tell the Inspector."

She gazed at me. Her face ashen, the dark shadows under her eyes making her appear gaunt. And when she eventually spoke, her voice seemed to be coming from deep inside a well. "That man said he's going to cut out my baby's tongue."

I tried to hug her but it was like hugging a cement post.

"Why would he want to do that?"

I shook my head and with one arm around her uncooperative body led her across to the couch.

"I don't understand what's happening." She perched on the edge of her seat and stared up at me. "Kat, you won't let Lofty win, will you?"

Oh, God, if only it was that easy.

I shook my head and began kneading my fingers into her shoulders, even though I knew no amount of massage would ease the knotted muscles beneath her jacket.

"Listen, Tan," I said, continuing to work on her shoulders. "Don't worry about Lofty. We'll work that out later. First, we need to come up with a plan to rescue Erin. Okay?"

"No. No. No." Tanya pushed my hands away, her voice rising in panic. "Just do as he says. He'll let Erin go if you do as he says."

"I don't think we can trust—"

"You *have* to follow his instructions, to the letter. Do you hear me? Otherwise...if anything bad happens to Erin...it will be your fault." Her ruinous eyes met mine then filled with tears. "And…and I'll never see my little girl again."

A slab of guilt the size of a basketball court lodged in my stomach. I watched Ben remove the mug from Tanya's fingers, slide it onto the coffee table next to the bloated gargoyle statue my sister sent me for my twenty-first birthday, and hunker down in front of her.

"Trust me on this, Tanya," he said holding her face in both hands. "There's no way you can believe a mongrel kidnapper. Even if Kat gives Lofty a sedative and he loses his race, how do we know he'll let Erin go afterwards? How do we know she hasn't seen this guy's face?" He kept his hands on her face as she tried to pull away. "We can't take that risk. I go along with Kat and say we find Erin and get her out of the kidnapper's clutches *before* Lofty races."

I caught Ben's eye and gave him a thumbs up of approval. In return he sent me a lopsided grin that had my heart skipping several beats.

Dan, his voice almost unrecognizable, spoke for the first time since we'd played the message on the answering machine. "And when we do find the bastard who took my kid, I'll put a hole in his head big enough to drive a semi through."

Ben straightened. "I know where you're coming from, mate, but we need to stay calm if we're going to get Erin back."

"Calm?" Saliva flew from Dan's lips as he fired his snarl at Ben. "Easy for you, Taylor. She's not your kid."

"Dan…" Tanya shook her head.

"Sorry. Sorry." Dan threw up his hands and sank onto the lounge, his body shrinking as though someone had recently deprived it of air.

"You're hundred percent right," Ben told Dan. "I can't begin to imagine how you and Tanya must be feeling right now." He paused, determination visible in the set of his jaw, the fire in his dark eyes. "But what I *do* know is—we must find Erin. And fast."

"I'm with Katrina and Benjamin," Scuzz told Dan. "It is imperative we find your little girl before anything bad happens to her."

"And do we agree—not a word to the police?" Ben's question was directed at Dan and Tanya.

"No police," whispered Tanya.

Another tense silence followed. It was finally broken by my dude-helper, Jake, who'd sloped through the front door as the Inspector left. With his long spindly dreadlocks falling over his face, he voiced the number one question on everyone's lips.

"So…where do we look?" He pushed his hair from his eyes. "No one's seen or heard a cat's lick of Erin. We've, like, combed the area totally man, and found nada."

Jake was right. All very well to say we'd find Erin, but we had no idea where to start. May as well hunt for a square grain of sand on the beachfront at Semaphore.

"Play the message again, Kat," advised Scuzz. "See if there are any clues to the little girl's whereabouts in the kidnapper's words."

Tanya scrambled from her chair, eyes wild. "No. I can't," she gasped. "I can't listen again. He's going to kill her—I know." A sob choked her words. "And I-I'll never see my baby again."

I held her in my arms, rocked her in time to a silent rhythm in my head. I'd never felt so helpless. And what made it worse—Tanya was right. If we didn't find Erin soon she might die. Hell, she might be dead already. The kidnapper could have killed her straight after he left his message.

Tanya clung to me, shoulders heaving, tears running unchecked down her face. She was my best friend in the world and yet there wasn't a thing I could do to ease her pain.

Ben gently removed Tanya from my arms, hugged her then steered her towards her ex-husband. "Dan, take Tanya home and look after her. If we haven't found Erin by the time Lofty races tomorrow night, believe me, he will come in stone motherless last. Kat will see to that. But whatever happens," he went on, his eyes bright as he watched the couple lean on each other and shuffle brokenly towards the door, "I promise we'll do everything we can to find Erin and bring her home, unharmed. You have my word."

"Mine too," I added, scrubbing at my eyes.

"And mine," put in Scuzz, his bottom lip caught between his teeth.

"Go home and stay by the phone in case we need to get in touch with you."

There was no cheerful "Mary had a Little Lamb" toot from Tanya's horn today. I imagined her driving home through a curtain of tears. She only lived in the next street, but even so, I worried about her safe arrival.

"Let's listen to the slimy maggot again." Ben reached for the play button on the answering machine. "Like Scuzz says, we might be missing something."

It didn't matter how many times we played the message the voice on the other end had the same effect on my bowels. After the fourth replay I shook my head and sighed. There was nothing to hear but a psycho, a terrified little girl, and a few scratchy background noises. We were wasting valuable time when we could be out searching for Erin.

"We know he used Erin's mobile phone," I said blocking my mind from the still playing message. "But is there any way to track where the call came from?"

"Yes," Scuzz answered, nodding at me. "But there's no time for that. And unless you know an expert in the field, we'd need to bring the police in on the case."

Ben frowned. "No police."

"Hang on dudes." Jake, who'd been concentrating so hard his eyes were screwed shut and the tip of his tongue poked from the corner of his mouth, held up one hand to shush us. He moved his head closer to the answering machine. "Hear that noise in the background?"

I forced myself to listen to the message again, trying to disassociate myself from the chill it espoused and concentrate on background noises instead. Yes, there it was. A grunt? And was that a squeak during the pause before Erin spoke?

But who or what had caused the sounds?

Head tipped to the side, Ben absently stroked his chin. "Could be puppies."

"Sounds more human to me." Scuzz frowned in concentration. "Perhaps the kidnapper had the little girl gagged before she spoke on the phone."

Jake, his eyes still closed, tugged gently on his nose ring. "That's pigs," he said. "I'm sure of it. My uncle owns a piggery at Port Wakefield and whenever we visit, it's not only the smell that drives us home early—it's the noise. Pigs never know when to shut up."

Of course!

"Good one Jake," said Ben doing a complicated dude handshake with my kennel assistant. "You're the man!"

Scuzz set the tape back to the pause before Erin spoke and we listened to the background noise again. It definitely sounded like the grunt and squeal of pigs. Did this mean the kidnapper had Erin hidden near, or at, a piggery?

I scrabbled under the phone table until I found the Northern area telephone book and with Ben, Scuzz and Jake peering over my shoulder, flicked the book open to P—then Pigs—and finally, Piggeries.

"Bloody hell!" groaned Ben. He stood so close I could feel his warm breath fanning the side of my neck. "I didn't know growing bacon was *this* popular. Got to be at least thirty piggeries in the North."

Scuzz pressed against me from the other side, his solid bulk comforting. "I think we should focus on the piggeries in a ten-twenty kilometer radius from home."

"Why?" The inflection in Ben's voice seemed to say, *what-would-*

you-know-about-the-situation-when-you've-just-dropped-in-from-biker-land?

"Because the kidnapper is a local."

"And how do you come to that conclusion?"

Scuzz lifted one great hand and started ticking points off on his tattooed fingers. "One…our kidnapper knows Kat has acquired a new racing dog. Two…he knows this dog will start favorite in its first race for her. Three…he knows Tanya is Kat's best friend, otherwise why kidnap Erin to use as blackmail against her? And finally, he knew where Kat kept her spare key."

Ben gave Scuzz a friendly punch on the arm then rubbed his knuckles. "Sorry, mate," he said. "I shouldn't have doubted you."

"But why is this all about me?" I wailed. Since the moment I'd given in and let Matt stay the night, my life had been on the downside of a roller-coaster ride.

"Maybe he's not happy about you investigating your friend's murder," suggested Scuzz.

Ben shook his head. "I've been right beside Kat all the way. If that was the case, why isn't he targeting me too?"

"Because he's a coward?" proposed Scuzz.

"Would the steward on the starting box know Mr. Big's identity?" Jake asked. "You know, man, the one they put in hospital?"

"Probably does." Ben nodded. "But you won't get him to talk. Barney's scared shitless. And after the beating he took, who can blame him?"

"What about Big Mick Harrison, the bookie?" I mused. "I guess we can't wipe him off our suspect list. His wife won't corroborate his alibi for the time Matt was murdered. He swears he was home in bed with her at 3 a.m., but she says he didn't get home until 4." Funny thing, although Mick had threatened me, my gut told me he had nothing to do with Erin's kidnapping. The man might be cheating on his wife or even a potential murderer but I couldn't see father-of-the-year ever hurting a child.

"Or what about George Summers?" Scuzz rubbed at his wispy ginger beard, his dark eyes thoughtful. "He said Erin was gone when he came to collect her. Don't you think that's a tad suspicious? Should I go lean on him? See if he has a friend who owns a piggery?"

"You could, but I doubt Summers has the balls to be Mr. Big," Ben told Scuzz.

"But he might know who is. Can't leave any stone unturned, can we?" I said picturing George wetting his pants as he watched the giant biker approach. "Can I come with you when you lean on George?"

Scuzz's lips twitched and then settled back to serious. "When you spoke to Erin on the phone, Kat, did you hear another voice in the background at any stage of the conversation?"

"Don't think so. Although, at the time, she was making me so mad I probably wouldn't have heard if a reincarnated Elvis started singing in the background."

"Think hard. She told you someone was at the door. Did you hear anyone call out? If so, was it a voice you recognized?"

I shook my head. "No. Sorry." And then I thought…maybe I'll never hear Erin's voice again. A steel band tightened around my chest threatening to cut off my air supply. *Devil's Spawn* might be a pain in the butt—but she was *our* pain in the butt. With her sassy mouth and the freckles she tried to hide under her mother's foundation and that air of bravado she carried like a flag. The steel band tightened another notch as I imagined a psycho getting his kicks from carving out her tongue. Maybe not stopping at her tongue. Maybe going further and slicing the knife across her throat.

Who was behind all this? Who was the faceless monster holding the greyhound industry to ransom?

For a moment I removed my rose-colored glasses, narrowed my eyes and peered across at Scuzz. What did I *really* know about Theodore Samuel Parkington the Third? The man-mountain with his shaved head and tattooed body. He'd arrived at Jake's door out of the blue, supposedly on his way to meet a half-sister he'd only recently discovered.

What sort of a fishy story was that?

I met his dark eyes across the room. No. Scuzz was with me when Erin went missing. Although, on second thoughts, he could have arranged for an accomplice to do his dirty work. And then I remembered his kindness, his fierce protective snarl when he thought an intruder was out to attack me.

Evidently unaware of the way my mind was defaming his character, Scuzz smiled at me, his gentle eyes showing concern. "Don't worry, Katrina," he said. "We'll find your friend's daughter. Even if we have to examine every inch of mud in every piggery listed in this telephone book."

Out of the blue I remembered his hot, unexpected, stomach-clenching kiss and returned his smile.

Ben might be the handsome yummy one—but hey—it was Scuzz the Biker who actually cared enough to notice me.

25

It was nine o'clock the following night. Darkness had come early. No great hunk of a full moon guided our steps. Nope. Just a sliver of a first cousin, so skinny, it may as well have stayed home in bed.

As I crept on hands and knees through the last pen of the last piggery on our list, I felt a tug on the waistband of my jeans and jerked to a stop. *Oh no!* There was a sucking squelching sound as I plucked my silver Nokia from the bog and held it up for inspection.

Damn. Damn. And double damn.

Now it too stunk of pig shit. Just like the rest of me. I sighed in exasperation as I rammed the phone back into the waistband of my jeans and cringed when the cold grainy slime slid across my bare skin. After a day spent creeping through pig sties searching for Erin, I figured it would take at least half a bottle of coconut shower gel to make me smell human again. Even my favorite jeans would be relegated to the trash can after today's adventure. No amount of scrubbing would remove that toe-curling stink from the denim.

There was a low oomph from behind me, and a soft, *Get away from me, you bitch!* I turned my head, and in the darkness could just make out the shape of my partner in crime sprawled in the mud, a fat mamma sow spread-eagled on top of him.

"No time for games, Pig Boy," I told Ben. "It's an hour to Lofty's race and we still haven't found Erin. Tell Doris you'll come back and play with her tomorrow."

There was another grunt, not sure whether it was Doris or Ben, so I switched on my torch. The face illuminated beneath the Akubra hat was streaked with mud and thoroughly pissed off.

"Pig Boy?" growled the muddy apparition with an indignant snort. "You'll keep." He let out another oomph followed by an anatomically impossible curse as the pig bunted him in the face. "Hey, McKinley," he hissed. "For God's sake get these bloody pigs off me before I turn them into bacon sandwiches."

Squelching on hands and knees towards him, I struggled to hide a grin. By now six baby piglets had joined their mamma. They were having more fun climbing on and sliding off Ben than toddlers on a slippery dip.

Between Ben flailing his hat and me *shooing* and pushing, we eventually convinced the pigs that Ben wasn't their new best friend. Doris, annoyed at the rejection, head-butted Ben in the groin before gathering her family around her. Then, with one last disgruntled grunt she waddled off in a huff to snuffle around in the feed trough.

It was time to regroup. After climbing over the sty fence, I peered suspiciously at a cottage huddled near the end of the driveway. No lights shone through the windows. No car parked out front. "What do you reckon?" I asked. "Are they asleep or have they gone out?"

Ben adjusted his hat and wiped at his face with the sleeve of his shirt. "Only one way to find out—but either way, mate, it looks like we've struck out again. If the kidnapper had stashed Erin here wouldn't you reckon he'd leave at least one goon to guard her?"

A cold chill swirled in my stomach and settled like a lump of indigestible porridge in my chest. "What if that one goon is lying in wait for us? What if he has his night-scope binoculars trained on us right now? What if—"

Ben snorted, stopping me in mid-rant and effectively switching off the panic button. "Night-scope binoculars? Jesus, McKinley, you've been watching too many *CSI* shows."

"Hey, don't knock *Crime Scene Investigation*, Benjamin. You learn more about solving crimes from watching that program than reading any dry-as-dust textbooks from the library." I glanced down at the muddy tire iron in his hand. "All I'm saying is keep your weapon ready. Okay? You never know when you might need it."

I'd brought along my own weapons of choice stashed in a side pocket of my back-pack. A can of heavy-duty hair spray to blind my opponent and a cute little knuckle duster I'd picked up for five bucks at the local church fete. Tongue in cheek, Ben pointed out there was only one hitch—both weapons necessitated I get within "hair-combing distance" to use them. But as I told him, it's almost impossible to buy a designer gun or a Samurai sword at a church fete these days.

Anyway, my words of warning must have hit paydirt because Ben took a firmer grip on his tire iron before turning toward the cottage. "Ready?"

"Ready when you are."

"If Erin's not here it means we're stuffed," Ben admitted. "No one else had any luck and this godforsaken hole is the last piggery on our list."

"Plus we're running out of time."

The night before, after a brainstorming session on how to stop Lofty from winning if we couldn't find Erin, we'd come up with two options that didn't entail injections or pills. The first included unobtrusively smearing Vaseline from human palm to dog's eyes before placing him in the starting boxes. The second entailed lifting one paw on the pretence of checking a pad and inconspicuously swapping a wad of chewing gum from human mouth to canine toes.

We'd settled for the chewing gum.

My dude helper, Jake, had the unenviable task of handling Lofty at the track. His instructions were clear. If he received three rings and a hang-up on his mobile before the steward called handlers to the kennel-house, Lofty ran on his merits. If not—Jake would shove the contents of two packets of bubblegum into his mouth and discreetly transfer the results to Lofty's paws while lining up at the boxes.

I pressed the button on my watch to illuminate the dial. Twenty minutes to kenneling. Twenty minutes left to find Erin.

Both the front and back doors of the cottage were locked, so we shone our torches through the first window. With no blinds or curtains to block our view, we could see dirty dishes and empty beer cans completely covering a scarred wooden table and spilling over into the sink. One plate on a table near the window had green mould sprouting from a leftover chop and I bet if examined at close quarters, livestock would already be in residence.

The next window revealed a bedroom. A single unmade bed and two sleeping bags on the floor suggesting three people lived in the cottage. The only other item of furniture in the room was a large built-in wardrobe. Could they have tied Erin up and stashed her in there?

Flashing our torch through the next window we discovered a space double the size of the other two rooms. It was furnished with a clapped-out sofa, several armchairs and a battered table, all looking like they'd been rescued from a local dumpster. Incongruous amongst the mismatched furniture was a huge state-of-the-art plasma television that took up most of the back wall.

Either locked or gummed up with dirt, the only way in through the windows was to smash the glass. Not a wise move if the owners of the cottage were merely innocent pig farmers.

"What now?" I asked as we scurried around the corner to the rear of the cottage. Whatever happened to that lovely principle where people trusted their neighbors? The back door was locked.

And then I noticed Ben's shrewd eyes assessing me.

"What?"

Oh no, he seemed to be comparing me to the size of a small open window high up on the wall at the back of the cottage and measuring me as a suitable breaking-in tool.

"Uh! Oh! No way, Benny boy! I am *not* climbing through there."

"Come on, mate," he cajoled. "I reckon you're skinny enough."

I took another step away from him. "And I reckon you're nuts."

"It's not like I won't be doing *my* share of the work," he said, his voice put-upon. Even petulant. "I'm the one who'll be pushing you through from this end."

"As I said—you're nuts," I told him, studying the width of the window and then the width of my hips. "The only way I'd fit through that window would be if I stripped naked and covered my body with Vaseline."

His only answer was a choking sound and I swear something moved in the crutch of his jeans.

Pushing that interesting tidbit aside for later perusal, I shone my torch on the window, checked my watch again. "Okay, I'll give it a go— but only because we're running out of time." I drew in a deep breath. This was such a bad idea. "You'll have to give me a bunk up because Spiderwoman I'm not."

To keep my mind off the fact that I was breaking and entering, while Ben elevated me toward the open window I focused on the image of me all slippery and naked and Ben in the same condition. And I didn't lose this delightful fantasy until I poked the torch and my head through the open window.

"Get a wriggle on, Kat. We haven't got all night, you know."

"Okay for you, Taylor," I hissed back at him. "You're down there. I'm up here. *And* suspended head first over a toilet bowl."

"As long as the lid's down, it'll be a cinch," he assured me, a definite chuckle behind his words.

"Well, it's *not* down," I snarled back at him. "And the smell's making me gag." I choked as another wave hit me. I turned my head away, tried to hold my breath.

"Mate, I promise on my brother's life, I won't let you go of your legs until you give me the signal. So there's no way you'll end up falling in."

"Some promise. You're always fighting with Nick."

"Just hurry up!"

Hesitantly, reluctant to entrust Ben with my bottom end, I eased both shoulders through the opening, turned side on and wriggled forward a few inches.

That's when my imagination took over….

What if I got stuck?

What if the police found me like this?

How could I explain to DI Adams that I wasn't really breaking in— I was only looking for Erin?

And when I finally blanked out that embarrassing scenario, an even more heart-stopping picture popped into my head. What if the owner of the piggery returned home? What if he was the murderer? What if he had a gun? Stuck in the window, unable to move, I'd be toast. Hell, he could shoot me right between the eyes and all I could do was watch him take aim and hope the bullet didn't disfigure my face so much my mother wouldn't recognize me when they called her into the morgue to identify my body.

Suddenly I felt Ben's warm hands move on my legs, distracting me, which was lucky, because my imagination had been scaring the hell out of me.

"Ready?" he whispered.

I gulped and cleared my throat. "Okay, knock yourself out."

One hand strayed from my upper leg and slid to my rear end. "Hey, I hadn't noticed before, but you've got a really cute butt, McKinley."

"Ben, will you keep your hands where they'll do the most good and push me through this damn window before I turn chicken? I'm not really cut out for this break-and-enter caper."

"Spoil sport." I could hear the grin in his voice and bit my bottom lip.

Why wasn't this dialogue taking place in a nice safe environment? Like at home. Where I could grab his back-handed compliment of having a cute butt and run with it. Preferably—at a gallop—to the nearest bedroom.

My mind in bed with Ben, still naked and slippery, I popped through the window. It happened so quickly I didn't even have time to scream. And so much for Ben's brother's life—my one-man support team let go of my feet and I only saved myself from drowning in Black Plague sewerage by twisting in midair and landing head first on a pile of dirty laundry.

"Sorry. Fingers slipped," whispered Ben from outside the house. "You okay?"

I stood up gingerly, feeling for broken bones. Except for my pride, everything seemed intact and still in working order. "No thanks to you."

"Your cute butt sort of distracted me. Sorry."

"So now you're saying it's *my* fault?"

"Stop being a drama queen and open the back door," growled Ben, cutting short my tirade. "We have fifteen minutes to kenneling."

By the time we'd unsuccessfully searched the inside of the house, kenneling time had been whittled down to ten minutes.

"What say we check out the sheds and the barn and if she's not there, we ring DI Adams?"

I nodded in agreement.

"You know, Kat," Ben said tapping the tire iron against the side of his leg as he spoke, "if anything happens to Erin, I'll never forgive myself."

"Don't beat yourself up," I told him. "I'm the one who's been playing at amateur sleuth. I'm the one who coerced you into helping me in the first place."

Ben tramped to the back door and slipped through. I trailed after him. "Yeah, but I was the one who insisted we leave the police out of it," he insisted. "If the police had been informed from the start, perhaps Erin would have been found by now."

"That's rubbish and you know it. The moment the kidnapper got a whiff of the cops, he'd have killed Erin, dumped the body and fled. We had no other option but to keep Detective Inspector Adams in the dark."

The property housed a large barn plus two smaller sheds the size of average household garages. Both sheds were locked, and when Ben hoisted me up to peer through the windows, all I could see was sacks of pig feed in one and a tractor or some such farm machinery in the other.

Please. Let Erin be locked in the barn, I prayed as, keeping to the shadows, Ben rattled the barn door, only to find it unlocked. We'd failed. No one would imprison a hostage in an unlocked barn. Now all we could hope for was that when Lofty lost the race, the kidnapper would collect his money then keep his promise and let Erin free. Some hope.

After sliding the heavy door open, Ben shone his torch inside. Twenty pens on either side, each wide enough for a pig to stand but not turn around or lie down in comfort. Under the fear for Erin's safety, I felt anger biting away at my insides and vowed never to eat bacon again. Living conditions for these porkers was on a par with battery hens. Evidently the pigs in the outside pens were kept for breeding and the ones inside were fattened for market.

We peered into the first pen. Immediately every pig in the barn woke up and began squealing in excitement. Probably thought it was feed time.

"Jesus!" hissed Ben. "I bet the guy who looks after this lot wears earplugs."

"Switch on the light, Ben. There's no windows in the barn so the most anyone will see from outside is a slit under the door. If Erin's in here we don't want to miss her in the dark."

Ben reached up with one long arm and yanked on a cord dangling from the ceiling. Instantly the big shed was bathed in artificial light, so bright, it made me blink.

"Okay, we'll check it out and then vamoose before the owners return."

It only took a minute to realize Erin wasn't in any of the pens. Hell, there was barely room for a pig.

Ben shook his head in defeat. "That's it then," he said and reached up to turn off the light. "We ring the cops and pray they find Erin before she's hurt."

That's when I spotted what looked like a large cupboard set smack up against the back wall.

"Hang on," I said grabbing his arm. "What's in there?"

"Probably more feed," said Ben, moving out of reach of an inquisitive pig that wanted to smell his crutch. "What else would they store in a pig barn?"

"If it's only feed—why is there a dirty great padlock on the door? There must be something they don't want anyone to find. Pigs are clever but not clever enough to need a padlock to keep them out of their feed cupboard." I grabbed Ben by the sleeve and tugged. "Come on, let's look for the key."

There was no garden gnome nearby. No key strategically placed on a large nail on the wall beside the cupboard.

And it was four minutes to kenneling.

"My Grandma always kept her spare key in a biscuit barrel," Ben informed me.

I was down on hands and knees searching the pit at the end of the sewerage drain for the key. I glanced up, gave him a *duh* look. "And that's going to help us because…"

"There's a biscuit barrel over on that shelf."

"Well, don't stand there catching flies," I told him deciding there was no key in the drain and scrambling to my feet. "Look inside."

Crowding up against him, I watched Ben lift the chipped china lid, draw out a large key and hold it in the air. He grinned.

"Okay, okay, you're a genius. Don't waste time crowing, see if it fits the keyhole."

The key slid easily into the lock and turned. Heart forgetting to beat, I held my breath while Ben unhooked the padlock, slid the bolt across and threw the door wide open.

"Aaaaaaaaaaargh!"

A dark whirlwind hurled itself through the open doorway. Head-butted Ben in the stomach and when he hunched over with an *oomph,* bashed him on the head with a great lump of wood.

I stared in horror as Ben staggered, let out a muffled groan and sank to his knees on the dirty cement floor.

26

"ERIN?"

The small creature stopped in mid-swing and stared up at me. Eyes hostile, hair matted, teeth snarling like a cornered animal.

And here I was expecting to find her a cringing wreck.

Bottom lip quivering, Erin slowly let the lump of wood slide from her fingers. "What took you guys so long?"

"Come here," I squealed, opening both arms wide. She threw herself at me. "Your father says he's going to lock you in your room until you're twenty-one," I told her, sniffing back tears and hugging her. She clung on tight, both arms wound around my waist, her small body trembling. "Thank God we've found you."

There was a low moan from the cement floor. I looked over Erin's head. Oh yes…Ben. Clutching his stomach with one hand and his head with the other, he stumbled to his feet and blinked.

"Jesus! What hit me?" Still holding his stomach, Ben bent over, scooped his hat off the ground and shakily returned it to his head. "Don't suppose you caught the number of the truck that ran over me, did you, Kat?"

I squeezed Erin harder.

"Sorry, Ben," she mumbled into my chest. "I thought you were one of them mean guys come to hurt me again."

"'S all right, kid. I'll survive." His face screwed in a grimace, Ben rubbed the side of his head and let his breath hiss through his teeth. "I think."

Erin gave Ben a defiant look. "I wriggled the leg off the bed."

"Clever girl."

Holding Erin close with one arm, I poked my nose into the cupboard and my brain frosted over. Jesus, with my claustrophobia I'd have been screaming and battering the walls within two minutes of being locked in there. The cupboard was smaller than a bathroom, and even with the lights on in the barn the space was dark—with the door closed and the lights off Erin would have been trapped in smothering blackness. I looked at my *pain in the butt* tormentor with renewed admiration. For two days that kid had been sitting on a tiny makeshift bed with one pillow, an army blanket, a plastic bucket for a toilet and the remains of a candle stump in a bottle.

Erin snorted when she saw me check out the candle. "The mean guy said I might burn down his stupid barn so he took away the matches."

I hugged her tighter. Never again would I call this little girl *Devil's Spawn*.

By this time Ben had staggered towards the barn door and cranked it open. "Ring Jake," he yelled over the noise of the pigs. "And then let's get the hell out of here, while we still can."

I glanced at my watch. Two minutes to kenneling. Scooting towards the barn door, I punched in Jake's number, let it ring three times then disconnected.

No chewing gum for Lofty tonight.

I'd just tapped in Tanya's number when Ben, who'd been scouting around outside, ducked back behind the barn door and grabbed me by the arm. His fingers so insistent, they almost cut off my circulation.

"A truck just turned into the driveway."

"Tanya!" I yelled into the phone. "We've found Erin and she's okay. Can't talk now. Gotta go."

Ben stole another peek around the door just as a strong white light illuminated the front of the barn. "Looks like three of them," he said.

"One guy's got a searchlight and another one's jumped off the back of the truck. Oh! Uh! He's coming this way." Ben withdrew his head so quickly it's a wonder the blood didn't burst through his ear drums. As he swiveled around to speak, the white-faced, incredulous look he gave me almost made me wet my pants. "Jesus," he whispered, eyes as big as Ferris wheels, mouth down around his knees. "He has a fucking machine gun!"

For a moment his words failed to compute. And then survival instincts kicked in, snapping my mouth shut and kicking my brain into top gear. We needed a distraction. And we needed it fast.

"Let the pigs out!" I screamed and began running along the aisle.

Fortunately, Ben cottoned on immediately. While I opened the gates on one side of the barn, he covered the gates on the other side. Erin, still surprising us with her fortitude, shouted and shooed the milling pigs toward the open barn door.

"Okay, I think we've outstayed our welcome!" I yelled. "Keep together, crouch down and use the pigs as a shield."

Grabbing Erin's hand I bent double and followed Ben, pushing through the sea of squealing pink until we were outside, running along the blind side of the barn.

Almost to the end of the building, I glanced over my shoulder and froze, heart rate hitting triple figures. The goon with the Big Momma of a machine gun had turned the corner and was aiming the lethal weapon at me. Time slowed and almost came to a standstill. As I thought, *why isn't my life flashing before my eyes* and answered my own question with—*probably because until now it had always been so bloody boring*—a hundred pound porker, intent on following his mates at any cost, smacked into Big Gun Man. Sent him sprawling in the mud, face first. Then as Big Gun Man flailed around on the ground, the gun fired a flurry of bullets into the air and another six pigs, screaming in terror, trampled the shooter even deeper into the mud.

"Kat!" yelled Ben, grabbing my arm and dragging Erin and me behind him. "Stop gawping and move!"

Earlier, Ben had parked his van in an empty driveway about a mile away and we'd approached the piggery by foot. Now, after a frantic 000 call to alert the police of our sticky situation, we took off through the scrub in the vague direction of the car. Ben fell over a log and I cut myself on a barbed wire fence, but torchlight was vetoed for fear of being followed—yet, if there'd been an Olympic event that included racing across country in the dark, I reckon we would have been awarded the gold medal.

Totally exhausted, we finally found the van and scrambled inside. My wheeze was louder than a freight train. Even Ben was gasping. Erin, although covered in mud, was the only one not breathing like there was no tomorrow.

"We going home now?" she asked clambering over me to position herself in the middle of the front seat.

"Sure thing, kid," Ben gasped and puffed and fished around in his pocket for his mobile. "But first we have to stop off at the police station."

"But I want to go home."

"Don't worry. I'll text your mum and dad. Get them to meet us at the Owen police station and they'll take you home from there."

While Ben sent off a text message to Tanya, Erin wriggled closer to me, finally dropping her head on my chest.

"You okay, love?" I asked, smoothing damp hair away from her forehead.

"Mmmm." She wiped her nose on her shirt sleeve. "Just wish I'd hit one of those mean guys 'stead of Ben."

"Me too, little mate." Ben, message dispatched, leant over and gently wiped a tear from Erin's cheek. "You sure pack a wallop, kid. Guess I'll have a headache for a week."

At that moment six police cars, sirens screaming, red and blue lights flashing, hurtled past the driveway, doing at least a hundred and twenty kilometers an hour.

"Let's hope the cops get there in time to catch the kidnappers," I growled turning on the car radio to listen to Lofty's race.

"Rotten mongrels," agreed Ben.

"Mean guys," snarled Erin.

By the time I'd tuned the radio into the racing station, greyhounds were being boxed for the eighth race at Globe Raceway. I crossed my fingers and grinned at Ben. In a disbelieving voice, the race caller was informing the betting public that Big Mistake had drifted to the extraordinary long odds of 6/1, while Forever Mine had shot into short-priced favoritism.

"The bunny's on its way." The caller's low-pitched voice held a note of anticipation. "And they're racing. Big Mistake jumps straight to the front...."

"Go, Lofty!" I shouted performing a sitting-down version of a Snoopy dance with my feet, hands, and head.

The further the race progressed, the further Lofty increased his lead, until he flew past the post ten lengths ahead of the field. My dance grew wilder and my grin broader.

"Woo! Hoo! There'll be a bowl of ice cream with your favorite topping for you tonight, Lofty, you big gorgeous boy."

"Well, that should make Peter Manning happy," Ben said slipping the key into the ignition. "Who knows, he might even throw you a decent trainer's bonus this time."

Bonus or not, Lofty was the winner and Mr. Big the loser. Still buzzing from the win, I grinned down at Erin. Her returning smile, barely twitching the corners of her mouth, plunged my euphoria into the vicinity of my boots. Erin had wriggled so close to me during the race she was almost sitting on my lap. What nightmare must this kid have been through?

"Do you want to talk about it, sweetie?"

She didn't answer, just played with the end of her ponytail as though it was the most interesting thing in the world.

"After you spoke to me on the phone, someone knocked on the door. Was it the kidnappers?"

She nodded. "I thought it was Dad's mate...you know...come to pick me up," she told me, her voice reed thin and coming in short bursts. "But when I opened the door there were two men there. They yelled at me and pushed me against the wall and I got real scared. I-I think they put a rag over my face. I dunno. I must have gone to sleep."

"And when you woke up?"

"I felt heaps giddy and my stomach hurt. I wanted to chuck. And...and it was dark...and...I really, really wanted my mum."

She buried her head in my chest, muffling the sound of her tears. As I rocked her trembling body I heard a soft expletive from Ben. "It's okay, love," he said, his voice strained, as though holding back a string of virulent swear words. He reached over and rubbed her back. "No one can get to you now. You're safe with us."

Erin slowly sat up, sniffed, and looked up at me through wide wet eyes. "And then the real gross one, the one with hair in his ears, he came in with this other guy. Said he'd cut my tongue out if I didn't do as he said. I was so scared, Kat. 'Specially when he showed me this real sharp knife he had in his hand." I watched, helpless as shivers jagged through Erin's body. But the torturous memories didn't stop her from continuing. "I told them my mum would beat them up if they hurt me. They just laughed. Then the gross one punched me in the stomach and made me spew up. And then...he locked the door and I was in the dark again."

Hot tears prickled behind my eyes. With teeth clamped in my bottom lip, I held her against me. What sort of lowlife scumbag mongrel terrorized a kid, punched her in the stomach and then locked her in a dark cupboard? Over the top of Erin's head, I watched Ben's eyes grow fierce, his lips grimace into a snarl and we exchanged a silent pact—if the cops didn't catch Erin's kidnappers, we would.

"I tried not to be scared," Erin snuffled. "I even thought up a plan." Suddenly defiant, she pulled away from me and turned toward Ben. "That's why I twisted the post off the bed," she told him. "My plan would have worked too. Wouldn't it Ben? I'd have knocked one of those guys out with the wooden post and escaped. Wouldn't I?"

"You sure would, Tiger. You've got a terrific right arm. Bet you'd be a baseball star. Bet you'd be the best batsman in the whole Little League."

That's when my crush on Ben slipped over the line into something warm and fuzzy and genuine. It was time to take this relationship one step further—even if it meant losing him as a friend if I got it wrong.

Determined to give it my best shot, I bent forward over Erin's head and planted a kiss full on his lips. They were soft and pliant. Surprised, he opened his mouth enough for me to slip my tongue inside. All things sexual immediately clenched and unclenched and then went haywire. Just like before, Ben's mouth was hot and wet and alive, tasting of strong peppermints and the promise of wild unfettered sex.

Oh my!

Prepared to settle in for a bout of blazing tongue sex, I groaned as Erin tugged on my arm. "Hey, come on, you guys. No sloppy stuff," she wailed, tugging harder. "That's so *gross!*"

Eyes slightly glazed, Ben eased away. "Um...not that I'm complaining," he said slowly running his tongue over his lips, "but what was *that* for, McKinley?"

"Just for being you..."

"Oh." He brushed one finger along the line of my cheekbone. "Don't suppose you'd like to um…*talk* about this later?"

"You bet I would."

He tossed me a *we'll-do-more-than-talk* grin and I returned his invitation with a cheeky *that's-definitely-okay-with-me* smirk. I could wait. Hell, I'd been waiting for Ben to notice me for two years. What was another hour?

Grinning like a horny teenager, Ben backed the car out of the driveway and set a course for the Owen police station.

27

A WHIRLWIND OF QUESTIONS GREETED US the moment we pushed open the swing-doors of the Owen police station. Didn't we know it was a jail offence to lie to the police? Why did we put Erin's life in danger by attempting to rescue her ourselves? Didn't we know we could be charged for breaking and entering?

And on it went.

After twenty minutes of interrogation, Ben's, *we'll-talk-about-this-later* grin and my cheeky *that's-okay-with-me* smirk had sagged at the edges and slid right off our faces. And we weren't even the bad guys. Hey, Erin was safe—wasn't that the most important item on the agenda? And why weren't these men in blue out hunting down the bad guys instead of intimidating victims? The only thing that kept me from losing it was Ben's cool hand in mine.

Earlier, when I'd first rung the station from the piggery, the Sergeant, realizing this was not only a kidnapping case but also a murder investigation, had radioed his superiors, DCI Stevens and DI Adams. Within minutes of our arrival they'd breezed in, Inspector Gorgeous, as smooth and suave as ever, and Columbo with bed hair and his coat done up on all the wrong buttons.

However, before the Big Guns took over, Tanya and Dan exploded through the doorway and immediately the police station turned into a three-ring circus. They scooped Erin into their arms. Tanya cried. Dan cried. Tanya cried some more. Then, while Dan harangued the police, insisting on taking their daughter home to bed, Tanya threw her arms around my neck. And with tears and mascara leaving wet black tracks on both cheeks, she apologized for doubting me.

Finally, to bring calm to the chaos, DCI Stevens allowed Dan and Tanya to take Erin home. On the condition they brought her to the Elizabeth Precinct the following morning at 8 a.m. to arrange for counseling, to answer more questions and to look through their mug files.

Yeah…that's right. The police had come back empty-handed from the piggery. By the time they'd picked their way through the sea of pigs stampeding across the roadway and flowing into nearby market gardens, the kidnappers had flown the coop.

It was past midnight before Ben and I finally made it out of the Owen police station and into the adjacent car park. While Ben angled back onto Port Wakefield Road and set the van's nose towards Two Wells, I fastened my seat belt and let out a sigh of relief.

"Remind me never to take up a life of crime," I told him. "We're the victims and yet I feel like I've been stuck in a microwave on high for the last two hours."

"More like on a raft with sharks circling."

That got a grin out of me. I could actually see the faces of two of the sharks. They'd been playing *good cop—bad cop* with us, back at the station. At one stage I'd half expected Columbo to pull out his truncheon and beat us over the head while DCI Gorgeous made us a "nice cup of tea" and offered to wipe up the blood.

"Well, at least the police didn't charge us."

Ben snorted. "They wouldn't dare. Remember it was the Keystone Cops who lost the crooks. Not us."

Mentally and physically exhausted, I let out another sigh. It had been a long emotional night. However, one vital question needed answering. Was Ben ready to take our newfound relationship to the next level—or were we still just good mates?

I leant my head back on the car's headrest and closed my eyes.

"Anyway, thank God it's all over."

"But it's not over," warned Ben. "That's the problem. The guys from the piggery are still out there and after snatching Erin from under their noses and setting the police onto them—I wouldn't expect an invite to their next Tupperware party."

"Maybe they'll jump a ship and go to Antarctica, or Siberia or somewhere equally far away and never return."

"And what about Mr. Big? At the time we were running from his hired guns, he'd have been at the track or a TAB outlet, laying big bucks on Lofty."

"Which means, right now, he'll have a big empty hole where his bank account used to be," I declared, and laughed as I thought of Lofty's brilliant ten lengths win. "With luck, if his goons got in touch with him, he might have done a runner too. Surely he'd realize the police are hot on his trail by now."

"Or he might be planning revenge." Ben took his eyes off the road long enough to throw me a speculative look. "In which case, it might be best if I stay with you tonight."

Yeees! "What about Scuzz?"

"Hey, I'm shattered," he growled, mock-offended. "Does this mean you would prefer the bodyguard's company to mine?"

One large warm hand reached across the car console and found my knee.

"Yes—I mean, no." All rational thought threatened to fly out the window. I took a quick breath, hung on with both hands and focused on getting this right. "I mean...it's not that I don't want you to spend the night. It's just that Scuzz will be there—that's all."

"And three's a crowd," Ben drawled, his lazy fingers massaging the inside of my leg. I did another silent, air-punching, *yesss*! That was definitely *not* the action of a mate. "How about we arrange for Scuzz to go bunk with his cousin?" His fingers crept half an inch higher. "Because *we* have unfinished business. Business that could take the entire night to complete."

My stomach swirled in anticipation and heat welled between my legs. Even my breasts ached to join the party. No way was I pretending to be coy after waiting this long for action. Hell, I wanted Ben to rip my clothes off and run those tantalizing fingers all over me. My hand reached for his thigh and instead, connected with something hard and stiff that pressed relentlessly against the front of his jeans.

Uh! Oh!

Wrong move.

Ben gasped, swore, and the car swerved sharply to the right.

I flicked my hand away and sat on it. Jesus, we were travelling at 100ks an hour along Port Wakefield Road and after surviving stampeding pigs and machine gun fire, crashing the car into a tree seemed a pointless way to die.

"Um…there's an all-night service station up ahead," I gulped, wriggling closer to the window, away from temptation. "Want to grab a coffee?"

"It's not a coffee I'm after." Ben's wandering fingers settled back on the steering wheel. "Look, I'm not sure what's happening here, Kat, but there's this weird electricity zinging between us. Never felt that with a woman before." He paused as though trying to sort his words out in his head before continuing. "See, we've been mates for a long time, and it's like—I don't know—in the last couple of days I'm seeing you for the first time."

"And I thought I'd have to dance naked on the hood of your car to get you to notice I was a female."

Ben's laugh was infectious. "Hey, don't let me stop you, mate."

"There you go again!" I yelled barely refraining from beating my fists against his chest. "I'm *not* your, mate!"

"You're not? Could have fooled me." He grinned that lopsided grin that got me every time. "Okay, okay, sorry. You're a woman. A beautiful woman. Even with mud and pig shit in your hair. But if I have to wait one more minute to verify your gender, we're going to end up in a ditch." He glanced across at me, his dark eyes hot and fiery. "What say we pull off the road?"

"And *talk*?"

He threw me an evil grin. "If you insist."

Before the car stopped I had the zip of his jeans undone and he had my T-shirt over my head. After that it took less than thirty seconds to get his chest bare and my jeans down around my ankles.

"Okay, Pig Boy," I gasped as his hand cupped the crutch of my panties causing a fire to stir down below. "What shall we talk about?"

"Pig Boy?" he drawled, his fingers edging aside the elastic of my bikini briefs until they found their designated target. A target that was already hot, slick and crying out for action. He leaned across the car's console, and kissed me, his lips hard against mine. "Didn't I warn you I'd make you sorry for calling me Pig Boy?" he murmured into my mouth.

When both his kiss and his incredibly agile fingers deepened, I lost track of the conversation and arched to meet him, moaning, writhing and gasping for breath. I wanted to scream out his name. I wanted to drag him on top of me and feel him thick and hard and hot inside of me.

His mouth still joined to mine, Ben threw one leg over the console, struggling to cram the rest of his body over, when the beam of a torch and a sharp knock on the car window broke through our sexual haze.

I blinked. Peered over Ben's shoulder. There was an unfamiliar face plastered against the glass. The face of an old man with thick spectacles, a bald head and a tremulous smile.

"Sorry to disturb you," he said, playing his torch through the couple of inches of wound down window. "I was wondering if you could tell me where we are. I'm looking for Wild Horse Plains. My wife and I are paying a surprise visit to our daughter and her family, but we seem to have lost our way."

"Fuck!" Struggling to get back into the driver's seat without doing damage to his masculinity, Ben swore under his breath while I felt on the floor for my abandoned T-shirt, covering myself as best I could.

"I don't suppose you have a cell phone?" the old guy went on, as if we were having this conversation at the dinner table on a Sunday afternoon. "I haven't a clue where the nearest payphone is and I should ring my daughter, Sally. It's very late and she may get a scare if we just roll up now and knock on her front door."

"Um…yeah…hang on a minute, mate." Ben tried to drag his jeans up over a ramrod straight Mr. Percy, cursing when the zip refused to cooperate.

"Oh dear, I haven't caught you at a bad time, have I?" Our intruder peered shortsightedly through the window. "Having a bit of a kip were you?"

A giggle rose up from my chest and threatened to choke me. Ben, still struggling with the zip on his jeans leant over and banged me on the back.

"Not a word," he warned, his own lips twitching as he gave up on the zip and pulled on his shirt.

I choked down the giggle and concentrated on my predicament. What to do? I desperately needed to pull up my jeans, but if I did, I might drop the T-shirt and reveal all. And that would be even more embarrassing. Unable to make up my mind, I continued to sit like a frozen packet of peas staring at the face at the window. Then, just as I'd decided to risk all and dive for my jeans, a querulous female voice came from somewhere near the roadway.

"Richard? Is everything all right, dear?"

Oh God, not another one.

"Yes, Madge. I'm over here. This nice young couple will give us directions. They've also offered to lend us their cell phone so we can ring Sally."

Madge didn't sound appeased. "Why didn't you wait for me?" she complained. "I told you I didn't want to be left alone in the car. Just because you've only got one gammy leg and I've got two, there's no need to show off, you know. Before my last hip operation I could beat you around the block any day of the week. And you know it."

"I'm sorry, dear, but I was in a hurry. I wanted to ask directions before this nice young couple drove away."

Another face appeared at the window, this time on Ben's side of the car. "Oh, dear!" the owner of the new face exclaimed. "And what do we have here?"

Ben growled and mumbled a string of oaths under his breath. I only caught the words, *bloody sideshow* before he bent forward and banged his head on the steering wheel.

"Disturb you, did he?" The woman tutted at us. "Don't worry, my dears. Blind as a bat is my Richard. I have to drive the car now because he can't see his hand in front of his face, so there's no need to worry about *him* copping an eyeful." She shone her torch on the bulge at the front of Ben's jeans. "Hmm…got a little present for the girlfriend down there, have we?" She peered more closely, her nose pressed against the glass. "Although in retrospect, it's not really what you'd call, *little*, is it?"

"Umm…my…cell phone…um…where did I put it?" mumbled Ben his face a bright cherry as he felt around on the floor. "Um…Kat, you got your phone handy? I seem to have misplaced mine."

"Nope. Not handy." I refused to move. My mobile was in the pocket of my jeans and my jeans were still around my ankles and if I moved I might lose my top.

"Richard, why don't you switch your torch off for a few minutes?" said Madge, a chuckle in her voice.

"Why? If I turn off my torch, it'll be dark and we won't be able to see a thing."

"Exactly." She swung her walker in front of her at each step, moved around the front of the car until she reached her husband, grabbed his torch, and switched it off.

By the time the torch came back on again, I was dressed and Ben had his mobile in his hand and was standing outside leaning on the side of the car. Within a few minutes he'd let the unsuspecting daughter know to expect a surprise visit from her parents and drawn a map showing the directions to Wild Horse Plains. And then, after helping Madge fold her walking frame and stow it on the back seat of their car, he stepped back and waved them off.

"Well, that was fun," he declared, sliding behind the wheel and blowing out a tightly held breath.

"Only if you're into self-mutilation or being eaten by maggots," I replied. By this time I'd decided making out in the car, on the side of the road, might be high on a teenager's to-do list, but I'd hold out for a nice comfortable bed. "Let's finish this at home, Ben."

Ben leant across the console and brushed his lips against mine, so lightly, so suggestively, I almost changed my mind. "Best idea you've had all night," he murmured, his voice low and husky.

The windows were steaming up and I had to fan my face. "Phew! Is it getting hot in here—or is it just me?"

He grinned and then, obviously satisfied he'd managed to turn my legs to jelly with one kiss, started the car.

"Your place or mine?"

"Better make it mine," I said. "If I don't show up, Scuzz will be worried."

"Ring him and let him know he's off duty…as from now," ordered Ben swinging the car back onto the road. "Tell him to hop on his Harley and go visit his cousin." He sent me a glance so sizzling hot that every one of my hormones began to sweat. "After all, we haven't finished our *talk* yet."

Flirting outrageously, I puckered my lips, sucked my finger and drew the wet digit slowly down his arm. "About that talk, Benjamin," I said. "What say we slow it down to crawling pace this time? Nice and leisurely and drawn out. We wouldn't want to miss out on all the good stuff by jabbering, would we?"

As though his throat had suddenly lost all its moisture, Ben gulped, and I watched his fingers strangle the wheel. He grabbed a shaky breath. "Make that phone call, Kat. Now!"

Ignoring the corresponding tightening in my groin I jerked the cell off my waist band, hit my preset home number. No answer. I tapped out Scuzz's mobile number, but all I got was his message bank. A fleeting sense of unease shifted like a heavy weight on my chest. Where was Scuzz? Why wasn't he answering the phone?

"Maybe he's outside checking for prowlers and switched off his mobile in case the ring tone alerts them," Ben suggested.

I clipped my Nokia back onto the band of my jeans and nodded. "Yeah, you're probably right. Scuzz takes his bodyguard duties very seriously. I'll try again when we get closer to home."

As the car hummed along the main road toward Two Wells I settled back and closed my eyes. This had been one hell of a night. I'd crawled through acres of mud and pig shit, broken into a house, been shot at by crooks with machine-guns...

And to top it all off, my good mate Ben had finally, after two years of me dreaming and fantasizing, noticed I possessed one less X chromosome than he did.

I smiled as I thought of the way his lips, hotter than road tar, had left me gasping for breath, the way his fingers, strong, agile, and hitting my G spot with ten out of ten accuracy, had me writhing against him, the way he moaned my name as I explored the warmth of his mouth with my tongue. *Oh! Uh!* I crossed my legs, told myself *to get a grip!* We were barreling along Downes Road. Another two minutes and we'd be home. Looking across at Ben's craggy familiar face, my smile widened. Oooh yeah. And the best part of the night was still to come.

"Where's that smoke coming from?" Ben's body tensed beside me. Frowning, he stuck his head out the open window. "Shit!" he growled, his voice seeming to scratch his throat.

I dragged my eyes from Ben's face to peer through the windscreen. Thick black smoke enveloped a property up ahead. I blinked, my breath caught in my throat and fear sliced a hole in my chest as I took in the flames leaping angrily into the night sky.

Three fire engines, sirens echoing and hammering in my ears, whooshed past, screeched through my open gateway and slewed to a halt in front of my burning kennel-house.

"*Nooo!*" Screaming, sobbing, I tugged on the door. "Please, God. Not my dogs!"

Before the van stopped, I leapt through the open car door and hit the ground running. All I could see through the thick choking smoke were tongues of yellow and red flames. All I could hear was the roar of the fire and the hysterical barking of terrified dogs.

28

A FIERCE ROARING FILLED MY EARS. I stumbled. Almost fell to my knees as I plunged through a blinding fog of smoke.

"Scuzz…where are you?" I screamed, but my voice got lost in the rage of the fire. Why wouldn't my legs move faster? It was like my brain had pressed the slow motion button and left me to plough through a sea of treacle.

Not content with devouring my kennels, the greedy flames snapped at the sky, demanding more. Heat punched me in the face. Two firemen, snaking thick hoses along the ground, yelled at me to stay back. I ignored them.

Only two thoughts filled my mind–finding Scuzz and saving my dogs.

Coughing and retching against the blanket of smoke that curled and blinded, I fought my way to the open doorway of the kennel-house. The only recognizable shape in the frenzy of flames inside was my luxury dog-treatment table. I'd spent more than I could afford on that piece of equipment, but with all the extra attachments it had made my work easier and I'd never regretted the expense. Now, the wooden surface bubbled and the steel legs were red hot and melting. To my overwrought senses, the table appeared to be writhing in agony. A shiver dumped down my spine yet the heat from the inferno was so intense I tugged my T-shirt over my head before lurching through the doorway.

If this was akin to the fires of Hell, from now on I'd be especially kind to the sick, the homeless, those who called me bad names and my mother, if she ever returned from her extended holiday. My eyes stung. My throat burned. My lungs were a tight clamp in my chest. But I had to find Scuzz. Save my dogs.

I hadn't gone more than three steps when a rough hand grabbed at my shoulder, dragging me backwards.

"Let me go!" I kicked out, connecting with a hard shin.

"No way." It was Ben and of course he didn't listen. The kick didn't even slow him down. And when I dug my heels in and refused to cooperate, he continued hauling me like a bag of garden refuse until we were well clear of the burning building.

"Jesus, Kat!" His eyes wild, his head huddled under his jacket, Ben tightened his fingers on my arm. "You got a death wish or somethin'?"

When I tried to shake loose from him, his fingers fastened onto my other arm and clamped tight. When I tried kicking him again, he picked me up and held me hard against his body.

"Damn it, Kat. It's too late! There's nothing you can do in there except commit suicide."

"Noooo!" I screamed, struggling to get free of his python hold, only to have it rack up an extra notch. "I have to find Scuzz. Save the dogs...."

"Kat, it's okay. Scuzz is—" Ben began in a soothing voice and ended with a groan—right about the time my knee connected with certain sensitive items around the groin area.

Breathing heavily, Ben's face contorted, but his grip didn't loosen. "Scuzz...is over by the ambulance," he gasped, his face going a strange greenish color. "They're treating him for burns."

"You're sure?"

Ben nodded, and then, just when I expected him to give me a blast for hurting him, he angled his head to the side and kissed me. A kiss so soft and comforting it was as though he was telling me how glad he was we were alive. I felt him relax his hold and, lips attached, slid through his arms until my feet touched solid ground again.

A mixture of guilt for the knee jab, euphoria that Scuzz was okay and the need for comfort had me deepening the kiss. After the first five seconds, guilt subsided and enjoyment kicked in. But not for long.

"What about my dogs?" I asked, my voice cracking and tears threatening to spill as I pulled away.

Arms still wrapped around me, Ben cocked one eyebrow and twisted his mouth into a grin. "Well, apparently, our mate, Scuzz, is a hero. He managed to save all but one dog and the only reason he couldn't save her is because the roof caved in before he could get back in."

Relief flooded through me at Ben's words. Scuzz was safe. All but one dog had been rescued. I should have been dancing for joy, but for some strange reason my legs had gone on strike and refused to do anything but shuffle. Add to that my throat was on fire and my chest hurt and all I wanted to do was cry.

Ben's dark eyes glinted yellow as he looked down at me, a reflection from the flames. "Now, sweetheart, can we *please* move right away from this fire? I admit, I did plan to be stretched out beside you tonight—but not on a slab at the mortuary."

"I don't understand any of this, Ben. Who hates me so much they'd want to kill my dogs? And why?"

"I don't know, babe, but I'm sure as hell determined to find out."

We found Scuzz perched on a hard green plastic chair beside the ambulance. His face was streaked with soot, his beard singed and his leather pants scorched. In stark contrast, spotless white bandages covered both his hands.

As we approached, Scuzz removed the oxygen mask covering his mouth and in the light of the fire I thought I saw a tear balanced precariously in the corner of one eye. I shook my head. Nah! Leather-clad bikers didn't cry. Especially a rugged, man-mountain with legs like two-hundred-year-old tree stumps and a knife strapped to his boots.

"How's it going, Scuzz?"

"Kat," he croaked. The single tear began its slow downward roll. I gazed at the phenomenon, mesmerized, unable to stop my own tears from bubbling to the surface again. The tear slid down his cheek, reached his chin and plopped onto his boot. "I'm *so* sorry," he whispered, his ruined eyes never leaving mine. "I couldn't save her. The little white dog in the end kennel. She was so scared, yet she didn't make a sound, not until the end and then…and then she screamed. One long, drawn-out, terrified scream." He shook his head, wiped his nose on the back of his hand. "I'll never get that scream out of my head as long as I live." His eyes beseeched me to understand. "I tried to reach her, Kat. Honest. See, I'd promised I'd come back…but the fire beat me and—"

"Oh, Scuzz…"

Bawling like a five-year-old, I threw my arms around the big guy's neck and hung on. "Bubbles knew you did everything possible to save her," I assured him, hiccupping as I patted the large expanse of leather jacket under my hand. "She wouldn't have blamed you."

"Bubbles? Was that her name? I called her *Little One*."

"Hey, she'd have known you were talking to her. *Little One* was her nickname." Weighing in at only 24 kilos, Bubbles had been the smallest, cutest, sweetest greyhound in my racing kennels.

Ben shuffled from one foot to the other, concern for Scuzz scribbled in anxious lines across his face. "You okay, mate?"

"I'll live."

Scuzz placed the oxygen mask back over his nose and mouth, took a few deep breaths then ripped it off and frowned up at us. A frown so ferocious, so dire, his eyebrow rings clicked together.

"We have to catch this maniac," he growled, top lip curling back in a wolf snarl revealing teeth jammed together hard enough to crack the enamel.

Ben's eyes narrowed and grew darker. "Bloody oath, we do." He took a step closer, bent down so he didn't have to yell over the noise. "Don't suppose you caught sight of the mongrel who lit the fire, did you?"

Scuzz nodded.

"Recognize him?"

Scuzz slowly shook his head. "Too dark." I could see frustration eating at him; hear it in the bitterness of his voice. "The son-of-a-motherless-goat took off into the bushes when he saw me coming. If I had been close enough to grab him I would have hurled the creep so far into orbit he would have landed in the middle of a meteorite storm." Scuzz shrugged his massive shoulders and stared down at his bandaged hands. "The kennel-house was on fire by this time so I couldn't chase him. All I could do was ring the fire brigade and evacuate the dogs."

"Thank God you did," I put in, affection for the big guy making it difficult to talk through the soggy lump in my throat. "You know, if I thanked you every day for the next ten years, it still wouldn't be enough for what you did tonight, Scuzz."

At that moment the ambulance attendant, a motherly woman dressed in bottle green overalls with luminous yellow strips front and back, came hurrying over. She paused to replace Scuzz's oxygen mask and check his bandages.

"You really should get checked out at the hospital, Mr. Parkington."

For a moment I couldn't work out who the ambulance attendant was addressing until Scuzz answered. "I told you before, madam," he said, one finger pulling his mask away from his face so he could speak. "No hospital."

With a slight shrug she lifted his chin and checked his eyes. "No need to get upset, dear. It's your call."

"I *hate* hospitals," Theodore Parkington the Third continued, his bottom lip protruding like a toddler ready to throw a tantrum. "Last time I was admitted the nurses avoided me and the doctor on duty selected the largest needle he could find to sedate me before I could even begin to explain my medical problem." He paused and I caught a fleeting glimpse of naked pain in his face before it was whipped away by the quirking of his lips. "Anyway, hospital sheets are way too scratchy for my tender skin."

I grinned. Glad to see the return of the Scuzz I knew and loved. "I could always drop your black satin sheets off at reception for you. Pack them in with the Panda Bear hot-water bottle and your Superman jammies."

"Not necessary. I am not going to the hospital."

The ambulance attendant reached out and patted Scuzz on top of his shaved head. I almost expected her to select a lollypop from a jar and hand it to him. Instead, she told the giant biker not to worry, he could rest in the chair for as long as he liked.

"While you're here," Ben said to the woman, "any chance of taking a look at my girlfriend?" He gently nudged me forward while I momentarily lost my breath at his use of the word, "girlfriend." "Kat's suffering from shock and smoke inhalation. Thought she was fireproof, didn't she?"

"Hello, Kat." The attendant's motherly smile broke out again. "Are you the owner of this establishment?"

I nodded at her. And then my shoulders sagged as I heard the last of the kennel-house collapse behind me. All that was left was a wet smoking husk. A tumbled mess of twisted iron and blackened wood. And with it went my livelihood, my dream of making it as a professional greyhound trainer. Mr. Big, thwarted by the rescue of Erin and the success of Lofty, certainly knew which button to press to bring me to my knees.

"Let's take a look at you, dear." The attendant climbed the steps into the ambulance before stretching one rubber gloved hand out to assist me. "I know it seems like your world has come to an end tonight, dear, but the main thing is no one died in the fire."

I straightened my shoulders and sent her a smile. She was right. I needed to be strong, not allow this lowlife to beat me. My kennel-houses could be rebuilt. Erin was safe at home. Scuzz's burnt hands would heal. "You're absolutely right," I told her as she placed a cold stethoscope against my chest. "The main thing is no one died in the fire tonight."

Scuzz coughed and his soft voice drifted out from beneath his oxygen mask. "Except for little Bubbles."

29

By the time i settled my traumatized greyhounds into outside runs and the fire brigade packed up their gear and trundled out of the gateway, it was almost two o'clock in the morning.

Weary to the point of exhaustion, Ben, Scuzz and I trudged through the front door of my house and into the kitchen where Tater and Lucky subjected us to a royal welcome. Nails clicked and slithered on the linoleum, bodies contorted into near-impossible shapes and tails lashed joyfully. Then, certain of our full attention, Lucky wriggled under the sofa and brought out her new hot pink beanie baby for Scuzz to inspect, while Tater did his usual *I'm starving* tap dance beside the refrigerator.

After distributing several slices of cheddar cheese to keep the locals happy, I slouched across to the window, leaned against the sill and gazed outside at the wreckage. Who was I kidding? It was all very well to get all pumped up, tell myself to act brave and not let Mr. Big win, but how could I possibly go on training greyhounds? All my equipment was gone. My kennel-house was a bomb site. Hell, I didn't even own a collar and lead any more. Perhaps my mother was right and I should give up this foolishness, as she called it, quit greyhound training and get a *real* job.

Trouble is, stuffing my butt in an office chair from 9 till 5 or flipping burgers at the local burger joint would drive me nuts within a week. I loved training greyhounds. I loved the freedom of being my own boss, the crisp air that made my ears go numb on a cold winter morning, the thrill of watching my beautiful dogs stretch out at the gallop and the challenge of guiding a young dog from the time he left the breaking-in establishment to the excitement of his first race.

Nose against the window, I let out a sigh that came from way down in my soot-covered sneakers.

Scuzz, chest wheezing like a chronic asthmatic, placed one bandaged hand around my elbow and shepherded me across to the nearest chair. "Come along, Katrina, you must stay strong." It was like he could read my mind. "If you give up now…you'll have that evil man laughing." The biker's huge frame collided with the kitchen table as he tried to ease his body into the chair beside me. "You need to look beyond tonight's nightmare and concentrate on the future. I have many friends who will rally around and build a temporary structure to house your dogs until a new kennel-house can be built."

Ben looked up from the floor where he squatted, all the better to scratch Tater's favorite spot, the little whorl behind his left ear. "There's more than enough iron and timber out the back of our block for a temporary kennel-house. We can use that."

"Good." Scuzz raised his be-ringed eyebrows at me. "So…I'm surmising you *are* insured?"

I nodded, thanking God for my share of race wins this year which helped keep the exorbitant insurance fees up to date.

"Good," he said again and then paused for another body wrenching coughing fit. "And don't worry about your dogs. The gentleman next door has already taken four off your hands. And by tomorrow I'm sure other trainers will offer to care for the rest of your team until you're fit to train again."

Of course Scuzz was right. Here was I wallowing in self-pity while Scuzz, recovering from a nightmare himself, was attempting to cheer me up. It was definitely time to develop a stronger backbone. As the motherly ambulance attendant had proclaimed, no human life was lost in the fire and all but one of my dogs had been saved. After all, what was an inanimate object like a kennel-house compared to that?

The phone chirped, scattering my thoughts to the rafters.

Ben glanced up at the clock and frowned. "Let it go to the answering machine."

As though swimming through deep mud, I pushed myself off the chair and stood up. "Might be an owner who's heard about the fire and wants to check on his dogs."

Ben, much to Tater's disgust, stopped scratching behind the little dog's ear and stood up. He opened the refrigerator door and hooked a carton of milk from a side shelf. "What say I make us a round of hot chocolate before we hit the sack?"

"I'll be in that. Thanks, Ben. You'll find a bottle of brandy at the back of the food cupboard to strengthen the brew."

Important details dealt with, I lifted the receiver and spoke into the handset, only to find it was Big Mistake's previous trainer, calling from Melbourne.

"Sorry I'm ringing so late, sweetheart," he said, his words slurring into each other. I rolled my eyes. *This* I could do without. Sounded like the guy had been partying on into the night. "Bloody good win by Lofty."

"Yes, we were rapt."

"And you'll win plenty more with that dog, sweetheart. He's a bloody champion."

"He certainly is."

"I told Peter when he left to drive home before the big race that Lofty would win the final of the Puppy Championships. And now he's bolted in first up for you too."

I frowned. Peter left *before* the big race? I thought he'd left Melbourne the morning *after* the race.

"The wife and I won a heap of money on the big ugly bloke tonight. Backed him with the bookies and couldn't believe the price he paid. Bloody marvelous!" The trainer's raucous laughter had me easing the phone from my ear. "Anyway, gotta go, sweetheart, 'cos me darling wife has just refilled me glass. Can't let me beer go flat, now can I?"

With that he hung up.

I shook my head, bewildered. Had Peter lied to us, or was this guy so drunk he'd forgotten what day of the week it was? I sighed, my brain too clogged with smoke, fear and unanswered questions to sort this out at the moment. I'd quiz Peter in the morning.

"Everything okay?" asked Ben, placing three giant mugs of hot chocolate on the kitchen table.

"That was Lofty's previous trainer. Says he won a packet on the dog tonight and it sounded like he's been celebrating."

"Typical," growled Ben running long fingers through his already rumpled hair. "Everyone won money on Lofty—except us."

I quirked an eyebrow at him. "Considering we didn't know whether Jake would be gumming Lofty's toes together, I guess backing the dog wasn't a huge priority for us."

He grinned. "Yeah, and we *were* a little busy at the time."

Scuzz lifted his drink awkwardly between both bandaged hands and sipped at the hot brew before he spoke. "It must have been tough for that little girl. You know, the kidnapped child."

"Erin? Jesus, she was amazing," Ben told him and pulled out the chair next to mine so he could sit at the table.

"Absolutely," I added.

"You should have seen her, Scuzz. She came out of that cupboard swinging like a terrier on steroids. Head-butted me in the stomach and almost took my head off with a dirty great lump of wood."

The memory of Erin in that claustrophobic cupboard had my stomach heaving. God knows how long it would take her to sleep through the night without waking to nightmares.

Needing to clear my head, I pushed my chair back and got to my feet. "Anyone want a biscuit to dunk in their chocolate?"

Both men replied in the affirmative so while Ben filled Scuzz in on our adventures at the piggery, I wandered off to the pantry. I still hadn't been grocery shopping but it looked like Scuzz, in desperation, had played the little woman. I smiled at the tins of fruit, cake mixture and king-sized boxes of Weeties breakfast food on the shelves. And there on the bottom ledge, next to a stack of tinned salmon, sat two packets of caramel Tim Tams. Exactly what the doctor ordered.

Nothing beats chocolate when it comes to treating shock.

Biscuits in hand, I wandered back into the kitchen where I could hear Ben now telling Scuzz about Matt Turner's safety deposit box.

"If we could find out what's inside that box, I reckon we'd know the identity of Mr. Big," he informed Scuzz. "We cracked the password, didn't we Kat?"

"Yep. T.A.B.," I answered, opening both packets of biscuits and placing them on the table.

Ben instantly snagged a Tim Tam, took a bite and dipped the remainder into his hot chocolate. "What say we go back and check out Matt's box tomorrow?"

"If Ms. Fusspot hadn't been so damn officious last time, we'd probably know the identity of the killer by now." I nibbled on a corner of the Tim Tam, briefly closing my eyes as the chocolaty taste spread inside my mouth. "And then Mr. Big would have been in jail instead of setting fire to my kennel-house tonight."

I looked across at Scuzz, sprawled on the table, shaved head resting on his folded arms.

"You okay?" I asked, squinting into his tired, red-rimmed eyes. He smelt of smoke and fatigue and his color under the ginger stubble reminded me of weak milky tea.

"Actually, I'm beat," he admitted, dragging himself upright which produced another bout of coughing. When he'd recovered, he scraped his chair away from the table and lumbered to his feet. "If it's alright with you, Katrina, I'll call it a night."

"Time we *all* hit the sack." I stood on tiptoe, wound my arms around Scuzz's neck and pulled his face down for a goodnight kiss, my lips scratching against the sandpaper of his cheek. "Don't worry about getting up early in the morning. It's my turn to cook bacon, eggs and tomatoes for *your* breakfast. Okay?"

"I look forward to it." His returning smile needed matchsticks to prop up the corners of his mouth.

"Good night, Scuzz. Sleep well."

I watched the giant biker bend his head to maneuver under the door frame and thought how lucky I was my unpaid bodyguard had been outside, on patrol, when the fire started.

But what if no one had been home?

As though he could read my *what-if* thoughts and decided to chase them away with what he did best, the moment Scuzz disappeared into the lounge room Ben favored me with one of his slow, leg-melting grins. "Hey, McKinley," he drawled. "About that *talk*…"

I returned his grin with a wide-eyed look of mock innocence. "What *talk* was that, Taylor?" I said and picked up the empty cups and placed them in the sink.

"Why don't you come over here and find out?"

I was bone weary, I'd need half a bottle of Coconut shampoo to remove the stink of smoke from my hair…but hey, if Ben didn't care, neither did I.

I strolled across the room until I stood behind his chair. With both hands planted on his shoulders, I leant forward and skimmed my lips along the nape of his neck, smirking when the fine hairs stood up and waved at me.

"You know you're asking for trouble," he growled.

My answer was to blow hot air in his ear and grin when he squirmed in his chair.

"Come here, minx." With one quick motion, he flipped me onto his lap and held my wrists together with one hand. Like wisps of fairy dust, the fingers on his other hand smoothed a stray tendril of hair across my cheek and tucked it behind my ear. And when his lips, soft and teasing, and tasting of my two favorite flavors, chocolate and caramel, touched mine, so gently, so intimately, I gasped against his mouth.

"Whew! Where'd you learn to *talk* like that?"

"Hold onto your fillings, babe. We haven't even started the conversation yet."

He swung my legs around so I sat facing him, straddled across his lap and then he found my mouth again. Not soft and teasing, this time his lips were so demanding and hot I could almost smell the sizzle, hear oceans roaring in my ears. Breathless, I arched against the hardness of his body and moaned when his tongue, deep inside my mouth, found and caressed every sensitive corner, every pulsating nerve point; even those I didn't know existed.

By the time our lips finally parted, Ben's shirt was unbuttoned, my top was hanging around my neck and every inch of my body ached with a heat so acute I was ready to start at his toes and eat my way up to his...

From the room next door, Scuzz's rattling breath, each one sounding like it was going to be his last, filtered through my sexual frenzy.

Oh, God. We couldn't do this. Not with Scuzz in the next room.

Reluctantly pulling away from the enchantment of the sweet store, I tried to steady my breathing while wriggling off Ben's lap. "Let's finish this tomorrow when we're alone." *The hardest words I'd ever said.* "Scuzz needs you tonight. He shouldn't be left alone."

Ben ground his teeth together, hissed a shallow breath and then slowly stood up. "You're right, of course, I'll sleep on the sofa in the lounge tonight," he said, and pulled my head up against his chest where I could feel his heart banging against my cheek, like a caged possum. "But what about you? Will you be okay on your own?"

I looked up and gave him a grin, weak, but still a grin. "Hey, I have two bodyguards, don't I? And there's always Tater and Lucky."

"Kat, you *do* realize that *talk* of our scan't wait much longer...or I'm going to explode like the fat man who ate one too many meat pies."

I giggled and nodded and had to physically refrain from rubbing against the truth of his statement when it pressed against my stomach.

In fact, it took another bout of coughing from the lounge room to convince me to walk away.

*****

The refrain from *Staying Alive* sliced through my sleep. I swum my way to the surface, cranked open one eye and squinted at the clock.

Ugggh… 4am….

I rolled over and reached for my tote bag, a dark blob on the bedside cabinet. Tinny and insistent, *Staying Alive* continued to bang away in my head, every note a sharp nail hammering into my brain. With one hand inside the bag I shuffled through the contents until my fingers closed around the rowdy piece of technology.

"Huh…" I grunted into the cell, still half-asleep.

"Is that you, Kat?"

I gave another grunt. Who else would be answering my mobile at 4 o'clock in the bloody morning?

"Sorry. Did I wake you?"

Didn't even deign to answer that one.

"I just heard about the fire so thought I'd ring to commiserate. How many dogs did you lose? And what about *my* dogs—any saved?"

I pinged my eyes open and mentally kicked myself in the rear. Peter Manning. Naturally he'd be anxious for news of his dogs. "Geez, Peter, I'm sorry for not contacting you. What with the fire and other stuff that's been happening around here, I just didn't…"

"No need to apologize, Kat," he soothed, all sympathy. "I understand."

"Bad news, I'm afraid. Bubbles didn't make it. My friend Scuzz managed to rescue all the other dogs but couldn't get to your little girl. She was in the last kennel and by the time he returned for her the roof had crashed in and it was too late."

"Oh well, it could have been worse. The bitch was insured so I'll be compensated for my loss." When I didn't comment on that bit of cold callous information, he continued, his voice more businesslike now, as though he had certain voices for different topics of conversation. "Anyway, the reason I rang is because I have something interesting to show you."

Hitching the quilt up to my neck, I dropped my head back on the pillow and sighed. I didn't care if he had a picture of Superman having sex with a lioness—all I wanted to do was switch off my phone and go back to sleep.

"Can I meet you somewhere?"

"What? Now?" I snuggled deeper under the bed clothes. "Can't it wait?"

"I have proof of who lit the fire tonight?"

"You do?" I threw back the quilt and bolted off the bed, stubbing my toe as my bare feet connected with the cold floor.

"Look, I can't say any more, my phone could be bugged. Meet me at the town end of your road in say, ten minutes? And come alone."

"But what about Ben and Scuzz?"

"If I see anyone with you, I'll drive straight off."

"But—"

"No one! You're the only one I can trust, Kat. If the wrong person finds out what I've discovered, I could end up dead."

I hesitated. This cloak and dagger stuff had warning bells ringing in my head. But Peter was one of my owners and if he had proof...

"I'll be there."

"Good girl," said Peter. "I'll be sitting in my car on the side of the road. You know, under the old sycamore tree. Pull in behind me and if it's safe and I haven't been followed, I'll show you the proof. If there's likely to be trouble, I'll flash my headlights when I see you coming. If that happens, do a U-turn and drive home, pronto."

"But why can't—"

"See you in ten minutes." And with that he hung up.

My first instinct was to say damn Peter's melodrama and go wake up the A team, but I knew that would prove futile. Unless I was alone the deal was off.

I dragged on jeans and a pullover, slid my arms into an overcoat and pulled a beanie down over both ears to keep out the cold and at the last minute, gut instinct had me reaching for my weapons—a trusty can of super-hold hair spray and my shiny brass knuckle-duster. I slipped them both into my coat pocket, told the dogs to go back to sleep and shut the bedroom door behind me.

As I tiptoed down the stairs, a cacophony of snores blasted from behind the lounge room door confirming the A team were deep in the land of Nod. I held my breath as I inched past and unlocked the front door.

The loneliness of early morning greeted me. And after the deafening noise and movement of the fire, the night laid still and cold around me. Everything was bathed in a silver light, compliments of a three-quarter moon that rode high in the sky. I took a deep breath, averted my eyes from the dark shape which was all that was left of my kennel-house and let the breath out slowly. One or two dogs barked sleepily from the outside runs and a sharp smell of smoke tugged at my nostrils.

Bypassing the gravel path on the way to my car, so as not to wake Ben or Scuzz, I started to jog. If I was late Peter might not hang around. He'd sounded freaky over the phone. Wired? As though he was in some sort of trouble—or close to a breakdown.

Two steps away from my car I blipped to unlock the doors and heard a rustle behind me. I paused to listen. Maybe it was that feral cat—the one who had been taunting the dogs to distraction over the last couple of weeks. I'd been threatening to sic Tater onto the skinny, mean-eyed pest but the damn cat almost laughed in my face when I told him.

Before I could turn around to investigate the noise further, a quick whooshing noise zipped past my ears. Something hard connected with the back of my head. I staggered forward, a searing pain spreading like a live crackling wire through my skull…

And passed out.

30

It was the thumping headache that woke me. I opened my eyes, slits at first, then when blackness greeted me—curling through and eating into my brain—I opened them wider.

Had I gone blind? Was I dead? I clenched my teeth and cursed my active imagination.

It's the middle of the night. Of course it's dark!

Next question: *where the hell was I?*

The interior of my head was a demolition site and if I didn't know better, I'd swear someone had filled it with prickly pear and well-sharpened roofing nails. I ran my tongue over my lips but the dryness extended inside my mouth and ran down my throat into my chest cavities.

I blinked and shook my head. *Shit! Shit! Shit!* A biting pain threatened to take off the back of my skull and gouge out sections of my brain. Bile spewed up into my mouth. I closed my eyes, sucked in big noisy breaths and retreated to that personal space deep inside that allowed me to experience the sensation without being directly involved.

It felt like an eternity, but finally the pain and nausea eased and I decided maybe I was going to live after all. Opening my eyes, I swallowed the bile and found my central core by sucking in slow, calming breaths through my nose and blowing out through pursed lips. Strangely, the air smelled stale and musty; of age-old wood and locked cupboards. Could the smell of Matt's body still be clinging to my bed?

That's if I was in my bed.

Momentarily, I stilled my breathing, listening for a clue to my whereabouts. No dogs barking—only the muffled sound of some dreary funeral dirge playing on the radio. I frowned. Couldn't remember leaving the radio on before going to bed and I sure as hell couldn't remember tuning into a station that played funeral music.

I reached out to change the station...and hit something solid.

Jesus!

Tentatively, I inched my fingers toward the other side.

Ditto...

I struggled to sit up and immediately bashed my head on something so hard and unyielding, stars lit up the smothering blackness.

Keep breathing.

Don't panic.

There has to be a logical explanation.

Ignoring the chunks of headache that were slowly peeling off inside my skull, I closed my eyes, took a deep breath and imagined I was floating on top of a red and yellow blow up mattress in the middle of a warm pool, enjoying the morning sunshine and listening to a tuxedoed waiter inform me brunch would be served on the patio in five minutes, madam.

Ah....that was better.

Now, where was I?

I remembered stumbling into the house after the firemen left, drinking hot chocolate laced with brandy, kissing Ben like there was no tomorrow, and then going to bed. Remembered being woken by a call on my mobile from Peter Manning telling me he had an important clue as to the identity of the person who'd set fire to my kennel-house.

I remembered grabbing my coat and car keys, shoving my trusty hair spray and knuckle-duster into my coat pocket and sneaking out the front door.

I remembered unlocking my car and then...

And then…and then what?

I dug deeper into my soggy brain. Nope. That was it. The last thing I remembered was activating the locks on my car doors and hearing a noise behind me.

Had I tripped and knocked myself out?

Had I been hit over the head?

Or had I fainted?

More importantly—where was I now?

Struggling to prevent the nightmare from freezing my senses and turning me into a screaming, dribbling mess, I investigated the barriers at my sides with probing fingers. Although solid, the obstruction seemed to be padded with soft material, smooth, cold and silky to the touch. I lifted my hands above my head and poked at what felt like solid wood, inches from my face. I reached out with my toes only to find another barrier a mere stretch from where my feet ended.

Oh sweet Jesus!

As comprehension sucker punched me in the gut, my breath went on strike and my chest cramped in sympathy. I opened my mouth to scream but no sound came out. I banged and crashed and bucked my body in a futile attempt to break free. I gasped for air but the more I gasped, the less air I could find. Like a wet sandbag dropped from a great height, my next thought floored me. Completely defeated me.

Had I been buried alive?

Whimpering, I closed my eyes. Hysterics crawled around in my head. I wasn't ready to die. Not by a long shot. I wanted to wave goodbye while celebrating my 100th birthday, dancing to rock-and-roll music and belting down one martini for every year of my life. Not like this. Not buried under the ground. Not tearing my hair out and choking on my last breath.

I pummeled the lid of the coffin with closed fists. Yelled, *let me out!* Sent a message to The Universe to inform It of my predicament and that no amount of positive vibes would help me this time—unless It intervened. Like right now.

But nothing happened. There was no voice of encouragement. No angel of mercy. No crack of lightning splitting the ground asunder and sending into orbit the wood and bronze and satin that imprisoned me. I was still trapped inside a coffin six foot under the ground with as much likelihood of survival as a spider coughing out bug spray.

With the painful wheeze of my chest assaulting my ear drums, I closed my eyes, crossed my arms like I'd seen in pictures of dead people in their coffin, and decided if I was going to die, I'd do it while thinking of Ben. My Ben, with his crinkly eyed smile. My Ben, with the toned body that I'd never ever get to see naked. At that thought, a spasm of anger shook me.

Determined to let out another lusty yell, I opened my eyes.

And blinked.

Painted angels were smiling down at me from above, with tiny rosebud lips.

I narrowed my eyes and peered more closely. Had I died and gone to Heaven? No, I was staring at a cream colored ceiling dotted with recessed lighting and painted angels. So where the hell was I? And who had opened the lid of the coffin?

For a moment I lay there, my depleted lungs sucking in ragged breaths of air. Sweat ran from my forehead, stinging my eyes. When no crazed killer appeared, attempting to rearrange my neck at the correct angle so he could cut my throat, I cranked the top half of my body forward and sat up.

Ears alert for movement, I scanned the room. Although dimly lit, I could make out several oak coffins lining one wall, lids sealed and topped with brightly colored flowers. Their brass handles and trimmings winked in the muted light from the overhead fittings. And to add to the somber atmosphere, a cloying smell of violets hung in the air while soft music purred from a nearby speaker.

Other than that—the room was as still as the dead who occupied it.

"Lusty pair of lungs you've got there, Kat."

As though hit by a switch, I flicked my head to the left and peered in the direction of the voice.

"My old man would not be pleased if he heard you shouting in his funeral parlor. When I was a kid he'd lock me in here for hours if I so much as sneezed amongst his precious dead."

Dim lighting made it hard to see clearly, but I could just make out a familiar figure sitting in a chair on the other side of the room, arms folded, legs stretched out in front of him.

"Peter?" I croaked. Relief, and what felt like hours of yelling making my throat scratchy. "Oh, Peter, you *darling* man. You don't know how happy I am to see you. Thank God you found me. Did you notice anyone suspicious hanging around outside? Sorry I couldn't meet you down the road like we planned. I don't know what happened but—"

Like a runaway bus slamming into a brick wall, my euphoria suddenly crashed and burned. I gulped and the sound echoed with a dry click in the back of my throat. For there, in Peter's right hand was the gleam of a little silver gun. And the gun was pointed at me.

"Peter? What are you doing? How did—" My voice, even scratchier now, cracked on a high note.

Peter smiled at me. A weird spaced-out smile that didn't reach his eyes. "You're an easy touch, you know, Kat. I rang from outside your house and within minutes you'd walked into my trap." He shook his head and made a tutting sound with his tongue. "In fact, you are so naïve there's no skill attached to tricking you at all. You need to wise up, question people's motives, stop trying to be Miss Nice Girl all the time or one day something bad will happen to you."

Huh? And a gun pointed at my head was a good thing?

He straightened the knot in his silk tie. "When you waltzed out of the house, alone, as instructed, it was merely a matter of hitting you over the head with a tire iron, bundling you under a blanket in the back of your car and driving to my father's funeral parlor." He made a sweeping gesture with one hand. "Perfect location for getting rid of my final complication, don't you think? It's always so deadly quiet in here." His mirthless laugh sent my heart into deep freeze. Dark spots danced before my eyes. And I thought I was in trouble inside the coffin? "As you can imagine," Peter continued, "my father's clients have never been very big on conversation."

When I didn't respond, Peter got to his feet, flicked an imaginary crease from his trousers, and strolled toward me. He came to a halt a couple of meters away beside a beautifully embossed mahogany coffin with crucifixes engraved in the wood.

"I'm sorry about this, Kat. I really like you and you're a great trainer," he went on shaking his head as though I were a naughty child, while using the nearby coffin as a back rest. "But you've been far too nosy. That idiot, Matthew Turner meant nothing to you, so why get involved? Why sniff around and complicate issues for me? If I'd known you were going to be such a pain in the butt, I would have finished you off when I eliminated Turner instead of allowing you to flounder around downstairs in the dark pressing your little music gizmo while I attended to business upstairs."

"But why did you...?" Once again, I couldn't go on. Speechless, I sat on a bed of pale blue satin topped with white lace and blinked up at him. Tire Man Pete—a murderer? *My* Tire Man Pete? Lucky and Lofty's owner? It just didn't compute.

"There was no way around it," he went on, settling down for a cozy chat. "Turner had the brains of a headless chicken. Do you know, he actually thought he could blackmail me? Said he had an audio tape of me on the phone threatening to break his kneecaps if Queen of Egypt won. He even threatened to send the tape to the police if I didn't give him a cut of the action. What a loser!"

His voice rose and I watched in horror as the man in front of me changed from the charming, well-spoken Peter Manning, I thought I knew, to an alien monster.

"And when I refused to cooperate, his bloody dog won and I lost fifty thousand dollars," he snarled, saliva gathering at the corner of his lips. And then he took a deep breath, let it out slowly and smiled at me. "So, naturally I had to kill the guy. What did he expect? That I'd allow him to walk away and blab to the officials? It's losers like Turner that give greyhound racing a bad name."

Peter Manning was in cuckoo-land. Although his trigger finger remained tense and the silver gun stayed level with my chest, his voice was utterly calm. We could have been politely discussing the need for rain after a hot dry summer.

Mesmerized by the deadly black hole at the business end of the gun, I gulped down a knot of dried spit and attempted to kick-start my brain. "But why, Peter? Why would a respectable businessman like you go from managing a tire company to—to murder?"

With his free hand he fingered the snowy white handkerchief in his breast pocket and smiled benignly down at me. "Money of course. It's *always* about money. My tire business was going bust and I needed a bankroll to get out of the country and start afresh."

"Couldn't you have asked your family for help?"

"Oh no." His frown deepened and the alien monster appeared in his eyes again. "My father would never understand. He has very strict rules about gambling. When I was ten, he caught me betting five cents on a game of marbles and beat me so severely I couldn't walk and then he shut me in the crematorium with a mattress and a bucket for two days to 'repent my terrible sin.' According to my father, gambling is a sin *worse* than murder."

He frowned and paused, his fingers picking distractedly at the cuff on his sleeve. Finally, he rammed his fidgeting hand into his coat pocket and continued talking. "So, I decided I'd invested enough money in greyhound racing over the years and it was time the industry repaid me. I deserved it. People can die waiting for a lucky break to come their way, you know, so I decided to push the envelope." His shrug was noncommittal. "It's called making your own luck."

"And murdering Matt and kidnapping Erin and beating up the starting-box steward—"

"All merely taking care of business."

He pushed himself off the heavily embossed coffin and straightened up, his familiar figure a direct contrast to the lethal weapon in his right hand. The same hand that accidentally king-hit me the day he and Ben fought outside Ben's kennel-house—what, three days ago—seemed more like a year. But how could Peter, my most generous owner, a man I'd known for five years, be standing here threatening me with a gun? It was impossible to get my head around. That is, until his trigger finger tightened and he lifted the gun and pointed it at a spot marked X, right between my eyes. Hell, this was real all right—this was totally fucking real. I let out a gasp as my heart, unable to batter its way out of my chest, flipped and dived somewhere in the vicinity of my toes.

I was going to die!

And then, for some strange reason, probably pants-wetting fear playing tricks with my mind, I thought, well, if Peter shoots me now, I'll topple back into the coffin and be all ready for burial. No fuss. No complicated funeral arrangements. All taken care of.

Mother *would* be pleased.

And then another thought, much stronger than the first, came gate-crashing through the panic, elbowing the pathetic one out the way. What about my new relationship with Ben? If I meekly allowed Peter to drill a hole in my head, what about all the fantastic sex I'd miss out on? Hey, I'd waited two years for that thick-headed mate of mine to notice I had boobs and other interesting female bits and I was damned if I'd let some crackpot with a gun prevent me from finishing off what Ben and I had started in the front seat of his car.

If I could keep Peter talking, maybe his father, or one of his assistants, might drop into the parlor to tighten the screws in one of the coffins, or change the flowers, or whatever it is funeral directors and their subordinates do when they're not burying people.

"So...Peter," I said to him. "What happens when the police find out you lied to them about being in Melbourne for the Puppy Championships the night you killed Matt?"

Once again Peter's smile didn't match the emptiness in his eyes. "Ah, yes, my alibi. Foolproof. I was in another state arranging to buy Big

Mistake for you to train—how could I have been in two places at once?"

"I wouldn't be too sure about the police not knowing the truth, Peter." I cautiously inched my left hand into my coat pocket. Peter was right. I was an easy touch. It was time I wised up and got rid of my *Miss Nice Girl* image. Stopped being naïve, trusting and so bloody *nice*. Peter hadn't even bothered checking my pockets for weapons before he stashed me in the coffin. How insulting was that?

"What do you mean?"

"Lofty's ex-trainer rang me tonight. While I was talking to him he let slip that you'd left Melbourne *before* the final of the Puppy Championship. He could do the same when the police contact him."

"What? That *stupid* idiot!" Peter's top lip curled back in a snarl, the beast threatening to resurface. "Christ! The world is full of morons. I gave Brett Tregenza enough money to buy him and his bloody family, an all-expenses paid trip to the Bahamas in return for that alibi. All he had to do was swear to the police, or anyone who contacted him, that I didn't leave until the morning after the big race. How difficult was that?"

"And what about the kidnappers?"

"Dickheads! I contracted the pair of them to convince a pig-headed steward to see things my way and they didn't even think to cover their faces." He sighed as though he'd hired his employees from a two-bit incompetent job-hiring agency and was close to striking the agency off his Christmas card list. "And tell me, Kat, who in their right mind would stash a kid at a piggery? I guess that's how you found the brat…heard the pigs in the background over the phone. Am I right?"

I nodded and put on this, poor-you, finding-good-crooks-these-days-must-be-the-pits expression to keep him talking. By now I had my left hand hooked around the can of hair spray and had started to wriggle the fingers of my right hand into the cold slots of my knuckle-duster.

"Nothing's going to plan." His face twisted into a spoilt, little-boy pout as he raked a hand through his hair, rumpling the ultra-smooth coiffure. "I had to book my flight to Spain two weeks earlier than originally planned because of you." His laser glare settled on the X between my eyes. "You've caused me a great deal of inconvenience, Katrina. I needed one final windfall and instead, lost a shitload of money at the track tonight. Why couldn't you stop that big ugly dog of mine from winning?"

"What? And miss out on your congratulations? You know me, Peter—always trying to please my owners." I bared my teeth and carefully edged the can from my pocket. Damn. He wasn't close enough. A shot of hair spray to the eyes from this distance would only make him smell nice.

Of course my sarcasm sailed straight over Peter's head. He frowned, his thick eyebrows just about meeting over the deep creases on his forehead. I could almost see the chaotic thoughts leaping back and forth in his head.

"I have to leave for the airport now," he told me. "It's only a matter of time before the cops pick up those moronic losers. And of course to save their own pathetic skins they'll sing like canaries."

I watched his trigger finger whiten and sent another quick SOS to the Universe. "If you're leaving anyway, Peter why bother killing me?"

"You know too much. I'll be out of the country before the Spagnetti brothers are caught, but it's too risky to keep you alive." He took another two steps closer and gave me a hurt look like a father having to spank a child for her own good. "It's nothing personal."

"Maybe not to you—but believe me Peter, it is to me."

"I'll even give you a choice," he went on in his sanctimonious fatherly voice. "I can pull this lever and send you and the coffin straight to the crematorium. Or I can shoot you first and then pull the lever. Either way, I'm afraid you'll be a pile of ashes by the time I'm settling into a comfortable first-class seat on my way to Spain."

Holy Catfish! All the wires in Peter's brain had blown apart. He planned to burn me to a crisp in his father's crematorium. And what's more, he didn't care whether I was dead or alive at the time.

Goodbye Miss Nice Girl!
Hello Bombshell Chick!
Muscles tensed, a hungry spider eying a fly hovering over her web, I watched Peter take one more step closer. *Come on baby…Come to Mama!* And then he took another step and his hand reached out for the pivotal lever that would drop me and my silk lined coffin into the fires of Hell.

No way, Jose!
With a battle cry worthy of a charging Aussie Anzac, I drew out my super-size can of extra-strong-hold hair spray, took aim, and hit the trigger.

"Take that you chest-stabbing, kid-stealing, dog-killing, son of a bush-pig!"

"*Aaaaggh!*" Peter grabbed at his eyes while obscenities, ranker than two-week-old garbage, spewed from his mouth. I felt the *zing* from a stray bullet whistle past my ear as I leapt from the coffin and brought my second weapon into play. When I'd spotted the gleaming brass knuckle-duster at a church fete's Bring and Buy sale and counted out five dollar coins for the pleasant-faced lady dressed in pale blue polyester who was running the stall, I knew my purchase would come in handy one day.

And today was the day.

Kapow! Before Peter could blink the spray from his eyes, I swung my brass-covered fist and let him have it fair and square on the point of his chin. He gave me this bemused *duh* look, as if to say, hey, that wasn't part of my master plan, and then his eyes crossed, glazed over, and finally, with a low moan, he dropped to the canvas.

31

"*Oooooh!* I reckon *that* must've hurt!"

I flicked a startled glance over my shoulder. Ben, his gorgeous face screwed into an exaggerated grimace, sauntered across the room toward me. Behind him, Scuzz, nose rings vibrating with every snort, tattooed muscles tense and ready for action, filled the open doorway.

Oh, what a beautiful sight. Relief kicked in and with it came the urge to break down and bawl, throw my arms around the A team and let them kiss and cuddle the horrors of the past fifteen minutes away. Instead, I dug deep and dredged up a cocky grin. "Hi there, boys," I trilled giving them a two-finger wave to complement my new *Bombshell Chick* persona. "Drop off for a couple of pints at the pub on the way here, did you?"

Scuzz hooted. "Good one Katrina. I told Lover Boy you could take care yourself." His lips quirked as he angled his massive head in Ben's direction. "But of course the cowboy was too busy wailing and cursing and stamping his feet to listen to me."

"We heard you take off," explained Ben, "but couldn't follow because your car was gone, my car was in the garage at home and the tires on Scuzz's hog had been conveniently slashed."

Scuzz growled deep into his ginger beard. "And whoever messed with my wheels is going to pay big time. Anyway, next thing, your man has his head under your next door neighbor's dash, hot-wiring his SUV. And when I protested, as any normal law-abiding citizen would under the circumstances, he informed me it would take too long to wake the guy up and ask for his keys."

"I was worried about you, babe." Ben's arms circled my shoulders hugging me to him. I let my head rest on the warm solidness of his chest and breathed in his outdoorsy smell as though it was nectar.

"Worrying is good," I told him and sniffed.

"We'd have been here sooner," Ben went on, smoothing my hair from my eyes with rough, work calloused hands. Hands that felt better than any suit-wearing lawyer, businessman, male model's wishy-washy softness. "But by the time I'd convinced Mr. Concerned Citizen that the guy next door wouldn't mind if we borrowed his wheels," Ben said scowling at Scuzz, "your car had disappeared from sight. We've been driving all over the neighborhood searching for it."

"During which time, Lover Boy has been growing more and more frenzied," added Scuzz.

"And we were just getting ready to call the fuzz, when we spotted your station wagon parked outside, of all places, Manning's Funeral Parlor."

I reached up and kissed Ben gently on the lips before pulling away and pretending interest in my untied shoelace. If I stayed in the warmth of Ben's arms a moment longer, I'd crack up, and maybe cry. And bang, there would go my new *Bombshell Chick* image.

A low moaning sound, eerie in the presence of so many dead bodies, echoed across the room.

"What's that?" Scuzz shot away from the coffin he'd been leaning on, so quickly he almost left his shadow behind. "Was that the guy on the floor or did it come from…"

Peter let out another groan.

"Damn," I said. "I mustn't have hit him hard enough."

Scuzz, a relieved smile playing at the corners of his mouth, tramped across the floor to check on Peter. Coffins and flowers shook in his wake. While Scuzz held both bandaged hands in the air and neatly bopped Peter on the head with his elbow, sending him instantly back to dreamland, Ben picked up the silver gun from the floor and emptied the bullets into his pocket.

"Looks like a Beretta," observed Ben. He twirled the gun on his finger a couple of times and then turned to me. "I can see you have everything under control here Kat, but can you please tell *us* what the hell's going on? Why'd you take off without waking us? What the blazes are you doing at Manning's Funeral Parlor? Who owns this gun? And why is it necessary to keep Peter in a constant state of unconsciousness?"

"It's all quite simple." I started to explain but decided even a *Bombshell Chick* needed comfort in times of extreme stress so snuggled into Ben's protective arms before continuing. "After you guys went to bed, Peter rang me. He said he knew who Mr. Big was and arranged to meet me at the end of the road." I looked up into Ben's anxious face. "He said he'd only tell me if I came alone."

"Oh, Kat, you didn't fall for that one? It's the oldest trick in the book. You should have woken me up."

"And me," declared Scuzz. "Because I know *all* the tricks in the book—and some the book hasn't got around to publishing yet."

I sighed. "Yeah, I know guys. Anyway, Peter must have been waiting for me and when I came outside he knocked me over the head. According to him he stashed me under a blanket in the back of my car and drove here."

"Always thought the guy was a pumped up slime ball," Ben growled. Eyes threatening dire retribution, he dug Peter in the ribs with the toe of his boot. "Lucky he's already unconscious or I'd knock him into the middle of next month."

"So...Sleeping Beauty must have slashed the tires on my Harley," Scuzz broke in, glaring at the prostrate figure on the floor. "I will be visiting your tire shop later today, mate. And while there, I'll be choosing some very expensive replacements from your stockroom."

"But why did he bring you here? To his father's funeral parlor?" asked Ben.

"I guess he had a key. And he reckoned it was quiet in here because his father's clients aren't very talkative."

"Not wrong there." Scuzz flicked a quick glance over his shoulder at the coffins displayed along the wall, evidently expecting a dissenter to sit up and take issue at our presumptuousness.

Clearly still trying to work out the facts, Ben frowned down at the silver gun clasped in his hand. "What about this?"

"It's Peter's. Peter Manning *is* Mr. Big," I blurted out. "He did away with Matt, arranged for Erin to be kidnapped, set fire to my kennel-house and was responsible for all the race fixing that's been going on. And tonight, he brought me here to kill me."

Scuzz's face went white under his beard. "In that case, when Sleeping Beauty wakes up, instead of putting him back to sleep, I'll rip his head off and use it to throw basketball hoops."

The color drained from Ben's face. His arm, cuddling me to him, tightened until I could barely breathe.

"Peter locked me in there." I pointed at the open coffin lined with pale blue silk and white lace. "And what's more, he had his heart set on cremating me."

"Mother of God," croaked Scuzz, crossing himself hastily.

Somehow, looking at it now, the coffin appeared smaller, narrower, more confining. And just as I was thanking God and The Universe for escaping its claustrophobic clutches, delayed shock pounced with the claws of a tiger. My breath caught in my chest, my stomach heaved, my legs turned into soggy rhubarb sticks…

And the door of the funeral parlor exploded open.

I jolted my head up. Surely I was hallucinating. I closed my eyes, counted to five before opening them again. Nope. All for real. Six sharp-shooters dressed in those bulletproof vest thingies, crouched at the door and they seemed to be aiming their state-of-the-art weapons at us.

"Police! Everybody freeze!" roared the leader, a big burly guy with a voice like a working steam shovel.

"And you—" Big and Burly went on, doing one of those jerky dance steps you see on TV cop shows and indicating Ben with a twitch of his gun hand. "—drop your weapon or we'll take you out!"

"Huh?" Ben eyed the gun in his hand as though it had suddenly turned into a writhing viper. His fingers flipped open and the gun hit the floor and bounced.

"Now, kick it to me," the leader ordered, his trigger finger clearly itching to contract.

This was fast turning into one of those black-and-white movie farces. If I didn't explain the circumstances quickly, who knows—one of us good guys might end up with a bullet to a vital part of our anatomy and they'd cart our killer off to the hospital as the poor suffering victim.

"It's not *his* gun," I explained as Ben obliged the leader by kicking the weapon in the direction of the door. "It belongs to the creep on the floor. Peter Manning. And he threatened to kill me with that gun. He also murdered Matt Turn—"

"No talking!" Big and Burly roared before addressing two uniformed policemen positioned behind the sharp shooters. "Contact DCI Stevens and DI Adams immediately. Inform them we've caught our suspects and have them immobilized."

Oh no—not Good Cop and Bad Cop again!

"Then cuff them and take them down to the station. The creep on the floor too."

Straightening to his full seven foot of craggy man-mountain, Scuzz eyed the approaching officer with raised eyebrows before extending both wrists, tattooed fingers facing up. When he spoke, his voice was polite, but laced with menace. "If that is what you *really* want to do, officer."

Like he'd smacked into an invisible force field, the police officer skidded to a halt. He perused the leather-clad biker, inch by inch, starting at his size 18 steel-capped boots and ending at his multi-pierced face. Turning a shade closely resembling sour cream, he shot Big and

Burly a questioning glance.

"I *said* cuff 'em!"

Handcuffs visibly shaking, the policeman took a large fortifying breath then continued towards Scuzz. When his steps faltered and he came to another halt, Scuzz snatched the cuffs from him, shook his head and fastened them on his own wrists.

Ben reached for my hand. "Don't worry, babe," he said and gave my fingers a reassuring squeeze. "We'll sort this out and be home before you can say *scrambled eggs*."

At the mention of *scrambled eggs*, I instantly felt ravenous. "This might sound weird, but I'd murder for a plate of eggs with lashings of bacon and tomatoes right now. I'm starving."

"You can make that two servings, babe." Ben wriggled his nose at me. "Although, with Stevens and Adams on the way, I have a feeling we won't be eating breakfast this morning."

32

THE BAD NEWS...BEN WAS RIGHT. Breakfast was a nonevent. It was 2pm before we literally fell onto our plates of scrambled eggs and bacon like they were gourmet dishes of caviar and truffles with a hot chocolate sundae to follow.

The good news was Peter Manning would probably be claiming the aged pension before he saw the outside of a jail. Not only would my evidence convict him, but Barney Thompson, the starting-box steward, realizing he was safer with the killer in jail than out, turned informant. Add to that, the Spagnetti brothers, captured stowing away on a cruise ship to Tahiti, quickly joined the queue and pointed the finger at Manning. In fact, once incarcerated, the brothers spilled information like buckets with no bottoms.

Funnily enough, after all our detective work, the contents in Matt's safe-deposit box did nothing to help put his killer away. Full of betting memorabilia, Matt had even stored his very first TAB ticket, procured at age sixteen—two dollars each way on a dog called Wun Wabbit—and the dog was evidently still *wunning*. But why he'd framed this losing ticket and stored it along with the rest of his racing documentation— for posterity or his grandkids or for future aliens to ponder over—I guess we'll never know.

Anyway, "life goes on" as is the theme of many books.

However, the morning Scuzz decided it was time for *him* to move on, even the dogs slunk around the house with their tails jammed between their legs. The day was sunny, sky the color of lapis lazuli—not that I know zilch about lapis lazuli except that it's a brilliant blue—and the air sweet. I sniffled. It should have been dark and dismal and raining buckets of cow's excrement to match my mood. For when Scuzz gathered his "accoutrements" together and wheeled his adored hog onto the driveway, I knew I was going to cry.

"Come here, Katrina," Scuzz crooned, holding his arms out for a hug.

Leather, soft as fine muslin, brushed against my cheek as I buried my head in his *Red Devil* jacket. Theodore Samuel Parkington the Third was one hell of a guy.

"Do you *really* have to go?"

"It is time I moved on, Katrina," he said, gently wiping a tear off my cheek with one large leather-clad finger before leaning closer for a goodbye kiss, which included a hint of tongue. "My bodyguard duties have been terminated," he told me as he came up for air. "Your temporary kennel-house is completed. Hey, you don't need me anymore." He paused, extricated himself from my arms and with a rueful twist of a smile, straddled his Harley. "It's time to hit the road again."

"But—"

"When I finally catch up with this mysterious half-sister of mine, I'll ring and let you know what she's like." He did one of his cute eyebrow wiggles and grinned. "Might even bring Summer here to meet you."

"That'd be great," I told him and gave a watery smile as I noticed the corner of a pastel pink pillow poking from the bedroll fastened to the rear of Scuzz's bike.

"Keep in touch, mate." Ben stepped forward to shake hands. "You're an ugly so-and-so but a good guy to have on side."

"You too, cowboy. And make sure you look after our girl."

Ben's eyes narrowed. "*Our* girl?"

"That's right. I'll be calling in on the way back from the West to check the situation out," Scuzz told him then turned to wink at me. "It's okay to give the cowboy a shot, Katrina, but if he's not up to it, I'll make you an offer you can't refuse when I return. Okay?"

"Umm…does this amazing offer involve black satin sheets and a hot-water bottle with a fluffy panda bear cover?"

"It involves whatever fantasy your little heart desires, Katrina."

Phew! Was that lust in all its lip-licking variations bubbling away in my stomach or a reaction to the gallon of tomato sauce I'd smothered over my eggs and bacon?

Behind me, Ben's growl came from low in his throat. Broke through my sudden hankering to play the game of *whatever fantasy your little heart desires* with Theodore Samuel Parkington the Third. Sheesh! Since leaving *Miss Nice Girl* in a cringing heap at the funeral parlor and transforming into *Bombshell Chick* sometimes I couldn't keep up with myself.

Like a lasso, Ben's arm shot out, circled my waist and hauled me possessively against his hip. "*Goodbye*, Theodore."

The rumble of the sensuous black and silver machine broke the stillness of the early morning air. "I'll be back!" Scuzz fastened his helmet and as he pushed off the ground with one foot, waved one hand in a farewell gesture.

"I'll be waiting!" I called out after him.

"No, she won't!" countered Ben, his arm tightening into a death grip. "She'll be too busy."

"Too busy?" I glanced up at his oh-so-familiar face. The face I'd spent long nights dreaming about. The face I could now hold and kiss and lose my mind over any time it took my fancy. "Busy doing what?"

"*Talking.*" Ben's grin sent an ache to my groin that screamed to be set alight, stoked and prodded and then soothed. Both *Miss Nice Girl* and *Bombshell Chick* were in complete agreement this time. "We seem to have become very adept at conversation."

The ache in my groin took over my senses and I bit back a rising moan. I couldn't get enough of this man. He was the bee and I was the nectar. He was the yin and I was the yang. He was…

Oh stuff it!

I grabbed Ben's arm and dragged him inside the house, undoing the stud on his jeans with my free hand. "Know what, Benjamin?" I said as the door swung closed behind us and I ran both hands up under his shirt, groaning as my palms met the hard smooth planes of his torso. "I think I can feel another discussion coming on."

"I'm all ears, babe." Ben's grin widened and he leant forward, kissed me soundly on the lips and then yanked my T-shirt up over my head.

As for Scuzz's concerns, the moment Ben's body molded itself against mine, I could tell, without even looking down, that he was definitely *up to it*.

Dear Readers

A former school teacher, competitive horse rider, and greyhound trainer, June Whyte has always dreamed of being an author.

She wrote her first full-length story (with chapters) when she was nine-years-old — *Donald McDonald in Texas* — a story involving a rather extraordinary boy who rode buck-jumpers in a rodeo.

And when she penned her first murder mystery, *Murder Behind Bars*, it resulted in her fifth-grade teacher questioning her home life.

Even now, in retirement, June's favorite spot is sitting in front of her computer, drawing on her knowledge of greyhounds and horses to create humorous mysteries for both adults and younger teens.

Her *Kat McKinley* greyhound series, starting with *Chasing Can Be Murder*, is laugh out loud funny, as is her *Chiana Ryan*, PI, Young Adult mystery series.

She's also written the cozy mystery series, *Vets2U*, which is similar to the TV show, Rosemary & Thyme — but instead of gardeners, Emily and Maggie are veterinarians. This series is for animal lovers — especially those who love horses.

For more information and news, go to:

www.junewhytebooks.com

Thank you,
June Whyte